PRAISE FOR

An Unreliable Truth

"A straight-A legal thriller, with a final scene as satisfying as it is disturbing."

—*Kirkus Reviews*

Crimson Lake Road

"Dark, darker, and then some. But readers who can take it are in for quite a ride."

—*Kirkus Reviews*

"In Edgar-finalist Methos's nail-biting sequel to 2020's *A Killer's Wife* . . . readers will be curious to see where Methos takes Jessica next."

—*Publishers Weekly*

A Killer's Wife

An Amazon Best Book of the Month: Mystery, Thriller & Suspense

"*A Killer's Wife* is a high-stakes legal thriller loaded with intense courtroom drama, compelling characters, and surprising twists that will keep you turning the pages at breakneck speed."

—T. R. Ragan, *New York Times* bestselling author

THE SECRET WITNESS

OTHER TITLES BY VICTOR METHOS

Desert Plains Series

A Killer's Wife
Crimson Lake Road
An Unreliable Truth

Other Titles

The Hallows
The Shotgun Lawyer
A Gambler's Jury
An Invisible Client

Neon Lawyer Series

Mercy
The Neon Lawyer

THE *SECRET WITNESS*

VICTOR METHOS

THOMAS & MERCER

Published by Thomas & Mercer, Seattle

www.apub.com

Amazon, the Amazon logo, and Thomas & Mercer are trademarks of Amazon.com, Inc., or its affiliates.

ISBN-13: 9781542038188
ISBN-10: 1542038189

Cover design by Faceout Studio, Jeff Miller

Printed in the United States of America

A child ignored by the village
will burn it down to feel its warmth.
—African proverb

1

Otto Murray woke up from a deep sleep to Allyx whispering, "Otto, our motion detector in the backyard turned on."

"Probably a raccoon or something," he mumbled, still hazy. He'd spent several hours working in the yard, raking up leaves, and just remembered he hadn't put the lid back on the trash can.

He was already drifting off when Allyx shook him and whispered, "It turned on again!"

"So what?"

"Otto, please. I heard there were break-ins in the neighborhood."

"Stealing skis out of the Sandovals' open garage isn't a break-in."

"I won't be able to sleep until you check on it."

He sighed. No use arguing with fear. "Fine."

After swinging his legs over the edge of the bed, he rubbed his eyes and stretched his neck.

The first thing he saw was Allyx's mannequin, which she used as a model while working on pieces of clothing she would sell around the neighborhood and at swap meets. A female mannequin with dark eyes and an uncomfortable looking tilt to her neck, giving her just enough of a deformed appearance to be disturbing. After they'd both retired, they'd needed something to fill the time. Otto had found fishing and hiking, and Allyx selling trinkets and clothing. The house was stuffed with unsold creations his wife refused to let him throw out.

"Things we do for love," he said as he tapped the mannequin on his way out of the bedroom.

"What?" Allyx asked.

"Nothin'."

He yawned while walking to the kitchen and debated whether to get a gun. It probably was a raccoon, but cougars and bears lived close to the West Mountains in Utah. A bear had even recently ripped off the door of a minivan to get to the McDonald's Happy Meal inside.

Now that's a break-in.

Just in case, he went to the den—which was one of only four rooms finished in the house, the rest being a work in progress since they'd only moved in a year ago—opened the brown gun safe, and took out his double-barrel shotgun. It wasn't as powerful or sleek as his pump-action Remington, but he preferred the classics. Things that held up over time were worth more than new things. Plus, when his father used to take him rabbit hunting, this was the gun he preferred to use, and it always reminded him of his dad when he got a chance to shoot it.

After loading the shotgun, he shuffled casually to the kitchen, yawning again, and squinted through the window above the sink. They had a large unfenced backyard that led to the mountains. Grass and trees surrounded the home, and beyond that was nothing but dirt and rocks. They'd bought the house on the cheap with the expectation they would finish it themselves, Otto having been a contractor, but he found it boring and slow work now that he wasn't getting paid for it. So he had an unfinished house with an unfinished yard in an undeveloped neighborhood. Still, for two empty nesters who didn't have many guests over, it was perfect.

He didn't see anything near the house and figured he had been right: raccoon. He wished one had still been there; having Allyx jump out of bed in fright after hearing a shotgun blast would be fair payback for waking him up.

As he turned away, the motion detector light came back on. He looked out the window again but didn't see anything in the yard. He went over to the back door and opened it. A slight trickle of fear touched his belly for the first time.

He scanned the yard from one end to the other and tried to focus on the sounds around him.

No crickets.

He could think of only two reasons for that: it was too cold, or a predator was in the area. Since the temperature had been almost ninety earlier that day, it wasn't too cold. But people attacked by bears had reported the forest going silent right before.

The motion detector clicked off. Otto stepped outside and looked up at the sky. Not much light pollution, and being higher up in elevation gave him the best view of the sky he could have asked for.

The motion detector light came on.

He turned, squinting, toward the light fixture at the corner of the roof.

"Hello? Someone there?"

The light clicked off. Darkness again.

Otto gripped his shotgun tighter and brought it up to waist height. His throat felt like sandpaper. He swallowed. Cougars liked to attack from behind, but bears attacked from the front. Sickening anxiety confused him as to what to do.

Then, relief washed over him. No one was here. The motion detector was malfunctioning. He recalled seeing some online reviews about false alarms being triggered with this system.

Despite considering himself a relatively tough guy, he had to admit these last few seconds had been a little scary.

He chuckled to himself and went back inside the house. As he shut the door, the motion detector light came on. It stopped him, and then he reminded himself that it was just malfunctioning.

"What is it?" Allyx called from the bedroom.

"The motion detector's busted. I told you to go with those other guys."

"They had worse customer service."

"What customer service? Just make sure our alarm works and leave us the hell alone the rest of the time."

He set the shotgun on the kitchen counter. He searched under the sink and then up in a cupboard until he found the smaller of his tool sets.

The light turned back on as he went outside, marched over, and set the tools down. When he went to open his tool kit, he realized he didn't have the key. It was one of those old sets from back when people fixed everything themselves and called experts in only when there wasn't any other choice. His dad's tool set he'd given Otto as a gift when he was a teenager.

When he was halfway back to the door, the motion detector light clicked off, then clicked on a second later. That sickening feeling came back and flooded his mouth with a sour taste.

"Is somebody there? Hello?"

Fear made his hands tremble, and he noticed for the first time that he'd left his shotgun on the counter.

The light clicked off. He stood still a moment in the dark and then continued toward the door. He had his hand on the knob when the light clicked on.

He decided he would go back to bed and worry about it tomorrow. Something bothered him, though. Before the light had gone out the last time, he'd seen . . . something. A shape. An outline. Something that stood out from the darkness but blended in enough that he couldn't tell if it was in his head. It was nearer the property line, toward a grouping of trees.

"Hello?" Otto put his hand over his eyes to shield them from the light. "This isn't funny, whoever you are. I'm calling the cops."

The shape moved.

It was a subtle movement, but noticeable. The shadow shifted to the right a couple of feet. As though it was a person taking a large step. But he couldn't see any legs.

The light clicked off.

Otto's heart thumped against his ribs, and all he could hear was his own heavy breathing. The darkness seemed deeper than it was a moment ago somehow, with just enough starlight to make out odd shapes floating past his vision.

As he scrambled to turn the doorknob, the blade pierced the back of his neck, and he felt pressure on his forehead where the shape pulled his head back to expose his throat. The steel felt like ice in his body, and then there was no longer ice, only warmth. Sucking breath did nothing but make him gurgle. He fell to his knees, his hands going instinctively to the wound, trying to hold back the blood.

The shape pulled out the knife in one powerful jerk, and then, grunting, swung it over and over again, plunging the blade into Otto's flesh.

———

Allyx called her husband's name a few times, to no response. Otto was a practical joker, had been since the time they had dated, and she had little doubt he was hiding behind some corner to shout "Boo!" at the right moment.

"Otto, this isn't funny."

After a few more minutes, she rose from bed. Her mouth felt dry and her throat itched and she thought about how mad she was going to be if this was a joke.

"I will be furious if you scare me. Do you hear me, Otto? Furious."

No answer, no noise. She went to the bedroom door and looked out at her hallway and the kitchen, a dozen feet away. She could see that the light from the motion detector in the backyard was on. Before she could take a step out of the room, the light turned off, and the sudden change made her gasp.

Then a noise caught her attention.

Whatever it was, it was somewhere in the house.

———

A guttural, primitive scream burst out of her as Allyx ran out the open back door, nearly tripping over the hem of her nightgown. She sprinted through the grass barefoot and into the dirt behind the house. When the light turned on, she saw her husband's body, torn apart and caked in blood, lying on its back. Milky eyes staring up at the night sky.

Headlights appeared on the overpass near their property, like eyeshine from an animal passing by.

"Help!"

The ground was uneven, and she slipped and fell, hitting the dirt hard. She rose to her feet and screamed for the car to stop.

The car turned onto a side road and was gone. Her words echoed in the empty valley, and she knew no one would hear them.

Her entire world became her feet pounding dirt and the sound of her hot breath as she grew more and more winded and tried not to think about the footfalls behind her and whether they were getting closer.

Then something shattered the rhythm of the predictable sounds. Like a bolt of lightning on a stormless night.

The first round tore through her shoulder, spinning her like a top. She slammed into the ground, dirt filling her mouth.

Sobbing, she tried to force herself up, but the blood flowing down her arm left her muscles weak. She managed to get to her knees, chanting, "No, no, no," as if the words would stop the bullets.

Another shot tore into her body, and she collapsed for good.

The taste of blood and dirt in her mouth made her gag, like sucking on a handful of pennies. She tried to push herself up to run again, but one of her arms wouldn't respond. All she could manage to do was flip herself onto her back.

The crunch of hard dirt grew louder as the shape approached.

"No, please," she cried, "please. I'll do anything you want! Please. I'll do anything!"

She looked up at the shape as the handgun rose. It wore a black hood that looked like a pillowcase with a drawing she couldn't make out on the front.

She opened her mouth to scream, but the round tore through the roof of her mouth and into her brain, and then there was nothing.

———

Bobby Larson had been driving Uber for four years now, and as far back as he could remember, the passenger in the back seat was the quietest he'd ever had. Even the quiet ones would answer a question if asked directly, but this guy . . . there was nothing.

Tooele, pronounced "Two Illa," which Bobby guessed was a Native American word, wasn't a city he was used to driving in, as he lived in Salt Lake City, a half hour away. Still, he had to admit, at night, it was beautiful with the bright stars and large mountains.

He'd brought a fare down here from the airport and considered himself lucky to have picked up another fare at two in the morning; he worked full time during the day as a short-order cook and could only get out driving at night.

Bobby had told the passenger it would be a lot cheaper to take a bus in the morning from Tooele to Salt Lake, but the passenger said it was fine.

"So we're right near State Street," Bobby said, looking over his glasses into the rearview mirror. "You got a preference on which side of the street I drop you off?"

No answer. Bobby shrugged and mumbled, "All right, dealer's choice, looks like."

"Not here," a low voice said from the back. "Up the street."

Bobby drove up almost half a mile before the passenger said, "Stop."

He pulled over and put the car in park. He was turning to ask the passenger to leave him a five-star review when he felt the muzzle against his cheek.

"Wha—"

The round ripped through his cheek, splattering bits of bone and ragged flesh over the windshield. Bobby's face hit the steering wheel, his glasses cracked and spattered with blood. He heard the back door open and then a few steps before he saw the shadow of the gun in front of him. The figure holding it wore a black hood, and Bobby could see the drawing in white on its front. A skull with an upside-down cross on the forehead.

The last thing Bobby heard was a loud bang.

2

Solomon Shepard startled awake. He usually didn't remember his dreams, but this one didn't fade when he opened his eyes. It involved shadows in dark corners that weren't entirely friendly.

It took several seconds for him to get his bearings.

Someone was knocking on the door. Only one person visited him anymore, and she should've been in school this early in the morning.

"Just a minute!"

He got on his hands and knees and searched for his cane. It had slid under the bed. He pulled it out and leaned on it. Wouldn't do to answer the door in only his silk boxers, so he slipped on a white T-shirt.

Russ lay sprawled out on the kitchen counter, his orange and white tail flicking lazily up and down.

"Seriously?" Solomon said. "Someone knocks and you don't even meow? What if someone broke in?"

The cat licked his lips.

Solomon had found him not more than a couple of blocks from his apartment. He'd walked by a garbage bin and heard a noise. Inside, he saw a litter of kittens. He rushed them to a vet. Russ was the one who wouldn't go to anyone else but him, so Solomon thought it must've been fate to adopt him.

Solomon answered the door, expecting to see Kelly asking for an advance on her pay for the groceries she was supposed to pick up. He couldn't remember the last time he'd opened the door for anyone else.

Billie Gray—who hated her actual name of Elizabeth—stood in front of him. The sheriff wore her blonde hair with pink tips pulled back. Instead of a uniform, she wore a suit with a skirt and her badge clipped to her waistband.

One of the last times Solomon had seen her, he was lying in a hospital bed with tubes sticking out of him, unsure if he would ever walk again. She'd dropped by his apartment a few times since then, but the demands of her job and the urge he had for solitude meant they had drifted apart. But seeing her face took him right back to where they had left off. Some people were like that, coming in and out of your life with nothing changing, while others changed right in front of you and drifted away.

"Got any coffee?" she said, as though they were just old friends who'd happened to run into each other.

"No, coffee kills. I got tea."

"Good enough."

———

They sat on his balcony and looked out over the Tooele Valley. Though he was in the city, he lived near its edge and could see the surrounding trees and hills and the long tracts of land covered in golden weeds that ran up to the mountains on the west side.

"I hope it's okay I just showed up," Billie said.

"I don't see you for a little bit, and you turn into a suit on me?"

"Suit?"

"The jacket and skirt. I thought you only wore jeans?"

"Oh, yeah. I had a meeting earlier. Political bullshit's half my job these days."

"You still hunting?"

She shrugged. "When I can, here and there. Been too hot this season." She took a sip of tea. "It's gotta be pretty pricey here with this view. How you still swinging a place like this?"

"Rent controls. The city's been playing around with them for a while. Don't think it'll last. The ultrawealthy Ivy Leaguers don't like us common folk stomping on their territory."

They were silent a moment. "Do you know why I'm here?" she said.

He shook his head as he took a sip of herbal tea. "No."

"You don't read the news?"

"Reading and watching the news shrinks your frontal cortex by a microinch every year."

"So, is that a no?"

He grinned at her perception.

"I occasionally take a look." He took another sip of his tea and put it on the side table between them. "Three dead two weeks ago. A couple retirees and an Uber driver. How certain are you they're connected?"

"Ballistics gave a ninety percent probability that the firearm that killed Allyx Murray is the same one that killed Bobby Larson, the Uber driver."

He glanced at her and then back over the city.

Eight years ago, when Billie was a detective sergeant, her father, Zachary, had worked a case together with Solomon that received so much media attention they became minor celebrities in their own right. The Eliot Nesses chasing an Al Capone. The media had painted the story perfectly to intrigue readers. The young, brilliant homicide prosecutor and the newly promoted tough-as-nails sheriff up against the most prolific serial killer Utah had ever seen: the Reaper.

The killer had been an enigma. Engaging in a murder spree that lasted, as best as they could estimate, for only two months but took the lives of ten people. The killer taunted police with a long, cryptic letter that began with *This is Reaper speaking*, detailed eight murders already committed, and promised more. Then, at the end, instead of a signature, a drawing. A skull with an upside-down cross on its forehead.

Because of the cross, law enforcement initially believed these were satanic murders, perhaps even committed by an entire cult. But Solomon had never thought so. Satanic cults were easy to catch. For them, the ritual around the killing was more important than the killing itself. Because of that, plenty of evidence was typically left behind.

Little evidence was found at any scene of the Reaper's. Victimology was useless in reconstructing his thinking. Some of the victims were shot, some stabbed. One suffocated, and another's skull crushed. One had gasoline poured over him and was set on fire while still in bed. There seemed to be no pattern, no method, and no coherence to anything the Reaper did. The only reason they even knew the murders were connected was because the Reaper claimed them in the letter with details only the killer would know. Every piece of evidence they had was given to them by the Reaper himself.

The county was gripped by fear. Gun sales tripled, women's mixed martial arts classes were full, and few girls on the college campus went out at night alone anymore. Men who had never owned a gun took concealed carry classes, and more than one person had been inadvertently shot by itchy trigger fingers.

Then, one day, the killings stopped, and the Reaper disappeared like a shadow.

"Nearly the same locations," Billie said. She unlocked her phone and set it on the side table between them. Solomon glanced down and saw a photograph of a man lying on his side on grass. There were so many stab wounds to his torso he looked like a butchered side of beef. The knife had gone through with so much force that Solomon could see the ragged flesh hanging down. In the original Reaper slayings, the first victims had been an older couple, Stephen and Betty Wagner, but the methodology was unmistakable: Stephen Wagner and Otto Murray had been killed in a nearly identical way.

They had never released to the public that Stephen Wagner had been stabbed eleven times before managing to get away and out of the house. Solomon held that detail back at the request of the victim's surviving children so that the grandkids wouldn't have that image in their heads.

Otto Murray appeared to have been stabbed at least eleven times.

When Solomon didn't say anything, Billie took one finger and swiped to the next photo, revealing a Caucasian woman in a field of dirt. She had been shot, her face frozen in an expression of pure terror and confusion.

Betty Wagner had been shot outdoors as well. Two shots to the back and one into the mouth that blew out the top of her skull. It appeared Allyx Murray had died in the same manner.

He looked away from the phone and to some trees in front of a building across the street. Behind the trees was the women's shelter, which he could see from his balcony.

"Why are you showing me these, Billie?"

"No one knows this case better than you."

He turned to her. "Why are you even working this? You're the boss now. Give it to Major Crimes and have them call in the FBI for help."

"I did. The consultant I spoke with didn't even fly out. He gave me a psychological profile and some background on the firearm used. They may as well have sent a drawing in crayon and it would've helped as much."

He inhaled deeply and looked up to the sky. The sky was painted purple and orange as the sun rose and burned away the thin mist that covered the city.

"You never finished this, Solomon. I know you think about it, and I know you always said you're a prosecutor, not an investigator. You bag 'em and I'll tag 'em and all that. I really do get it. But, I think we can catch him faster if you help."

13

He shook his head. "I'm sorry. I can't help you. Besides, you guys would expect that tacky gold watch you gave me back, and I lost that thing like three years ago."

She grinned and then took her phone and stole a quick glance at the woman in the photo. "When was the last time you left your apartment?"

Solomon sipped his tea. Purposely taking longer than he needed to. "What does that have to do with anything?"

Billie leaned forward and said, "When?"

"A long time."

There was a pause before she said, "Like two weeks or two years?"

"What does it matter? I can have everything delivered, there's more TV shows and movies than I could ever watch, more books than I could ever read, I get my pension and disability from the government . . . I don't need anything else."

"You need purpose and other people in your life. Hermits don't live very long."

"Hell is other people."

"I don't believe that for a second."

"That's the great thing about the truth. It's true whether we believe it or not."

She watched a group of teenagers walk past the building five stories below, laughing and teasing each other. "The Reaper killed without leaving anything behind and then disappeared like a ghost. And now he's back. How many more obituaries do we need to see until the next time he disappears?"

"Don't run a game on me, Billie. I was there. I was in that first task force when a photo of a six-year-old girl had to be hung on the murder board, and I was there when the lab, *your* lab, lost the DNA samples recovered from the saliva washes. Nobody wanted this guy down more than me and your dad."

"Then why won't you help?"

"I don't think I can go back to that way of thinking. I don't want to."

She rose. Solomon didn't move when she lightly placed her hand on his shoulder. He hadn't touched or been touched by another human being in years. Such an odd sensation. A small jolt went through him, and he wondered if it was static or the touch itself. Some energy that came with human contact that humans grew accustomed to and no longer noticed.

"You know how to reach me if you change your mind."

He watched her leave.

When the sheriff was gone, he took his cane and returned to the bedroom. In his closet, on the top shelf, was a transparent plastic bin. He pulled it down with one hand and put it on the floor before opening the lid.

It was the only file he had kept from his days as a prosecutor.

Written in bold lettering across a thick brown accordion folder was the word REAPER.

3

Solomon took the folder out to the balcony. It was as close to leaving his apartment as he had come in the past six months. The outside world was more and more becoming an abstraction, almost like watching scenes on television.

He blared music at around lunchtime. A band whose name translated from Norwegian as "Death by Bleeding." He didn't hear the knocking at his door until he went into the kitchen for a drink.

He looked through the peephole and saw Kelly standing there. He opened the door and said, "Where were you? I was about to start eating paint chips."

"Holy hell!" she shouted. "Turn this down."

Solomon got the remote to the stereo and turned it down.

"Why are you always listening to that garbage?"

"Hey, Norwegian death metal's a pure art form. Music should be a catharsis of all your negative emotions. Nothing gets out the negative emotions like people screaming in Norwegian."

She placed a bag of groceries and another one of cheeseburgers on the counter and said, "Everybody from California's moving here. You know how busy it's gotten out there? It takes an hour to go anywhere now."

"What are you, a hundred years old? Isn't complaining about traffic a little too jaded for a sixteen-year-old?"

She faced him and held out her hand palm up. He glanced at the scar on her cheek, a cut that went from her cheekbone to her jawbone. It had faded but could be seen from up close, and he knew she was insecure about it and felt bad for looking.

"Just for that, you have to pay me an extra buck."

"For what?" he said.

"Consider it a rude comment tax."

He shook his head as he pulled out his wallet and said, "Kids these days." He gave her the cash and began looking through the bags to ensure everything was there.

"So, who was that hot chick I saw come outta your place?"

"That was like four hours ago. How'd you see her?"

"Skipped school and looked out when I heard someone knocking on your door. I didn't think you knew anybody else."

"You're not exactly Ms. Extrovert yourself, ya know. And why are you skipping school so much? I loved school."

"That's 'cause you're a nerd," she said, taking an apple out of a bag and having a bite. She leaned on the counter. "So? Who was it?"

"Just an old colleague."

"Oh, yeah? What'd she want?"

"To talk about an old case."

"About someone you put in jail?"

He shook his head as he put a box of cereal in a cupboard. "No. That one we never caught."

"Then why was she here?" She gave a quiet gasp. "Oh my shit! Is it about those people that were killed?"

"You're too young to know about stuff like that." He took a five-dollar bill out of the cash in her hand. "No peanut butter or jelly in the bag."

"Oh, come on, I just forgot. I need that for gas money."

He sighed and gave it back to her. "I love peanut butter and jelly."

"Yeah, well, that's life." She took another bite of apple and with her mouth full said, "So who got away?"

He leaned back on the counter and rested the cane against the cupboard underneath. "Long story."

"I wanna hear it. What happened?"

He shrugged. "Some guy killed a bunch of people eight years ago and then just stopped."

"See, how do you know it was a guy if you never caught them? You think a woman isn't strong enough to kill?"

"Easy, tigress. He sent us a letter with information about himself."

"I'm kidding. What kinda letter?"

"A nasty one that isn't for children's ears. I'll give you another five if you run back to the store and buy me some peanut butter and jelly right now."

"No way, man. I got shit to do. I'll swing it by tomorrow after school." As she left, she held up two fingers without turning around. "Peace."

Kelly lived down the hall. Her stepfather, Travis, was a high-functioning alcoholic who was home so little Solomon had only seen him a handful of times in the years he'd lived in this building. Her birth father had died of a heart attack, leaving her twentysomething mother to raise a toddler alone. Kelly had once told him she had forgotten what her father's face looked like. Solomon thought he'd never seen someone look so sad.

The sun angled through the window over the sink to paint a square bisected by a cross on the floor. He could see dust swirling in the sunbeams and thought about how it was a miracle that a person inhaled dust and dirt all day and still managed to breathe.

He'd left his phone on the kitchen counter. It vibrated with a text message from Billie. **You need to get out of that apartment for at least a walk or something.**

The text made him think of the photo of the man torn apart and his wife staring up at the sky with glassy eyes. He wondered if Billie had sent the text because she was worried about him or because she knew that was the image that would pop into his mind.

He inhaled deeply and felt the smoothness of the phone in his hands while he thought of what to say.

Thanks, he replied. After a brief hesitation, he texted, Do you really want me to go for a walk or did you just want me to think about the victims?

Both. And I'm asking for a favor as a friend. You can't say no.

It took a moment with his thumbs hovering over his phone before he could reply. The fear that bubbled inside his guts felt like ice water. So cold it sucked his breath away. He had to swallow because his mouth went dry when he remembered the images from eight years ago. Images that made nightmares.

Then he recalled the sleepless nights, the hours staring at the murder board and trying to see patterns, any patterns, and feeling the conflicted thought that he didn't want anyone else to die but knew they'd have to if they were going to find this man.

He blew out a breath through pressed lips and typed, Send me the reports. I'll take a quick look.

Anxiety tightened his chest. He had just agreed to go into a world he'd thought wasn't a part of his life anymore, and there were things he was going to have to see that he didn't want to. It wasn't so much the gore; he could acknowledge the gore and still keep working. It was something else. A sense that something was off balance in the world.

That sense could lead to imbalance in his life, and if it got severe enough, he knew he wouldn't survive it this time.

4

Solomon rested his cane on the chair next to him and opened his laptop. A tuna sandwich with chips sat on the side table, and he took one bite and put it back, disgusted. He wished Kelly had brought the peanut butter and jelly.

Before digging in to what Billie had sent, he picked up the stack of papers next to his chair. Copies of the original Reaper murder book, forensic and toxicology reports, hundreds of photographs, witness statements, and profiles sent in from every mediocre academic in the country who wanted to be the one who, when the Reaper was eventually caught, had given the police the profile that most closely matched the killer's. They could then get their per diems on all the cable news shows as experts on criminal psychology.

Hundreds of pages of leads. All for nothing. Law enforcement had been no closer to catching the killer on the last day of the investigation than they had been on the first day.

He looked down to the street and saw the DoorDash delivery to the shelter. Every Wednesday evening after dinner, he sent a few dozen donuts for the kids who stayed there with their mothers. He liked watching them sit on the front steps and laugh and talk while they ate. Even in atrocious circumstances, children could make the best of it. He wondered at what point in life adults lost that skill.

Solomon picked out photos of the first two victims, retirees named Stephen and Betty Wagner.

The pathologist had guessed an extraordinarily sharp hunting knife was used on Stephen Wagner. Something possibly made by the Reaper himself for maximum efficiency.

The Wagners were killed in their home near Tooele Canyon, a home long since torn down and replaced. The address had changed because of all the development over the years, but it was the same location where Otto and Allyx Murray were killed. A place out of the way, with few neighbors around. Just a handful of homes dotted the barren landscape up there.

Then, in his original spree, the Reaper had killed a cab driver near the city center.

Ahmad Rasul, a middle-aged man with two kids, was shot to death with a 9mm handgun less than an hour after he'd picked up a fare. Ahmad was 180 pounds and healthy but had been caught so completely by surprise that he didn't get a chance to even shield his head with his arms. Solomon remembered going to the scene and seeing the emergency lights of the cab flicker in the darkness. Possibly a joke from the killer to law enforcement. *Careful, hazard.*

The firearm used by the original Reaper, a Ruger 9mm, would eventually be linked to seven other murders: an entire family of five, the Farringtons, and a young couple at a lake who had taken the day off work to spend together on the water.

No valuables taken, no sexual assault, no torture. Nothing. No motive other than the killing itself.

Solomon had been the screening prosecutor on the original case eight years ago, and it was the most frustrating case of his entire career. True monsters like the Reaper were so rare and difficult to catch that luck was the primary factor in stopping them. Without luck, law enforcement could work their entire lives on the case and never close it. Solomon had nightmares about the Reaper showing up at his funeral.

As a prosecutor, he couldn't do much in the investigation, but he did have a unique type of knowledge to bring to the table. A social worker who worked with the prison population before going to law school, he'd learned more about violence than he thought possible through his hundreds of interviews and counseling sessions. He'd later written a book on a new system of behavioral forecasting and categorization using tools he'd learned from his statistics background.

Billie's father, Zach, had come to him for help back then.

Zach had said Solomon thought in a way that could be useful. Solomon denied it, saying he did nothing different from anybody else, but Zach just looked at him from across his desk, and they knew it wasn't true.

A breeze flapped some of the pages, and he tried to grab them before they flew away. One slid under the bars of the railing and floated gently five stories down.

Solomon watched it land in the branches of a tree. He debated trying to get it, but decided he would ask Kelly to retrieve it for him instead.

He flipped through some of the old witness statements. Most murder cases seemed to be solved by witnesses rather than forensic investigation, but the only witnesses here were after the fact. People who came across dead bodies and called the police.

But Solomon had believed that there were *always* witnesses to crimes: not to all crimes, but at least to the worst crimes. The world was too complex and crowded a place for complete secrecy anymore. Sometimes witnesses just didn't realize they were witnesses.

Solomon pictured the killer as a shadow. A black mist without form. His job was to slowly start pasting pieces to the shadow, giving the formless shape. But they had so little useable evidence he wasn't sure that, even if they did have a suspect, they'd have enough for a search warrant.

Flipping through the files, Solomon came to more photos of Betty Wagner from eight years ago and stared at them a bit too long. Then, using his laptop, he pulled up the pictures of Allyx Murray that Billie had sent. The two women looked nothing the same: Betty had blonde hair and Allyx brown. Allyx was thinner with slim, delicate features, and Betty was thick with a round face.

He closed the photos and pulled up a news story about the recent murders. Allyx Murray had been fifty-two years old.

There's a couple more things I want to look at, he texted, but that's all, Billie. Just look.

Thank you, was all she replied.

He lowered the phone and stared at the page of white paper stuck in the tree. The wind blew it free, and it swirled before drifting to the pavement below.

Taking a deep breath, he pushed himself up with his cane and faced his front door. He didn't remember when the last time was that he had stepped out of the door.

He took a package of Pop-Tarts from the kitchen and focused on eating to distract his brain while he went out into the hallway.

The hallway smelled like the fresh flowers in the vases by the elevators. As a dirt-poor kid in foster care, what, Solomon wondered, would he have thought if someone told him he'd live in a place like this one day?

The air was warm and held a tinge of car exhaust, but the breeze felt cool against his face and he stood in front of the building and closed his eyes until the breeze stopped. Something seemed different about being out here and not just on the balcony.

He picked up the fallen paper and stared at it. It was another grainy photocopy of a crime scene photo, somewhere outside the Wagners' house.

"You okay, Solomon?"

He turned around to see Kelly's mother in workout clothes sipping on a water bottle. She was about to head in.

"Um," he said, glancing down to the photo, "yeah, Maria. Thanks. I'll be fine."

As the words came out of his mouth, somehow, he didn't believe them.

5

Billie Gray rose from bed around six a.m. and groaned. It seemed like every morning, she was reminded she was getting older. Thirty-five didn't feel like twenty-five, and twenty-five hadn't felt like twenty. She was just old enough now to feel the tug of what youth felt like and how much she had changed.

Dax was on his side snoring, wearing his boxers and no shirt. The bedsprings creaked as she rose and went to the bathroom. His toothbrush and shaving cream and razor were there, a new addition he had only left behind a few weeks ago. Billie moved them to some shelving on the wall and out of view.

She handled her toiletries and then took a shower and changed into jeans and a white shirt with a red jacket. She had colorful tattoos on both arms and didn't like having to sometimes cover them up to give a more professional law enforcement appearance. She put on her holster with her 9mm and then clipped her shield to her waistband. Dax was still soundly snoring. She loved the way he slept, with his mouth open. It was the way a child would sleep.

By the time she got to the bedroom door to leave, he said, "Where you goin'?"

She turned to him as he sat up and put on his glasses.

"Duty calls."

"I thought it was your day off?"

"It is. I'll be back by dinner."

She blew him a kiss before stepping out into the hall. Then she poked her head back in and said, "Don't forget to pick up some potatoes and sour cream. I need them for dinner tonight."

"I won't," he said, getting out of bed and stretching his arms above his head.

Billie got into her Ford truck and started it. Whiskey Myers played through the speakers, and she hummed along as she pulled out of her driveway and headed for the freeway entrance. A burger joint called JCW's was down the road near the entrance, and she stopped at the drive-thru and asked for a bacon cheeseburger and a Diet Coke.

"Um, ma'am, we don't serve the lunch menu this early."

"Just ask your manager. She knows me."

A second later, the manager got on and said, "Sorry about that, Sheriff. I'll bring your order out when it's ready."

"It's no problem. Thank you, Joan."

Billie drove downtown while she ate. Tooele wasn't what it used to be, and she was glad she lived in the remote suburbs. The city was packed, and graffiti was prominent on nearly every building. Pioneer Park, a patch of grass and playground in the center of downtown, was riddled with needles, used condoms, and empty bottles of booze. So many crimes occurred here that the police rarely came out for calls on nonviolent offenses anymore.

"Damn it," she mumbled when a blob of blue cheese dripped onto her lap. She cleaned it the best she could with napkins and then wrapped up the rest of the burger and put it on the passenger seat.

When she got out of her truck in the Sheriff's Office parking lot, a little boy on a bike cutting through the lot nearly hit her door, but she managed to grab his handlebars just in time.

"Easy, kiddo," she said. "Better to go slow and not get hurt than show off, right?"

He ignored her and rode on.

As she walked into the building, Solomon texted.

Can you come by at around ten?

Ten at night?

Yeah

Why? I have a minute now

We can't do what we need to now. Come at ten

She let out a long breath and checked her watch. Well, she had a lot of paperwork to catch up on anyway.

———

Solomon ate a TV dinner of steamed vegetables and steak with a glass of red wine. He had worked halfway through a second glass by the time Billie rang his doorbell.

"Lemme grab my phone and we'll go," he said as a greeting.

"Go where exactly?"

Solomon didn't respond. He got his keys, stepped outside his apartment, and turned to lock his door. "I wanna see it."

"See what?"

"The scene."

She strolled next to him in silence down the hall, the only sound his cane as it tapped on the hardwood floors.

When they were in her truck, he put his cane between his legs and rubbed the handle, which was made of silver and shaped like the head of a lion.

Billie put on a country station, and Solomon rolled down the window and let the warm night air wash over his face. He had sold his car after he got out of the hospital because it did nothing but gather dust. So to be back out speeding through traffic had an exhilaration to it he'd never noticed before. Though his guts were balled up in a knot, and he was fighting a growing sense of a panic attack coming on.

There were no streetlights in the Murrays' neighborhood. Nothing but the moon to illuminate the way to the few homes that were there. The ground was dirt sprinkled randomly with weeds and tall grass, occasionally broken up with long gravel patches or trees.

"I'm curious about something," he said.

"What?"

"Do they still talk about me at the County Attorney's Office?"

"Not really. Occasionally they'll say something to one of the new people."

He looked out the window. "What do they say?"

"That you were stabbed by a defendant while you were giving an argument to a jury and that you once wrote a book about math or something."

He chuckled. "Or something."

They came to a wide clearing above a ravine and a dried streambed. About a hundred yards away was a home. It was a cookie-cutter house and appeared quaint in the moonlight, surrounded by grass that abruptly ended and turned to dirt.

They got out of the truck, and Solomon pulled up the scene photos on his phone. Billie got out a powerful flashlight, and he compared the images to the areas on the ground he was looking at. Allyx Murray's body was found about a hundred feet from the house. She had gotten far, almost perhaps gotten away. He wondered if Otto Murray fought the attacker to give his wife time to escape.

Billie said, "The first vic was killed here, near the motion detector light. Eleven stab wounds, but the pathologist said one particularly forceful one was the killing blow through the throat. Probably the first one. He died from suffocation, but he would've bled out soon."

Solomon didn't like her not using their names and calling them *vics* but didn't mention it.

"He really surprised them," she said. "The first vic didn't even have time to get defensive wounds because his hands never came up to protect him. Just like Stephen Wagner."

Solomon opened the flashlight function on his phone and swung it one way and then the other, attempting to see if anything had been left on the ground. A futile search, he knew, because the Scientific Investigation Section of the Sheriff's Office likely searched for hours, but he did it anyway. "So, sheriff, huh? You always told me you wanted to go back to grad school."

"I went back for a semester before I realized it wasn't for me."

"Why?"

"I don't know. Academia seems so stale. Like it doesn't have much to do with the real world."

"I think that's the point."

He knelt and looked more closely at some disturbance in the nearby weeds. They appeared to have been pushed down by someone stepping on them . . . or from the wind, or an animal, or a dozen other things. There was nothing left to analyze here but randomness.

"We went through this place with a fine-tooth comb," Billie said.

"Never know. Some people's fine-tooth combs are a little finer than others'."

He scanned around the tall grass for a few minutes while she stood by, giving him light.

"Can you show me the path Allyx Murray ran before she was shot?"

When they got near to where Allyx Murray's body had been found, he looked at the photos of her footprints in the dirt. Unfortunately, the criminalists had done a poor job with the images. They should have had several floodlights in every shot, and it looked like they didn't have any.

Either short on resources or burned out, and apathy was seeping in. Most people in the forensic investigation fields only lasted about seven years before rotating out and finding something else to do.

Solomon tripped and nearly fell over when his foot slid into a hole. "Are you okay?"

"Yeah," he said. It took some effort to bend down and pick up his cane, and he felt embarrassed in front of Billie. "This place is like swiss cheese," he said. "The ground's nowhere near even."

Solomon held up the photograph on his phone. He was about ten feet from where Allyx Murray had died. In the photo, both of her eyes were open. Most murder victims died with their eyes open, fighting to hold on to that last bit of light.

Her face had blue veins thrusting out from the pressure of the cranium bursting and gave her a zombie-like appearance. He didn't want to think of her that way, so he would have to find a picture of her alive to get this image out of his head.

"She was shot three times, and they found three shell casings, right?" he said, looking past where the body had fallen to the house. The shutters were all closed. Relatives of murder victims always closed the shutters in a murder house.

"Right."

"Grid search everywhere near here?"

"Grid search and dozens of deputies going through the tall grass. No other casings."

He blew out a breath. "So sprinting in the dark on uneven ground, he still hit a moving target with every shot he took."

"We're compiling a list of known felons in the area with Special Forces or sniper training. Something my father didn't take a good look at last time."

"He thought it was just luck, not training. I agree. We shouldn't be so quick to assume military training. Some people are just natural deadeye shots. One of Japan's archery champions had never picked up a bow until three months before she broke every record in the country."

"A savant murderer. There's a comforting thought."

"Wait, stop." Solomon looked off to the right at a large tree. The leaves were gone, and the tree looked to be dying, if not dead already, but had thick branches. The moonlight wasn't blocked, and he could see even without the flashlight now. "What is that? Up in the tree."

They moved toward it. The Murrays' bedroom window looked out at it, and Solomon thought at night, in the dark, the tree would have appeared like a gnarled, twisted creature reaching out for the house.

It took Billie a second to see what he was looking at, a marking on the bark about nine feet off the ground. Billie shined the light on it. It was an upside-down cross on the thickest branch. A branch thick enough for someone to sit on.

"How did you see that?"

"A bigger fine-tooth comb, I guess."

"No, really."

He had the urge to climb the tree, to sit where the Reaper had probably sat and watched the house that night. Waiting for the Murrays to fall asleep. "When someone hears noises in a forest or canyon, they look around but not up. During human evolution, most of our predators were on the ground, so we haven't evolved to search up for threats like other primates. Investigators are the same. They don't always search up."

He snapped a photo.

"He must've carved it out of boredom," Billie said. "I wonder how long he was up there?"

"Probably as soon as it got dark."

She glanced around and then focused on the symbol again. "I read in the original file that my father thought that symbol was satanic, but he said you didn't agree."

"I don't. It's the Petrine cross, the cross of Saint Peter. He didn't think he was worthy to die in the same position as Christ and asked that he be crucified upside down. It's only recently been adopted by satanists, but it's a lot older than any of that. The Babylonians would kill people to observe their screams while they were dying. They thought the gods communicated the future through the dying. This symbol represented the death ritual to speak to the gods."

She scanned the tree up and down as she slowly walked around it. "You're just a ray of sunshine today, aren't you, Solomon?"

He grinned. "You're the one who brought up the devil."

Solomon took the pen out of his pocket and put it between his teeth to chew on. An old habit he had forgotten about until this afternoon, when he'd found himself reading the Reaper files again and chewing down a pen he'd fished out of a drawer.

Billie said, "I'll get SIS out here in case he left any other presents for us up there. And I'll run the symbol down and see if there's any local groups that use it that aren't connected to satanism. Busywork is better than no work." She ran her light over the empty field. The gray dirt at the edge of the beam made the area appear like the moon: empty and lifeless. "You think it's him, Solomon?"

"I don't know. Maybe. But why copy his first crimes again? Wouldn't he have evolved, or at least pretended he'd evolved, in eight years?"

"If it is him, wouldn't he want us to know? What's the point for him if he doesn't get the recognition? The easiest way to get our attention would be to just commit the same crimes again."

Solomon looked around. The dead tree gave him an ominous, claustrophobic feel. As if the air pressed in on him and stuck to his skin.

"If it is him, he might've been able to stop killing for years. He may be the most dangerous type of person there is. The type who needs to kill but can wait."

The wind blew over the branches. Some older ones crackled from the pressure. Loose dirt on the ground swirled and spun and then drifted back to the earth.

"It's been a long day," she said as she turned the flashlight off. "Mind if we pick this up tomorrow?"

"You go. I'm gonna stay out here a little longer."

"I can stay with you."

"No, it's fine. I haven't been out in a bit, and it's a nice night. Call me a romantic."

She seemed hesitant to leave, and he said, "You don't need to look out for me. Really. I'm fine."

"Are you sure?"

"I'm a big boy, promise. You go. I need to be here alone. Catch the old scent or whatever. I can grab an Uber home."

"Well, if you insist, I won't say no. I guess I'll see you tomorrow at the briefing."

"What briefing?"

She walked away with a grin and said, "Oh, didn't I mention it? There's a briefing at the Justice Center in the morning, and attendance is mandatory. Even for temporary employees."

"Employee? I'm a friend doing a favor."

She took out her keys and said, "See you tomorrow, Solomon."

He grimaced as she drove away. Meetings and briefings. The two things Solomon had hated about his old job. More even than not having a working bathroom on the same floor and taking the stairs to the floor above every time he needed to go. It was odd to think about that complaint now as he pondered how good it would feel to run up stairs again.

He watched until the red taillights were swallowed by darkness. When the lights were gone, the stars and moon lent a pale bluish glow to the surroundings.

Nothing was here of the Murrays anymore. Solomon's father had once said ghosts wandered in empty valleys at night. It gave the place a dark feel, and he didn't want to be here now.

He summoned a car and went home.

When he got to his apartment, he printed out a photo from the file. Allyx Murray's driver's license photo. She had a broad smile with her long hair pulled back, revealing a symmetrical face with just the right amount of makeup. She'd likely been stunning in her youth, and Solomon wondered if her killer had noticed her beauty, too.

He put the photo next to his computer, where he would be sure to see it.

6

It was early morning when Solomon opened his door to Billie shoving a large tea in his hand.

"What time is it?" he said as she brushed past him into the apartment.

"Seven."

"I haven't been up this early since high school."

"You should go to bed earlier," she said, walking to the window. "You can get more done in the mornings." She looked out at the street. "Briefing's been pushed back until tomorrow. I had something I thought you'd want to come along for, though."

"What?" he said before taking a sip. The tea burned his tongue, and he spit it out.

"Sorry. I like it sizzling hot," Billie said, staring at something down on the street below.

"That's like lava boiled inside a microwaved Hot Pocket," he said, rubbing his tongue against his cheek as he set the cup down on the kitchen counter. "What are we doing?"

"We're going to visit an old friend of yours. Bigfoot Tommy."

Anxiety hit his stomach, like something slick and cold had crawled down his throat. That was a name he hadn't heard aloud in years.

Thomas Cole Addison, better known by his road name, Bigfoot Tommy, on account of his massive size, was one of the scariest people

Solomon had ever met. His mother was known in local biker culture as an "ole lady." Meaning a woman taken as the personal property of one of the bikers. The ole ladies were given patches stating they were the club's property and naming the individual biker who had claimed them. Kids were the primary duty of the ole ladies.

Sometimes they were good mothers, and other times they abandoned their children to the club and let the gang raise the child. Unfortunately, Bigfoot Tommy had been raised by one of the most violent biker gangs in the southwest United States.

He had been a suspect in the original Reaper case. His Harley had been spotted in front of the Farringtons' home the night the couple and their three children were murdered. Bigfoot Tommy was brought in for questioning. Billie's father did the interrogation himself but couldn't break him, and neither could the FBI. Tommy was too far gone into the club to ever speak to law enforcement.

Bigfoot Tommy fit the profile of a ruthless killer gone off the rails. Severe mental illness, early childhood abuse, and brain injuries throughout his life from motorcycle accidents. A perfect storm of interior and exterior factors in creating a killer. Solomon had tried to prosecute him before for another crime, but the victim changed her story and the case was dropped.

Despite using R and I to survey Bigfoot Tommy and his crew for weeks, they'd never found enough evidence to affirmatively link him to any of the murders.

Solomon got dressed and then met Billie out in the hall. "And what's our old pal been up to?" he asked, locking his door.

"He's on parole for something new."

"Why am I not surprised?"

"I seem to remember hearing something about the last time you two talked. It apparently didn't end well."

They walked down the hall toward the elevators. "We almost came to blows. Though considering he outweighs me by a hundred pounds, it would've been the world's quickest fight."

35

She chuckled. "This is why women make better cops. We don't get into pissing matches with everybody." She looked him over as they waited for the elevator. "I think you should wear a tie."

"Why?"

"It gives you gravitas with guys like these. You can't look like them. They won't take you as an authority."

He grumbled something and said "Hang on" before going back into his apartment and throwing on a black sports coat and a gray tie.

Once they were in the truck, Solomon kept fidgeting with his tie. He hadn't worn one since he had quit, and it didn't feel right on him now.

He flipped through the court documents and police reports on Bigfoot Tommy's most recent case to distract himself as they drove. Tommy had tried to kill one of his underlings suspected of skimming profits from the prostitution rackets. Bigfoot Tommy hung him upside down naked and cut him with a machete. The underling's girlfriend had called out for help from other club members, and Tommy attacked his own men while high out of his mind on meth. One biker held up his hand to block the machete from swinging down into his head, and it split his hand in half.

Not a single person, even the man who had been hung upside down and tortured, would testify against Tommy. So he pled to a lesser charge of felon in possession of a dangerous weapon, which violated his parole, and he was locked up for three months before being rereleased.

Bigfoot Tommy lived on the city's outskirts near massive copper mines and vast fields of nothing but tall grass. It was a colossal house with about the most dilapidated lawn Solomon had ever seen. Yellowed grass and dirt overtook most of it. Motorcycle parts the rest.

A short biker with dark glasses sat on the porch steps smoking a joint. A girl who was clearly high and nodding off sat next to him.

"Smoking kills," Solomon said as they walked up the lawn to the house.

"Shit, everything kills."

"Amen, brother."

The man spit. "I know you cops. Y'all look the same. Unless you have a warrant, piss off."

Solomon looked at Billie and said, "I knew I shouldn't have put the tie on." He turned back to the man, who was passing the joint to the girl. Her hand shook as she inhaled a puff and held it before blowing it out. It had an acrid chemical smell, like burning plastic. He knew the marijuana had been sprinkled with heroin or crushed pills.

Billie said, "Tell Thomas to come out."

"Why?"

"It's better we speak with him directly. And if we don't speak with him here, we can speak at the station. But it's easier to talk to him now."

He nudged the girl next to him, and her eyes went wide as she shoved him back, fully awake now.

"Go get Tommy," he barked. "Tell him the cops are here."

She cursed at him and said, "Get him yourself."

"I swear if you don't get your ass up and—"

"And what? Huh? Do it and see what happens, you loser." She shoved him again and stormed into the house.

"Trouble in paradise?" Solomon said.

He put the joint out and stuffed the remainder of it into a vest pocket. "She'll get him. Just gotta throw a hissy first."

A moment later, Bigfoot Tommy was standing at the front door.

Solomon pondered whether it was possible for a grown man to keep growing, because he thought Bigfoot Tommy looked even bigger than the last time he'd seen him. Over six foot five and puffed up with muscles that bulged under a black vest with no shirt, he had a bald head and white goatee that revealed he was older than he looked. Even indoors, he'd been wearing sunglasses, and he took them off as he came over. A sign that he would look them in the eye without fear.

Tommy chuckled and folded his arms, and Solomon thought he looked like the Jolly Green Giant.

"Counselor," he said politely.

"Bigfoot."

"I heard you got shanked in court. Laughed my ass off. Gotta always watch your six, brother."

Solomon held up his cane. "Yeah, but now I get this conversation starter to carry around with me. Chicks dig it."

"I remember you bein' funny." He shook his head and made a snap sound with his cheek against his teeth. "Shit, though, I was hopin' it put you in a wheelchair."

"Yeah, well, I'm sure a lot of rapist tweakers were disappointed."

Bigfoot Tommy tilted his head like a dog seeing something curious. Solomon knew he had no fear of the badge or prison. And a man who wasn't afraid of prison was a man who had already been through something worse.

Solomon felt a shard of fear and got angry at the fear. But he swallowed it down and didn't show anything on his face.

"You know why we're here, don't you?"

Tommy nodded. "Them murders I heard about was the same as the ones you tried to put on me."

"I knew you wouldn't disappoint me, Bigfoot." Solomon leaned on the cane. "Do I even need to ask where you were that night?"

"I was here all night, and there's thirty people who'll tell you the same."

"We didn't tell you the date yet."

He grinned. "Whenever it was, I was here. Go ahead and ask these two."

"That doesn't really interest me. What interests me is poking around your house a little. If you've got weapons in the house, specifically handguns, I'd like to take a look at them. If you got nothing to hide, you've got nothing to lose letting us search."

"I ain't stupid. I'm on parole and ain't supposed to have guns. You ain't searchin' shit. I'm callin' my lawyer. Now you got somethin' to arrest me for or not?"

"No," Billie said. "We don't. Thank you for your time." She took Solomon's arm. "Let's go, Solomon."

"Yeah," Tommy said, "listen to your bitch."

Billie tightened her grip. "Come on, let's go."

"Hey," Tommy shouted, "you pretty hot. You ever thought of makin' some videos? We got a studio inside."

Solomon pulled away from her. He stepped up to Tommy and stared into his pupils. "I know you raped that girl, no matter what she changed her story to. But, I swear to you, you'll go down for it eventually. And you'll never see the outside of a cell again."

Tommy leaned forward, a grin coming over his prodigious face. "You got something on me, then use it."

The two men glared at each other a moment, and then Solomon turned away and headed back for the truck. He heard Tommy shout something like, "That's what I thought, gimpy," and then laughter from the couple who had sat out on the porch steps.

"Man, I hate that guy," Solomon said as he got into the passenger seat.

She sighed. "He's a lost cause."

He leaned his cane between his legs as she started the truck. Bigfoot Tommy stood on the porch and watched until they had turned around and driven off.

Solomon said, "I don't know. Seems like if he wanted someone killed, he'd send that guy on the porch to do it. He wouldn't risk doing it himself. Especially a couple of retirees and an Uber driver with nothing valuable. He would have a motive for killing, and I'm not sure there is one here."

"Maybe. I told you, busywork is better than no work."

Solomon watched a man in a white sweatshirt on a cell phone absentmindedly rushing across an intersection. He nudged a woman out of his way on the other side and almost made her fall. He ignored her and kept walking as she shouted at him.

"You had breakfast?" Billie asked.

7

They were seated at a diner near the courthouse. One they used to have lunch at all the time while discussing cases when Solomon still worked across the street.

The place had changed. The menu had gone from barbecue to vegan salads and sandwiches, and the walls had a fresh coat of white paint. The tables were new as well. The diner looked like it had just opened. The only thing that betrayed its age was the floor, marked up from decades of chairs scraping against it.

Once they had ordered with the server, Solomon said, "Your dad would always tell me about how he didn't want you to follow him into being sheriff. He really didn't want this life for you. So what made you dive in?"

"I don't know, honestly. I just knew that grad school wasn't for me. There was something so . . . reactive about it. Police work is proactive. You feel like you're actually doing something."

He smiled. "Making a difference, changing the world . . . yeah, I had the same illusions. It's not feasible for one person to make that much of a difference, though."

"If you really believed that, you wouldn't be sitting here with me."

The server brought their drinks. Billie set her phone down on the table and pushed it out of her view to the side. "After seeing him today, I don't think Tommy's our man. He's too obvious. The person we're after is cold and calculating. They left almost nothing at the scenes and have taken a lot of precautions to not get caught."

Solomon nodded. "Tommy feels he has so much power, he has nothing to be afraid of. If he wanted someone dead, he'd be far less clandestine about it, and there would be more witnesses. There's always a witness." He glanced at the couple sitting at the table next to them, arguing over some comment made in the conversation earlier. "I did notice something interesting in the file, though."

"What?" she said, taking a sip of coffee.

"The Uber driver, Bobby Larson. He was killed six blocks from where the cab driver was killed eight years ago. The Murrays were killed in practically the same spot as the Wagners. Why not kill Larson in the same spot as the cabbie? Why six blocks away?"

"I'm sure you've got a theory."

"My theory is that he couldn't kill Larson at the same spot because there were people there. Which means someone might've seen him. Maybe somebody walking by, like someone who lives in the neighborhood. We need to canvass every house and apartment building within a few miles."

She hesitated instead of replying, and he knew what was wrong.

"What's the budget on this?"

"I'll get decent resources, but wanting to canvass dense city blocks is going to take more men than I have to spare."

"Then let's call up the police academy. Those noobs need some real-world experience anyway."

She shrugged and took another sip of her coffee. "Not the worst idea."

The server brought their omelets. Solomon took a few bites. He closed his eyes and made a moan of pure pleasure.

"You cannot believe how much better food tastes fresh from the grill at a restaurant rather than ordering it and having it dropped at your door."

"When was the last time you went out to eat?"

The waitress came back just then and said, "How is everything?"

"Really good, thank you," he said. Glad for the interruption.

Solomon inhaled the omelet, but Billie just moved some of the food around on her plate.

"You not gonna eat that?" he asked.

She pushed the plate across to him. "All yours."

As she watched him pour Tabasco over the omelet, she said, "My father said you have some interesting theories on criminal psychology."

"You didn't read my book? I'm hurt."

"It's on my shelf. It's pretty dense."

He shrugged as he took a bite of hash browns and spoke with his mouth full. "Depends what you mean by interesting."

"My father said he doesn't really understand them."

He grinned. "Zach's a practical guy. Theory doesn't interest him much."

A moment passed where he ate but didn't say anything.

"So, are you going to tell me?"

He leaned back in the chair and watched her for a second. "Can I ask you something? Why are you out here? People become sheriff so they don't have to do crap like this."

"I asked you a question first."

He soaked her remaining omelet in Tabasco. "I don't think all psychopaths have similar characteristics. The *DSM* doesn't even recognize psychopathy as a disorder. It's labeled antisocial personality disorder. But that doesn't capture the different shades of the disorder."

"Shades?" she said as she put some sweetener in her coffee.

He nodded. "One percent of the general population suffer from psychopathy, but if you look at the different professions, there's much higher and lower numbers. For example, CEOs have four percent, politicians six percent, and law enforcement seven percent. So to say that someone suffering from psychopathy who's homeless and can't hold a job is the same as the CEO of a Fortune 500 company is myopic. So, I wrote my book recategorizing the different shades of psychopathy. Category one to thirteen. But I had to add a different category in a later edition."

"Category zero. I do remember that."

"Yeah, category zero. Someone born with no remorse, high intelligence, and a controllable urge to kill. Killing only when they have the least likelihood of getting caught. See, we only know about the serial murderers we've caught, so modern criminal psychology extrapolates what all serial murderers must be like based on the ones we have in custody. But how many are too smart to get caught? We'll never know. But I have a hunch their pathology is far scarier."

"Where does the Reaper fall?"

"Category zero. No incentive to kill other than the killing itself. A person who only wants the world to die. Every culture has a term for a person like that. The earliest reference I found was *umilac*. It's an ancient Sumerian word that doesn't have an equivalent translation. The closest thing we have is *boogeyman*, but that doesn't compare to the implication the Sumerians were trying to get across. It roughly translates to *bleeding soul*. It's the rarest type of human being there is."

"How does that help you—"

Billie's cell phone vibrated, and she said "Excuse me" as she picked it up. After a few seconds of conversation with whoever was on the other end, she said to Solomon, "I need to run." She took out a laminated swipe card and slid it to him. "That'll get you in and out of the office I set up for you."

"I don't think the good people at the County Attorney's Office would appreciate me popping in to—"

"Not at the County Attorney's Office. You are officially a 1099 consultant for the Tooele County Sheriff's Office."

"Officially? So does that officially come with cash?"

"Two hundred dollars per day."

He went to say something, and she quickly added, "And no, we won't give you an allowance for alcohol."

He took the card. "Everybody asks that, I take it?"

She grinned. "Yes. But I would've gone to two fifty. You need to be more assertive, Solomon."

8

When Solomon got home, he went to the silver-plated mailboxes—the rich couldn't have just any metal, of course—in a room on the first floor and retrieved his mail. Bills, a few advertisements, a request for donations as an alum of Cornell University's criminology program. He put a few in the recycling bin before heading up to his apartment.

He took a brief shower, letting cold water make him shiver. He preferred quick, cold showers that had him in and out without long periods of contemplation.

After his shower, he fed Russ, then got some cheese and fruit and was watching television when he heard shouting coming from the apartment down the hall. Kelly's apartment. Travis was shouting at the top of his lungs, and Maria shouted back. Giving as good as she was getting. Solomon went to his door and looked out the peephole. Kelly sat outside in the hallway near her door. She had on earbuds, and her head was leaned back against the wall. Her eyes held something that instantly made him feel sorry for her: she looked much older than her sixteen years.

Solomon opened the door. Kelly looked up at him, her eyes red and puffy. They stared at each other for a second, and then Solomon motioned with his head and opened the door all the way. Kelly rose and came inside.

They ate popcorn and drank Dr Pepper while they watched a show about a murder in a small town where the sheriff was the sole suspect. Solomon sat in the recliner, and Kelly sat cross-legged on the couch. When the show was over, she held her soda can and ran the tip of her finger around the lip.

"My mom told me she and my dad never fought even once," she said. "But with everyone she's been with since, it's like a war." She wiped her nose with her sleeve. "My mom's never been happy. Do you think some people are born unhappy?"

Solomon put the bowl of popcorn on a side table. "No, I don't believe that. I think the goal of life is to change money for time, not time for money. Because we all run out of time first. People don't realize that and waste their lives, and by the—excuse the pun—*time* they figure it out, it might be too late. Their lives are on autopilot."

"Ew. Don't do puns again." She hesitated a second as she took a sip of her drink and then returned to staring at it. "Is that what you do? Exchange your money for time?"

"Well," he said, glancing to his cane, "I've got a lot more time than most nowadays."

She played with the can and made it crinkle as she gripped it. "Why don't you go out anymore?"

"I went out today."

"Yeah, but before that was like months ago. And the store's not that far. Why do you have me go?"

Partly, it was that Solomon didn't like leaving the apartment. Once, his chest had constricted into a panic attack, and he had to sit down on the curb for a full half hour before things got back to normal. There was another incident when he was walking down the hall and nearly blacked out when he couldn't see his apartment anymore.

That was part of the explanation, the part he didn't mind Kelly knowing about. What he would never tell her was that he needed an excuse to make sure Kelly had money. He had heard her stepfather shouting at her that he wouldn't give her a dime for anything, but she was getting a 4.0 GPA and didn't want to risk it declining because of a job that took up too many hours. Her grades were her plan to get out of here.

"Is it because you got hurt? Is that why you don't go out? Is all that shit back?"

He used his cane to stand up. "I don't think it ever left."

She sniffled as Solomon got a box of tissues off the kitchen counter and handed them to her.

"Thanks," she said, taking a few and blowing her nose. "I've been hurt really bad before, too. It sucks. You're so mad, but there's nothing you can do. You just wanna hurt them back so bad that you forget everything else." She looked at him as he sat on the arm of the recliner with both hands leaning on his cane. "You told me someone in court hurt you, but you never talk about it. What happened?"

His upper lip suddenly felt dry, and he quickly slid his tongue over it, memories flooding his mind like they were being poured in from the outside. Memories he didn't want. But sometimes, it felt like he had no partitions in his mind. Every thought mixed with every other thought, and sometimes it was distasteful.

"It was a defendant in a case. Nasty dude."

"What'd he do?"

Solomon softly tapped the tip of his cane against the hardwood floors. "I was talking to the jury with my back turned to him. He ran up behind me with something sharp he'd made in his cell and stabbed me in the back, in the spinal cord."

"Whoa. Did it hurt?"

He grinned. Only a child would ask a question like that. "Not at first, but later, yeah. A lot."

She crumpled the tissues in her palms and didn't speak for a little while. "Can I sleep here tonight?"

"Kelly—"

"I know, teenage girl sleeping at a middle-aged man's house—"

"Middle age? I'm in my prime, young lady."

"Whatever, geezer. You were alive before there was internet. Which blows my mind, BTW."

"Yeah, back then, you couldn't just read anything with a few clicks. You had to follow smart people around and hope they said something intelligent." He went to a closet in the hallway and took out a blanket and pillow. Tossing them on the couch, he said, "You get the couch."

He turned the lights off and headed to his bedroom.

"Solomon?" she said from the couch, already underneath the blanket. Solomon could see from the moonlight that she was staring out the window, her face lit a dull blue along with the rest of the apartment.

"Thanks," she said, and he could tell she meant it.

He stood watching her. He felt sorry for her and had to constantly hide it. To be pitied was one of the worst feelings in the world. He knew it better than anyone.

"No problem." He tapped his cane once against the floor and then limped into his bedroom.

9

The briefing Billie had sprung on him two days ago had been rescheduled for this morning. The county attorney had a prior engagement he couldn't get out of the previous morning. Solomon figured that probably meant an appointment with a donor to his reelection campaign or a television interview.

The Tooele County Justice Center wasn't as large as the County Attorney's and Sheriff's Offices of many cities, even in Utah, but it was bigger than Solomon remembered. It also housed the offices of the city council and mayor in the same building, and it looked like another building had gone up next to it for emergency services.

The current county attorney, Knox Scott, who was a section head when Solomon worked here, stood at the head of the conference room on the third floor speaking on a cell phone. With feathery red hair, freckles, and abnormally pale skin, if he wore a white suit, it was difficult to tell where the suit ended and his skin began.

Solomon stood at the doorway. He recognized some of the faces but didn't recognize a lot more. Criminal law, from either side, was a demanding profession. The lawyers saw and dealt with the worst humans would do to their fellow humans. Unlike other people, who could turn away, they had to force themselves to look and keep working despite whatever they felt.

Most lawyers couldn't hack it for long and switched to something less stressful, like small claims, collections, personal injury, or social security benefits. Fields where they wouldn't have to be reminded what people were capable of doing to each other. Being a social worker with the prison population hadn't been much different.

The conference room was a good size, meant to hold two dozen people. Solomon remembered they'd used it as the Reaper Task Force HQ in the original case. Boxes were piled up against the walls then. Folders overflowing with paperwork that spilled onto the floor and a general stench of sweat and coffee.

The conference room was spotless now, with a flat-screen television taking up the space where a whiteboard used to be. High-backed black leather chairs had replaced beat-up upholstered ones. The floor-to-ceiling windows were freshly cleaned, and the carpet vacuumed. It felt sterile: like it was being shown to potential tenants rather than being a real working space.

Solomon leaned against the wall. He noticed a couple of the prosecutors looking at his cane, and he held it between his hands, lightly tapping the tip on the carpet.

A young prosecutor, a kid with shaggy brown hair and a disheveled suit, offered him a seat.

"Prefer to stand, thanks. I can sneak out of here faster if I need to."

"Not a fan of meetings, huh?"

"Let's just say there was a lotta Angry Birds played at the meetings I used to attend."

"Angry Birds?"

"Yeah. The game where you shoot birds at pigs? I'm not that old, am I?"

The kid stared at him blankly, and Solomon shook his head. "College really has killed this generation's spirit, hasn't it?"

"All right, everybody," a voice boomed from the front of the room. County Attorney Knox Scott stood with his cell phone in hand. "Let's have a seat."

The prosecutors still standing took spots at the table. A few detectives sat with Billie on folding chairs near the back of the room.

"Tell us you got something, boss," a man with a gray beard near the middle of the table said.

"We got something." He pushed a button on a remote, and the television on the wall behind him came to life. "It was received at the offices of the *Herald-Tribune* last night, and they rushed it over to the Sheriff's Office."

On the screen was a photo of a handwritten letter. The script was elegant. Somewhere between Asian calligraphy and medieval copperplate writing. There was deep beauty to the symmetry, and Solomon guessed it took a long time to write even short paragraphs so exquisitely.

The original Reaper letter was written in the same handwriting. Four pages' worth, complete with literary and artistic references that would make any English professor proud.

The new letter said,

> This is Reaper speaking. I wanted to make sure you trusted me because we're going to have to trust each other now. The envelope this letter came in was sealed. The seal has Mrs. Murray's blood in it. Test it and you'll see.

A few people shook their heads in disgust, a few seemed almost titillated, but most appeared like they weren't paying attention. They had to fill a seat at an all-staff meeting and then get back to the stacks of case files on their desks as soon as they could.

Victor Methos

Knox said, "Sheriff, where are we on testing the blood?"

Billie glanced at Solomon before saying, "The crime lab is doing a rush analysis. We should have the preliminary results by tomorrow afternoon."

"Just keep me in the loop. Peter, where are we on witnesses? We found anyone who saw anything at the Murray or the Larson scenes?"

In the back, a detective in a flashy blue sports coat said, "No one yet. A lot of folks just don't wanna talk. They're scared their name could be all over the news the next day."

"I don't care. Larson was shot while parked at the damn curb next to an apartment building. Somebody saw something. Keep at it. Go in the middle of the night if they won't answer during the day. Talk to them three or four times, and let's make sure they don't know anything."

Before he could stop himself, Solomon said, "You don't have to harass them to get them to talk. There's better ways."

The room went quiet as everybody turned to him. Suddenly, his face grew hot. He hadn't spoken to a room filled with so many people in so many years that it felt physically painful to him. His chest constricted, and breathing became difficult.

"Mr. Shepard," Knox said with a wry smile, "the sheriff didn't tell me you'd be joining us."

"Probably didn't want to ruin the pleasant surprise."

"I'm sure. So, you were saying something about telling my detectives how to do their jobs?"

His heart beat faster, but he tried to keep his face passive. "I'm not telling anybody how to do their jobs. I'm just telling you what I know. Those people, if they did see anything, are scared. You hit them up four or five times, and there's no way they tell you anything but to piss off, even if they remember something later."

Knox, without taking his eyes off Solomon, said, "For those of you who weren't here at the time, Mr. Shepard was the assistant chief section head of the Major Crimes Division before he retired. He even wrote a book on the categorization of murderers that I believe went on to sell at least a hundred copies, isn't that right, Mr. Shepard?"

A few people grinned but didn't laugh. The attention focused on Solomon felt like a laser burning into his skin. The tickle of sweat forming on his brow distracted him, and he tried to focus on that. Knox had absolute glee in his eyes.

Once deputy county attorneys hit their six-month mark, they could only be fired for cause, and the county council had to approve it. Knox had tried to get him fired twice and failed both times.

People in the office said it stemmed from a conflict of personalities, but Solomon knew that wasn't it. He'd racked up several significant convictions on cases with a lot of press, and the reporters wanted to interview him more than Knox, his direct supervisor, who came across as stiff and unlikable.

Also, Knox's wife had hit on Solomon on more than one occasion. After a few drinks at the office Christmas party, she'd confided that he looked like one of her old boyfriends from high school who had died in a car crash. It creeped Solomon out, but he'd never had the heart to say anything.

Knox hadn't visited Solomon in the hospital, just sent an unsigned card via his paralegal.

Solomon felt the constriction in his chest again. "Excuse me, I need to use the restroom."

He was out in the hall in a flash, sucking breath like he had been underwater. He sat down on a bench against the wall. Billie came out. She sat across from him on another bench and didn't say a word. Not until his breathing had calmed.

"Not the welcome you expected?" she said.

"No, that's about what I expected."

"He's a terrible person and a worse prosecutor, but he knows how to get the county council to give us funds when we need. That's an invaluable skill."

He leaned his head back against the wall. "What the hell am I doing, Billie? I don't belong here."

"You have invaluable skills, too."

He scoffed, "Yeah, right. Panic attacks in a roomful of lawyers and cops doesn't really qualify as a skill."

"My father is probably the most critical person I've ever known. He's not a man who compliments easily. And he asked you to be the screening prosecutor on this personally because he knew you could help."

"Whatever your dad thinks he saw in me that could help with this was random chance, not skill." He rose. "I'm sorry, I can't do this anymore."

10

Melinda Toby was sitting with her feet up on the front desk at the nurses' station when she received the call. The high school again. Her stomach dropped. This was the third call in two weeks. She glanced down the corridor to make sure no one was around.

"Yes?" she said with a tinge of hope in her voice that it was something mundane.

"Melinda, it's Brooklyn. I'm afraid there's some trouble."

"I figured." She sighed.

"Can you come down after school for a conversation?"

"You know what, Brooklyn, you guys call me down to that damn school every time he does something even a little bit disobedient, knowing I have work."

"We don't mean to drag you down here all the time."

"It sure as hell feels like it." She took her feet off the desk and leaned her elbows on it, one hand going over her eyes. A futile attempt to prevent the headache she knew was imminent.

"Just tell me. What now?"

"I'm afraid it's serious this time. During his PE class about an hour ago . . . well, it's probably best you come down."

She hung up without saying goodbye and grabbed her purse before heading out of the hospital.

South High School was a long way from her home and just as far from
the hospital. But it was the only school that would take Braden. He'd
been kicked out of three high schools, and homeschooling had become
a real possibility, but the schedule just couldn't align with how many
shifts she worked. So the only other option was South High. A place
for kids to go who couldn't go anywhere else.

The building was old and had a majestic look incongruent with the
surrounding neighborhood of liquor stores and gas stations. Like a relic
from another age that the city had forgotten to tear down.

Melinda parked and went inside, checking for stains on her scrubs
and finding none. A long hallway led to the administrative offices. The
receptionist saw her and said, "She'll be right out."

Melinda sat on a couch against the wall. A boy sat near her, looking down at the floor. He appeared maybe fifteen. He looked terrified.

"What are you here for?" she asked, attempting to be friendly.

"They said I cheated on a test."

"Oh. Did you?"

He nodded.

"It's okay. Everyone cheats a little sometimes."

"My dad . . ."

Though he didn't finish the sentence, Melinda could guess what was
coming next. The boy was almost shaking.

"Melinda, thanks for coming down." Brooklyn stood in front of
her. She was a smaller woman with short hair and a blue suit that looked
too big on her. Melinda had always felt she looked down on her but
could never tell why.

Melinda rose and adjusted the strap of her purse over her shoulder.
"Didn't seem like I had much choice."

Brooklyn ignored the comment and led her back to the principal's
office. They sat across from each other, and Melinda took in how much

messier the office appeared than the last time she had been here. Boxes and papers were stacked everywhere, with decorations overstuffing the walls wherever there was space. An odor of lemon air freshener to cover up sweat produced from a recent heat wave.

"It's not good this time. Someone was badly injured."

"Who?"

"His name is Garrett Nooms. We have an archery class here. An elective as part of the PE requirement. But the arrows are soft rubber, like Nerf guns." She cleared her throat. "Braden made a modification to it, and it . . . hit Garrett in the eye. He's at the emergency room now, and they're not sure if he's going to keep his eye or not."

Melinda was speechless.

"What happened?" she finally asked.

"Braden says it was an accident. That he was aiming for the target, and his hand slipped and shot the arrow far to the right. It's possible, so I don't want you to think he's flat out lying. But in speaking to the other students in the class, it seems unlikely it was an accident. But even if it was, with the modifications he made—"

"How could he modify it? What does that mean?"

Brooklyn cleared her throat and interlaced her fingers on her desk. "He peeled the foam away and then taped a sharpened sliver of pen on the end. He said it was so he could shoot the trees behind the school, but . . . we were very clear that modification was not allowed. He says that Garrett was too close to the target, and the arrow went wide and hit his eye."

"What did Garrett say?"

"Pretty much the same story. Almost too much so."

"What do you mean?"

"I mean down to the exact details."

As two mothers, they didn't have to probe any further as to what was meant. There was more going on here than the adults would likely ever know about.

"I'll, um, get Braden and we'll go down to the hospital and apologize. And I'll cover the boy's medical bills."

"I'm afraid that won't be enough. The police were called. I gave them your contact info and they said they would be in touch."

Melinda swallowed and felt dizzy.

"You all right?"

"Fine," she said, rising and nearly tripping over the chair. "Just please have Braden come out to the parking lot."

She got to the front steps and thought she might vomit. Inhaling a deep breath with her eyes glued to the sky as a class of seniors walked by, all she could think was, *Not again.*

11

The streets shimmered under the moonlight. Solomon hadn't even noticed that it had started sprinkling rain. He'd been staring at the sidewalk as he shuffled along the city streets. Something he hadn't done in so long that it felt like being on the surface of another planet.

He stopped in at a bookstore on the corner. The smell of old books in the used section took him back a long way. To libraries from childhood where a book could take him out of wherever he was, no matter how horrible, to someplace better.

He browsed the sociology and true crime sections, then the philosophy and conspiracy theory sections. He noticed his book on a shelf next to a biography of Charles Manson.

A bearded man next to him flipping through a book about the Armenian genocide whispered, "I wouldn't get that one" as he nodded toward Solomon's book.

"Really? I heard it's brilliant."

He shook his head. "*They* keep track of who buys what books and that's on their shit list. They don't want you knowing the truth. You buy that book, you might as well set up a bull's-eye on your back."

The man reached out and grabbed Solomon's wrist.

"They'll come for you, too. And you'll have to decide whether to join or get put into a body bag."

He let go of Solomon's wrist, turned away, and wandered off to another section while mumbling to himself.

"He's harmless," said a woman with brunette hair stacking books down the aisle.

"I had a foster father who used to say the people you think are harmless are the ones crazier than a shoeshine in a shitstorm."

She chuckled. "No, he really is harmless." She stopped what she was doing and looked at him. "I think he gets lonely and comes here to talk with people. Wish that's all it took to make somebody happy, huh?" She put the last of her books on the shelf. "I'm Angela, by the way."

"Solomon."

"I like that name." She smiled. "See ya around."

"Yeah, see ya," he said as he watched her walk away. He wanted to say something, maybe even ask her if she wanted to grab some tea or a drink. But the words wouldn't come out. It'd been so long he wasn't certain how exactly to ask without sounding creepy.

He left the bookstore. The man was outside now, sitting on a stone bench. As though they shared a secret, he nodded once, and Solomon nodded back before summoning an Uber.

12

Billie finished up some paperwork at the office and stretched her neck and arms. It'd been a fourteen-hour day, and her feet felt like she'd been walking on hot coals. She slipped her shoes off with an exhalation of relief and rubbed the cramp in her calf.

Someone came to her door, and she looked up to see Knox Scott with a file in his hand. He tossed it on her desk before sitting down across from her.

"Picked up the blood results for you on the way down. Blood on the envelope is a match to Allyx Murray."

She nodded, knowing it would be. "You could've texted me that."

"I suppose."

"What do you really want, Knox?"

"Maybe I like the glow of your charming personality?"

She leaned back in the seat. "My feet hurt, my legs hurt, I've got cramps, I'm starving, and I've cried twice today for no reason. I want to go home. So just tell me why you're here."

"You know why I'm here," he said, straightening a framed picture on her desk. "Why didn't you tell me you were bringing Shepard in?"

"I didn't know he would accept."

"You should've asked me."

"You're not my boss, Knox. I don't answer to you."

He grinned. "Calm down. I didn't come here to argue. I'm not your boss, and you're not mine, but we can make each other's lives miserable. Mutually assured destruction. So, I'm not looking to get into a pissing match. I want to know why."

"My dad said he's the best homicide prosecutor you ever had. That he knows how these guys think."

"That's not a benefit, Elizabeth. That's what your father never got about him. It clouds his thinking so that he gets obsessed with cases he should deal on and deals on cases he should take to trial. That's why I told the county council to let me fire him."

"Is that why, or is it because your wife got drunk and tried to sleep with him and he turned her down?"

His face flushed pink, but he remained motionless. "That's not what happened." He stared at her a moment. "You've never liked Michelle. Why?"

She inhaled deeply, debating whether to tell him to get the hell out of her office. "Some people just don't click."

"Suppose so," he said, smirking. He ran his finger along the edge of her desk and then made a point of looking at the dust on his finger before wiping it off. "I don't want him anywhere near this prosecution when we find this man."

"He's a consultant for my office, not yours. Relax, Knox. You won't be seeing much of him."

He nodded and stood. "I better not. Mutually assured destruction. Don't forget that."

When he left, she got out a tissue and wiped the section of her desk he'd run his finger over.

Billie grabbed her jacket and headed out of the station. The parking lot didn't have good lighting, and at night it was tough to see into the far corners where she liked to park. She could hear two patrolmen talking in between cruisers. They didn't seem to notice her as they laughed about something, but she couldn't make out exactly what. Though she did hear the words "That's what happens when you work for a woman."

Billie swallowed down the embarrassment; it wasn't the first time she had heard deputies or detectives speaking about her behind her back. She walked by, forced a smile, and waved. They waved back, and one of them said, "Night, Sheriff."

"Night."

Police culture wasn't all that different from military culture, Billie had been told. The ideal was to be macho and tough and not afraid of anything. Act first and think later. Women, in general, took the opposite approach, and it didn't sit right with many of her deputies and detectives.

Detectives would ask for approval to raid a known drug den, and Billie would instead put it under surveillance for a week or two. A prostitution ring moved into town, and her deputy sheriff and section chiefs would want to round up all the prostitutes and force the pimps to bail them out. Instead, she set up careful stings to arrest the pimps and traffickers and leave the girls alone, which took longer and involved weeks of surveillance but so far, she felt, had achieved longer-lasting results. Her approach had nevertheless earned her a lot of animosity from those who preferred to do things the way they'd always done them, and she was never quite sure what to do about it.

The fact that she had attended a year of graduate school and appeared like an intellectual to many didn't help.

It was nearly ten when she parked in her driveway and got out. All the lights in her home were off except in the master bedroom. As quietly as possible, she snuck in and kicked off her shoes.

Dax was sleeping on his side with the covers down by his knees. Billie turned off the light and shut the bedroom door so he wouldn't wake.

She could hear the television from the living room as she went to the fridge and pulled out some leftover pasta and a soda. Dax frequently forgot to turn it off: something that drove her crazy, as she'd grown up in a home always on a tight budget.

They hadn't gotten used to each other's rhythms. He'd asked to move in, and she had said she'd prefer to take it slow, but it seemed like he was always here now anyway.

She turned off the TV and took her food and soda to her office.

On the east wall of the small room was a whiteboard. Hanging on the left were photos of all the Reaper's victims, and on the bottom right were Otto and Allyx Murray and Bobby Larson.

The photos of the Farringtons always caught her eye first. An entire family, five people, dead for no reason anybody sane could understand. Their two youngest were boys, four and six years old.

She took a few bites of pasta and then popped open the soda before leaning back in the desk chair and staring at the photos. Only one phrase kept running through her mind, the exact phrase that always did when she was confronted with crimes that seemed incomprehensible.

What do you want?

"You okay?"

The voice startled her. She turned to see Dax standing in his boxers at the door. His hair was pressed down on one side.

"I'm fine. Just tired. How was your day?"

He came in and sat down on the couch, picking up a signed baseball that she kept on a stand near the sofa. "Same." Dax looked at the photos up on the whiteboard and stared at the one that showed Bobby Larson slumped against his steering wheel with a massive hole in his face.

"Do you really need those up at home?"

"It's the job."

He tossed the baseball from one hand into the other.

Dax had been married once before, and occasionally she caught him falling back into patterns he'd explained had led to his divorce. He'd been too possessive in his youth, and his wife, who had been his high school sweetheart, left him one day and moved to another city. "Well, maybe the job should be something else," he said.

"Seriously? You want to argue at this hour?"

He glanced at the mangled and bloody bodies. "Do you enjoy seeing that all day?"

Billie didn't answer right away. "If I did, I wouldn't do what I do." She rose and sat down next to him and took his hand. "Sometimes it feels like too much, but you don't understand what it's like. When we first knew this was the Reaper or someone copying the Reaper, I went into the office at midnight to get some work done because I couldn't sleep."

"I remember."

"What I didn't tell you was when I walked into the room I'd set up for the task force, every detective was there. Every one. No one had gone home. Whatever that thing is that made everybody stay, I have it, too. I can't just leave."

"Yeah, but you're the boss now. You don't have to do this anymore. It's not your responsibility."

She looked up at the photos on the board. "Everything's my responsibility."

Dax planted a kiss on her head before standing. "Don't stay up too late. You didn't sleep much last night."

When she was alone, she thought, *Didn't sleep much . . . if you only knew.*

The truth was she hadn't slept at all last night. Maybe an hour. Instead, she'd come down to the office and done precisely what she was doing now: stared at the photos on the board and hoped something would jump out at her. Some idea, some connection . . . something.

The result was always the same: nothing.

The one thing they had going for them was the Farringtons. The home they had been killed in was still up and lived in, though the police had moved the family who lived there now out to a hotel. The couple who died at the lake after the death of the Farringtons seemed random. Like the killer had simply gone to the lake and killed the first people he saw. Despite constant surveillance and undercover officers posing as swimmers and boaters, they hadn't turned up anything yet. She was terrified she would get a call one day that someone had been killed at the lake while it was still under her surveillance.

So far, the killer was following the original Reaper pattern, and they at least knew where the next killings were supposed to occur: the Farringtons' house. The copycat or whoever it was would have to know that they were prepared for this next move, so how he would get into that house to kill the family kept her from sleeping at night. Once, she'd pictured him showing up to the hotel and killing them there. That night, she drove to the hotel parking lot and slept in her truck outside.

She looked at the photos on the board one more time and then let out a deep breath as she turned to her plate of pasta. She wasn't hungry anymore and rose to put the dish in the sink.

13

Solomon checked the clock twice in an hour.

The third time, near midnight, he realized sleep wasn't coming. He got out of bed and for a second forgot he had to use his cane. It happened every so often, and it stung each time when he remembered.

He put on jeans and a T-shirt and left the apartment. Kelly's place was quiet as he walked by. Once on the street, he enjoyed the night air as he waited for his car. One of the stores on the corner that was out of view from his balcony had changed from a hardware store to a Vietnamese pho restaurant.

Has it really been that long since I've come outside?

Time slipped away from him when he didn't interact with other people. It was like the days and nights melted into each other in one clay block, one day not appearing any different from another.

The car arrived and was driven by a man who spoke the whole time, obviously trying to keep himself awake. He talked about life in his old country and how his father had been a surgeon but worked at a factory when they immigrated here. He spoke of vast fields of tulips, painted crimson and gold. About skies so blue they could hurt your eyes.

"Now," he said in his thick accent, "is nothing."

Solomon stared at the street as he pictured blue skies turning red and fields of tulips withering and dying. The earth opening up and swallowing people who would never be seen again.

"Here?" the driver asked.

"Yeah, that'll be fine."

"You want I wait?"

"No, I don't know how long I'll be."

Solomon got out of the car. It was warmer here than it had been in his neighborhood. He waited until he couldn't hear the engine anymore and then took the short hike to the overpass behind the Murrays' house. Two couples had died right here, eight years apart. Solomon had once heard from a paramedic that while she was helping load a man who'd been hit by a car into the ambulance, the man somehow appeared behind her. Bloody with ragged flesh over his face. He was staring wide eyed at his own body. The paramedic glanced at the body, and when she looked back, the figure was gone. Solomon was nervous whenever he was at murder scenes that he would see the victims standing near him with wide eyes.

How long, he wondered, did the maniac watch the Murrays struggle before killing them? Was he instant, efficient like a snake? Or did he savor it and take his time, tasting their suffering for as long as he could?

Solomon walked to the overpass. He didn't like the sound of his cane against the old cement. It felt like an intruder on his thoughts.

He leaned against the railing. From here, he could see the Murrays' house. All the shutters were closed and the lights off. Soon, he would see a FOR SALE sign in the yard. Neither of their daughters would want to own the house.

Solomon inhaled deeply and closed his eyes. The air here was still and hot, like the initial waft of air when opening a heated oven. He felt his shirt cling to him with sweat, and his heart raced as a sudden wind blew against his face. He pictured Allyx Murray sprinting through dirt, struggling with bare, bleeding feet to escape as wind hit her face, too.

The maniac had run after Allyx.

The moment the thought struck, Solomon unlocked his phone and looked up the weather forecast on the date of the murders. It had been 103 degrees that night. The killer must've been sweating.

Did it trickle down and leave evidence on the victims, or did he wipe it off himself first? Everyone either wiped their sweat off immediately because it bothered them or didn't care and let it soak into their clothes to dry. If he didn't wipe it all off, could some of it have dripped onto the victims?

Solomon felt a shot of adrenaline, and it made his heart race again. His hands would have trembled if he had let them, but he held them together over his cane to prevent movement. This was a moment he had felt before: the first connection between him and the killer. The first fact in the entire case that the killer hadn't purposely given them. The pinch in his chest was the electric current he imagined now linked him to this man.

Billie picked up on the third ring.

"Do you know what time it is?" she said matter-of-factly, like she had been expecting his call. Her voice was alert. He wondered if she had insomnia like he did.

"When are the funerals?"

"Why?"

"It was hot that night, and he'd be sweating. He would've wanted to watch them suffer. They'd be in pain and confused. He'd want to enjoy that rather than just ending it fast. If he stood out here and watched them die for even a few seconds, sweat could've dripped onto Allyx Murray or her husband. There's a professor out of Columbia that's doing some work on using secretions in our sweat to identify suspects in crimes. Everybody's skin secretions are unique, and it doesn't matter if the sweat dried or not." He hesitated when she didn't say anything, and then he added, "I know it's not much, but—"

"No, it's good evidence, Solomon. I'm just tired."

"Who do you have running forensics at SIS these days?"

"Nicole." He heard a dish being put in a sink. "I'll give her a call."

"No. Don't get me wrong, she's great, but Davis is the best. We didn't even know sweat could be used as an identifier until a few months ago, and he stays current on the literature. And we gotta do it tonight. On the off chance there's sweat there, it's already degraded and we can't wait another day."

She sighed. "He's going to be thrilled."

Solomon smiled and said, "Actually, ring me in third line. I wanna hear him screaming at you."

"I'll forgo that little humiliation, but thank you for offering."

"Okay, fine. Then next best thing: send a deputy down to wake him up. He'll have a harder time saying no face-to-face."

"I'll see what I can do, but there's no guarantee he's going to help."

14

Within twenty-four hours of being handed off to the mortuary after the police gave the clearance, corpses needed embalming or could present a public health hazard from the gathering bacteria.

Billie was already waiting for Solomon when his Uber pulled up. The owner of the mortuary had sent his son down to open the place for them. He was a tall, wiry young man with darkly tanned skin everywhere except the white circle around his neck where his necklace blocked his tanning light. He wore shorts and a Hawaiian shirt. Solomon thought he had picked the wrong profession to match his appearance.

"You really think Davis can find sweat after this long?" Billie said.

"I don't know," Solomon said. "But the only chance is if they haven't washed the bodies."

The young man opened the mortuary doors and said, "We were gonna do it in the morning and start the embalming. You're lucky you called tonight. 'Nother few hours and the morning shift woulda started. You ready?"

"We're waiting for someone."

"Oh, okay. I'll just be up front."

The two of them stood outside, listening to the crickets. The mortuary was in an upscale neighborhood, and Solomon figured the victims' families had money. It was high on a mountain overlooking the valley, and the lights sparkled like stars. Far in the distance, he could see the faint glow of the artificial light reflecting off the Great Salt Lake.

An older model Cadillac pulled to a stop in a handicap parking stall.

Davis Browning looked every day of his seventy-one years and got out of the car with a scowl already on his face. The few lights in the parking lot gave his face motion it didn't really have. He was wearing a thin tan coat, though today had easily reached a hundred degrees.

"Can't believe you did that," he said to Solomon and Billie both.

"What?" Solomon said, looking surprised at his anger. "I wanted to see an old friend."

"You sent a deputy to my house to wake me up. Woke up Sheryl, too."

"I knew you'd say no on the phone."

"Damn right I would have."

Billie said, "Solomon wanted the best on this. You are the best, aren't you, Davis?"

He rolled his eyes. "Don't run games on me, Sheriff. I was out here peeling corpses off the streets while you were still playing with Barbies." He checked his watch and said, "Well, I'm here. Where are they?"

———

Billie's office had a couch against the wall that sloped in the middle from nights when it wasn't worth going home with so little time left before sunrise. Solomon lay on it now and stared at the ceiling. Billie handed an iced tea to him and he said, "Your dad had this office decorated like a barbecue restaurant. I'm glad you brought some class to the place."

She sat down on the edge of her desk. "I don't know about class, but I am glad I got rid of that painting of the bull mating with a cow."

"I don't know, nothing really says *country sheriff* like a bull nailing a cow."

She smiled as the phone rang. She put it on speakerphone. "This is Sheriff Gray."

"Sheriff, this is Davis. I was hoping we might be able to get some trace evidence off the bodies. No such luck."

Solomon said, "Davis, you're breaking my heart."

"Well, then this'll get you to fall in love with me again. I managed to track down the nightgown the victim was wearing the night of her death. If any perspiration hasn't completely degraded, I may be able to get something for you."

"See?" Solomon said. "You are the best. Totally worth waking you up over."

"Uh-huh. Don't think I'm not billing for this. And I want gas and meals."

"Meals?" Solomon said. "It's like two in the morning."

Billie said, "You get me a match, and I'll buy you caviar and champagne, Davis."

"Yeah, well, we'll see about that."

15

The café was busy as Solomon stood in front of it. It reminded him of those little Parisian cafés where Hemingway and Zelda Fitzgerald sipped coffee and argued over Tolstoy. He remembered Hemingway once said that it was the best time of his life because he was both really poor and really happy.

Solomon had grown up in extreme poverty, the son of an eccentric professor who drank himself to death. His mother was an artist and didn't have many sources of income, so she ran a séance business talking to the dead relatives of clients who'd seen her ad in the phone book. One of the last things he remembered his mother saying before her suicide was that she had a degree in philosophy and this was what people with philosophy degrees had to do.

The café had a window at the front for walk-up orders. As Solomon stood in line, he saw a slim figure hurrying past him at the periphery of his vision. Kelly. She wore sunglasses and apparently hadn't noticed him as she walked by, so he loudly said, "What're you doing here, young 'un?"

She turned, but there was no surprise on her face. She had seen him; she just didn't want to acknowledge him. "Gotta hurry. My mom's waiting for me," she said as she backed away.

It was too late, though. He'd already seen what she was hoping he wouldn't notice. A deep purple-blue bruise under her left eye, big enough that her sunglasses couldn't hide it.

"Wait a sec," Solomon said. "Kelly, wait a sec."

She stopped in place. He went up to her and lifted her head gently by the chin, and removed her sunglasses.

The black eye was bad. The white of her eye was a deep purple from the blood that had seeped in. Her nose was slightly swollen, and her cheek looked red and tender.

"Do you know how hard someone has to get hit to cause hemorrhaging in the eye?"

"It's nothing," she said as she pulled away.

"I can take care of it with a phone call, Kelly."

"I've already told you I don't need help."

"Obviously," he said, motioning to her eye.

She folded her arms, staring at him now. "So, what, you're gonna get him arrested? Then what? How long is he gonna be in jail for? Long enough for me to turn eighteen and move away?"

Solomon said nothing.

"Yeah," she said, "didn't think so. With his money, he'd be out in a few days, and he would come home and beat the shit outta me and my mom."

Solomon watched her a moment. He didn't think it was fair to have to make this kind of decision at her age.

After a few seconds, her face softened, and she said, "You look good in jeans." She brushed something off his shirt like a mother preparing her son for school.

"I clean up nice sometimes." He glanced at the tables on the veranda. "Come on, I'll buy you a latte."

———

They walked into the café and were seated outside. A young family close by talked about a recent trip to Italy, and a couple ate in silence at the table next to them.

"Are you happy?" Solomon asked after they were seated.

Kelly shrugged. "I don't know. What does that even, like, mean? I'm happy when I drink a latte. Is that happiness?"

"I don't know. I just know that some people are happier than others, and there's some rules you have to live by if you want to be one of those people. The first of those rules is that you cut toxic people out of your life. No matter who they are, friends or family. You can't heal when someone is holding you in place. And toxic blood is not thicker than water."

She gave him a quizzical look. "So, are you asking to go out with me or something?"

"Kelly—"

"I'm kidding. I get it: don't be around shitty people. But I have to protect my mom. Right now, there's two of us. If I moved out and he took all his shit out on just my mom, I don't think she could—"

For the first time, Solomon saw the emotion in her eyes. She had a fierce exterior, but he'd known from the minute he met her that she was protecting a soft core with a hardened shell.

"Would it be okay with you if I talked to your mom? Just explained some of her options?"

She shook her head. "You really think she doesn't know she's getting the shit beat out of her every night and that it's wrong? She knows. She's just not gonna do anything about it."

"I can be very convincing."

"It won't do anything, but if you want to, fine. Travis doesn't get home till eight. Talk to her before then."

The server brought two drinks over, and Kelly stirred some extra sugar into hers.

"I used to come here when I was a prosecutor and would just watch people," he said, staring into the amber-colored tea in his cup. "I thought that if I could hear how real people talked and what they thought about things, it could help me win jury trials."

"Did it?"

"Hell if I know."

She grinned and sipped her drink, glancing at the family the next table over. After a few moments, she said, "So, you like never talk about yourself."

"Nothing really to talk about."

"Whatever. I bet you're crazy interesting."

"Not really."

"Okay, then let's play a game. You have to tell me something about you that nobody else knows, and I'll tell you something about me that nobody else knows."

"That sounds like the type of game that lands people in jail."

She laughed, and Solomon noticed she laughed with her entire body, bending her head back and then covering her mouth because she couldn't control the volume of her voice.

"Don't be a prick. Just play."

"You know, you've got quite the potty mouth, young lady. You may wanna tone it down a little there, Andrew Dice Clay."

"Who's Andrew Dice Clay?"

"He was the one that swore like . . . never mind. Before your time."

She set her latte down and put in more sweetener. "So?" she said.

"So? Oh, right. Hmm . . . something embarrassing about me . . ."

"No, not embarrassing. Something that nobody else knows about."

He thought it over. "There's nothing."

"Bull—"

"Ah ah."

She groaned. "Fine. Bull crap. There, I didn't swear. Now just tell me something so we can play the stupid game."

"I'm not kidding, Kelly. There's nothing. If you keep no secrets, no one can have anything to use against you. No leverage."

77

"Everybody has at least one secret. That one thing they don't want other people to know. *Everybody* has one. We think other people wouldn't like us if they knew the real us because of that one thing."

The pen came out of his pocket, and he lightly chewed on it. "I think I caused my mother's suicide."

She sat in stunned silence, clearly debating whether he was messing with her or not. Solomon leaned back in his chair and said, "That was way too heavy for this moment, wasn't it?"

"Ya think?" she said. "I was expecting, like, you smoked pot and went swimming in the ocean or something."

"Is that your big secret? Getting high and swimming?"

She looked down into her latte. "No," she said quietly. "Some of us have some real shit baggage, ya know?"

"Yeah," he said softly. "I do."

She blinked as though pushing away a thought and then looked up at him again. "What happened with your mom? Or does it still bug you to talk about it?"

"No, I don't mind talking about it. I got so used to telling it as a kid it doesn't bother me anymore. She just wasn't happy. No matter what was going on in her life, she could never see the joy in it. When my father drank himself to death, it got even worse. His death really came outta nowhere and caught her off guard. It was a downward spiral after that."

"And you think it's your fault?"

He thought a moment. "I think raising two bad kids on her own was more than she could handle."

"Bullshit. Everybody's sad and lonely. Doesn't mean you leave your kids to raise themselves. Both your parents can suck it."

Solomon took the pen out of his mouth; he'd chewed it down enough that it jabbed his tongue. "That's how the cookie crumbled. What can you do?"

"I don't like the way you say that."

"How else would I say it?"

"It's trauma. Trauma's not easy to talk about. You should take that shit more seriously."

"You sure you're sixteen? You seem like an elderly therapist sometimes."

She smirked and took a drink of her latte before saying, "You were right when you used to come here. All you need to do is watch people and they'll tell you everything about themselves by the way they act."

"Ain't that the truth." He tapped his cane on the cement beneath his feet. Occasionally he liked to hold it and feel the vibration of the strike going through the wood and up into his hand.

"So what happened after she died?"

"Social Services took me and my brother. Foster care wasn't much better than being alone, but it put a roof over my head and some food in my belly, I guess."

"Do you ever see your brother?"

"No."

"Why not?"

"What good would it do either of us to remind ourselves about the past?"

She thought it over a few seconds. "That's sad as f—I mean, that's really sad. But, thanks for telling me."

"So you play this weird game with everybody to learn their deep dark secrets?"

"Only people I think are cool."

"Man, do you have the wrong guy, then." He let out a breath and somberly said, "He's dangerous. You know that, right? He's gonna really hurt you or your mom one day."

She tapped her fingernail against the side of the glass. "I can take care of myself."

"Everybody thinks that, but very few people can."

"Then let me move in with you."

"What?"

"Let me move in with you. My mom won't even care if I'm gone."

"First of all, I doubt that, and second, Kelly, you're sixteen. You can't live with me."

"Why?"

"Because it's not appropriate."

"Are you shitting me? Appropriate? I'm your assistant, right? That's what you said you were hiring me for. Assistants move in with their bosses all the time."

He shook his head and didn't exactly know how to explain why it was inappropriate. It wasn't even that it was inappropriate, objectively, but Solomon had grown up in a different generation. A generation that had certain protocols that you just didn't violate. And there were things from childhood ingrained in you that never left. It felt sometimes like your mind and brain were two different things, and in a fight, your brain always won.

"I know it doesn't seem like a big deal, but you're still a kid. You can't live with someone who—"

She rolled her eyes and stood up. "Thanks for the drink. You can shove it up your ass."

"Kelly, wait. Come back."

It was too late, as she'd already stormed off. Kelly was, in a very real sense, his only friend. What would life be like if he didn't even have her?

"Kelly," he said, standing now. "Would you just wait a sec?"

She flipped him off without looking back.

16

The conference room in the Sheriff's Office was meant to hold twenty people but had twice as many in there now. Billie had pulled detectives from other cases to get as many hands on deck as she could.

"Okay, everyone, let's have some quiet," she said. "Dr. Browning has the latest update on the Reaper. Dr. Browning, you're up."

Davis rose from his chair with a groan as though breaking bones and stood in front of a pull-down screen. The image opened to a close-up of a woman's nightgown in bad lighting.

"You can see here with the sulfide powder I dusted Mrs. Murray's clothing with that we have a blemish on the left side of the epigastric region. Some of the locations were odd and didn't correlate with sweating from the victim's glands, so I believe this came from your perpetrator."

A male detective in the back said, "We can tell it's his sweat from the DNA, right?"

"It is a misconception that DNA can be retrieved from perspiration. DNA must come from nucleated cells, and perspiration doesn't contain any. Occasionally, forensic technicians have found skin cells caught in perspiration, but the samples were so degraded in every case that none of them were introduced as evidence at trial. Not until this year have we been able to extract identifying information from the perspiration itself. In fact, if this case were to go to trial, you would be the first in the nation to use perspiration as evidence in a criminal case."

"How does that even work?" the detective asked.

"We secrete sweat during the day and deposit it on anything we touch. This sweat is unique to the individual, much like a fingerprint."

"How?"

Davis looked annoyed. "There are three metabolites that appear in high concentrations in our sweat. The combination of these three metabolites varies from person to person. The likelihood of the exact combination of the three metabolites being the same in two different individuals is virtually zero."

Solomon said, "Virtually?" just to mess with him.

Davis breathed out through his nose loudly and said, "I'm going home now. Don't call me again until I have to testify in court. And make it a Friday. I don't enjoy getting up early on Mondays."

Billie rose and said, "Thank you for your help on this, Doctor." She looked to her deputies and detectives and saw that not all the faces were friendly. "So, let's send that out to all law enforcement agencies in the state. And I need three volunteers to check every postal worker, UPS driver, trash collector, and anyone else who has that area as their route. Maybe he scoped out the location before the murders and someone remembers him."

She had a few more instructions and then dismissed them after getting volunteers. Some of them had sour faces, as they always did when she gave them orders. It made her feel obligated to say something, but she always held back. What would it help to demand respect? Respect had to be earned, and she had no idea how she could earn the respect of men who believed she'd only gotten her job because of who her father was.

As she pulled out of her parking space a short while later, she glanced in her rearview mirror and saw one of the deputies say something and grab his crotch, and then both men laughed.

Billie put her truck in park. She tapped her finger against the steering wheel before opening the door and getting out. Then the thought came to her, like it always did when she was about to lose it, that her father wouldn't approve. Her father was soft spoken, with sympathy for everyone. He'd once even let a woman he arrested for drug possession stay in the room above their family's garage for a few weeks to get back on her feet. He always said the key to being a good leader was kindness. That anybody could get their men to fear them, but only real leaders could get their men to love them. For the entirety of her life, she didn't remember him even raising his voice at her.

She swallowed down her anger. The two men were looking at her awkwardly, and their smiles began to disappear.

"I saw you had something to say to me, Deputy."

The man cleared his throat and glanced away. "No, just makin' a joke 'bout something, Sheriff."

"Oh, okay. I love jokes. What was it?"

"Um," he said, glancing to the other deputy, "it was an inside joke."

"Great. Even better. They're usually funnier. What was it?"

He cleared his throat again.

Billie moved to get back into her truck. "What's that expression, Deputy Matthews? 'Say it to my face like a man,' right?"

They exchanged a look and then she got into her truck and drove away, a grin coming to her lips.

17

The balcony was where Solomon spent most of his time, and he sat out there now.

The months he hadn't left his apartment, he always told himself he was just becoming a homebody. But he knew that since he had been released from the hospital, something was different. He stopped driving after his injury. Then he stopped spending time with friends; then he stopped calling people. He told Knox he wouldn't be coming back to the office . . . and eventually, he locked himself in this apartment.

He went to the kitchen, where he'd stacked various files and papers, and got a thick folder filled with documents before coming back to the balcony. They were long police narratives, mostly linking witnesses. *This person told us about this person who told us about this person* . . . leading the police from one interview to another. And that was how they knew a case was cold: when there was no one left to talk to.

A photo was wedged near the bottom of the file. A copy of the original letter the Reaper had sent to a news station. The letter ended with the Reaper's symbol, a skull with an upside-down cross, the handwriting and drawing done so precisely Solomon wondered if the killer was an artist.

This is Reaper speaking.

And partway through:

> You will find a homicide at 537 Monroe Avenue.
> The family is dead. The little girl died last.

Solomon remembered a detail from the detectives' reports: they had found indentations in the carpet near where the body of ten-year-old Sarah Farrington was found. The four legs of a chair. The Reaper had put a clear plastic bag over her head and then sat down above her in a chair so he could watch her face as she fought for air until she died.

Solomon read the rest of the letter and then set it down and put his hands behind his head. He stared out at the block of the city before him and saw some weeds breaking through the sidewalk's concrete, lit up by an old streetlamp that was cracked. It gave the weeds a yellow hue that made them appear otherworldly. A shade of color he had never seen before. Four words kept running through his mind over and over:

This is Reaper speaking.

18

It was late when Billie knocked on his door. Solomon was still up, watching television, and, for a split second when he heard the knock, thought the Reaper had found him.

But when he looked through the peephole, he saw Billie standing there with beers.

"It's like midnight," Solomon said.

"Couldn't sleep. Figured you couldn't either."

"You figured right. Come in."

"Actually, I'd like to go for a walk."

———

Solomon's objections to a walk at night in a crowded neighborhood were overruled with the argument that the sheriff didn't need to feel nervous going out in her own county. So he found himself strolling next to Billie, sipping a bottle of beer. The moon was a sliver, and the street lighting was dim. They passed under the streetlamp where Solomon had seen the yellowed weeds earlier. From his balcony, they looked like life itself: breaking free through barriers not meant to be broken. But up close, they looked dead and wilted. Soulless.

"You know if you wanted to get me in a romantic situation, all you had to do was take me to Fat Burger."

"Fat Burger shut down, actually," she replied before taking a sip of beer.

"Seriously? I loved that place. The food was greasier than my skin when I was thirteen, but it was delicious."

"Ew."

He grinned. "I had an acne problem. Some of us didn't come out perfect from the loins of Zeus."

"Oh, please. I was such a fat little kid I was bullied all the time. Made me tough, though."

"All having a bunch of acne did was make sure I never had a date."

"No, that's probably more because you're a smart-ass."

They stopped at an intersection. Above them was a large tree. The moonlight coming through the branches painted pale white tattoos on the pavement.

They rounded the block and talked about anything other than the case. Sports, news, weather, Bitcoin, their favorite television shows . . . he found she was easy to talk to. A trait her father had in spades as well.

"Do you have that one case?" Solomon asked. "I don't know what you'd call it now. Every agency calls it something else. That one case that you never forget. That always seems to stick to your ribs."

She nodded. "I do—a twelve-year-old boy who killed his six-year-old neighbor. When I interviewed him at the Children's Justice Center, he said that he wanted to go home and was sorry for what he did. I told him he'd done awful things and couldn't go home, and he started crying. I think about him all the time. Two lives ruined so pointlessly. It just made me believe for a long time that maybe life is random, and there isn't meaning to all this suffering."

They were silent a beat before she said, "What about you? What's your one case? I can't imagine anyone other than the Reaper getting you out of that apartment."

Solomon felt the sound of his cane was too loud against the pavement. He tried to soften it but found he couldn't.

"You don't have to talk about it if you don't want to."

"No, it's fine," he said, staring down at the pavement. "You're right. It's this."

"Why? I'm sure you prosecuted other men just as heinous."

He shook his head in a gesture indicating he was as in the dark about it as she was. "The letter he wrote was, I guess . . . I don't know. He had so much insight into himself and life. I thought he might be a professor of literature or philosophy, one of the humanities. It was so alien that someone with so much intelligence and insight decided the best use of their gifts was to kill. It messed with me. I couldn't get it out of my head for a long time."

"Wow. And I just came to your door and dredged all that back up. I'm sorry."

"Don't be. It was destined to happen. You can't escape your past, no matter how much you want to."

They didn't speak again for a while heading back to Billie's truck, but it was about the case when they did speak.

As they talked, she looked down to the concrete. Solomon realized she was avoiding stepping on the cracks in the sidewalk.

"You must really love your mother to care about her back that much."

She chuckled, and he could hear a relaxation in her he hadn't heard before.

"My mom was the best. On Sunday, we'd make dinner, and she let me taste it first before my brother could. I mean, it was nothing, a few extra minutes I got to spend with her, but it's what I remember most."

"Is she doing any better?"

She shook her head. "No, she's getting sicker. It used to be every once in a while where she wouldn't remember me, but now it's almost every time. So I have to remind her who she is and where she is when I see her."

"Have you talked to your dad about moving her into a home?"

"No, I won't do that to her."

"You're not *doing* anything to her. You're making sure she gets the help she needs."

"My dad hasn't left her side for a minute since he retired. She has everything she needs."

They stopped by her truck, which was parked at the curb in front of his building.

"Thank you for helping me with this," she said. "Even if it is 'that one case' for you."

"What are friends for?"

As Billie drove away and her taillights disappeared, Solomon stood on the sidewalk and watched. He felt terrible that she had to work all day seeing the rot that humanity could do to each other, and then, when she went home, a place that should have felt safe, she instead had to deal with more heartache and pain.

As he turned to his building, he could hear the faint echoes of a man shouting. It was coming from the fifth floor, his floor. Travis, screaming at his wife over some perceived slight that he wouldn't remember in the morning. Solomon's father had been the same before the alcohol killed him.

He watched them through their open window, and then Kelly's mother noticed the window was open and closed it.

As he neared his apartment, he stopped and listened at the door. The fight was over money. Dishes shattered against the floor. A table or television was tipped over; then it went silent before a door slammed. Solomon heard stomping and realized too late it was coming toward the front door.

Maria opened the door and gasped when she saw him standing a foot away.

"Sorry," he said placatingly, taking a couple of steps back to avoid potentially getting punched in the face. "I didn't mean to scare you. I'm just heading back to my place and heard the noise."

She shut the door behind her. Her eyes were red and puffy, makeup smeared on her cheeks from the tears that had washed it away. "Sorry," she said. "I know it bothers you sometimes."

"You don't have anything to apologize for."

The two of them stood in silence, Solomon staring at the tip of his cane as he gently tapped it on the floor.

"You don't have to stay," he finally said. "You know that, right?"

She leaned against the wall with her hands behind her back, fighting the tears. "We have a lot of history together. When I was strung out and could barely feed Kelly, he took care of us until I was clean and could stand on my own. I told him I would do it for him if he needed it, and I'm trying. I'm trying so hard."

"So you told him you would do it, so what? You didn't sign a death pact to let him kill you over it."

"He's not gonna do that. He just needs to start his meetings and medication again, and it'll go back to the way it used to be."

"Drugs and alcohol are not his sicknesses, Maria. They're a symptom of his sickness. I know these men. I've studied them. You can never predict what they'll do."

She shook her head. "I know him, he's not like that. It's just the alcohol."

"You know I used to be a social worker at the prison, right?"

She nodded as she wiped some tears away. "Yeah."

"I did some research there on men that had been diagnosed as psychopaths. I would show them a series of pictures of a kid starting a fire with matches and then running away when the curtains caught on fire. I asked them to arrange the images in chronological order. It was straightforward. The matches, striking one, the fire, the fire jumping to the curtains, yada yada. And guess what? They couldn't do it. Do you know why they couldn't do it?"

She stared at something in the distance rather than at him. "Because they don't understand consequences."

He nodded. "If you're smart enough to know that, you're smart enough to know he could kill you one day."

She wiped the last of the tears away and said, "I appreciate your concern, Sol, I really do. But he was there for me when nobody else was. I won't abandon him when he needs me most."

Maria walked away to the elevators. Solomon watched until the doors closed. He knocked on Travis's door. Then he pounded on it with his fist.

Travis opened the door quickly as though he intended to hit whoever was standing there. When he saw it was Solomon, he snarled, "Go back to your apartment. This is none of your business."

"Where's Kelly?"

Bulky from fat and some muscle leftover from high school and college football, Travis was much bigger than Solomon. Kelly had told him that Travis worked as a pharmacist and liked to brag about money when he was drunk. Solomon wondered if money made people worse, or if people were already that way and only felt comfortable showing it when they had money.

"I know you've been spending time with the brat." He shoved Solomon on the shoulder. "Stay the hell away from her."

"Gladly. As soon as you stop beating her."

"I haven't laid a hand on her. And if she tells you I have, she's lying. That's one messed-up kid. You can't believe anything that comes outta her mouth."

"Funny. I was just thinking the same thing about you."

Travis stepped face-to-face with him. So close that Solomon could smell his breath, and it reeked of booze. "If I see you again, I'm not just kicking your ass, I'm calling the cops, too. Weird single man spending all his time with my teenage stepdaughter. How do you think they're going to respond to that?"

The door slammed in Solomon's face. He stood there and swallowed down his anger. He raised his hand to pound on the door again and stopped himself. He had upset Travis more than the guy already was, and Solomon thought about what Kelly had said—that trying to intervene would only make it worse for her and her mother.

He went to his apartment and shut the door behind him.

19

The only scary part of Jennifer Garrison's drive home was the patch of road between Elm and Vine Streets. It looped around a small canyon where there were almost no streetlights. The homes here had been built more than forty years ago, but her father, a carpenter, had told her they'd been built to last.

Usually, she wouldn't have been able to afford anywhere near this area on her own. But her roommate from college, Huong, had inherited the home from her grandmother and rented out the five spare bedrooms to her friends. Jennifer being the first one she had called.

Slowly, as the years passed, the friends drifted off, and the bedrooms emptied. Eventually, Huong had gotten married and was planning children and wanted someplace with better schools. So she sold the home to Jennifer at far below market value with a promise that she would take care of the place as if it had been passed down through her own family. Considering that Jennifer was one of nine children, she guessed that her view of what something looked like passed down through the family was different from Huong's.

Jennifer had taken tenants in at first, but after years of a noisy house at all hours, she wanted to see what it was like without roommates. So a few months ago, she vacated all the rooms and lived by herself.

Now, as Jennifer pulled up to the large empty house and parked in the driveway, she wondered what exactly had seemed so exciting about being alone in this house. It was massive and dark, like some medieval castle. But maybe the view made up for it. It overlooked the city from the east, and she had a clear view of the entire Tooele Valley.

It was a beautiful house on gorgeous property but always had a hint of dread to it. She'd heard from neighbors that someone had committed suicide here decades ago.

She entered the first two digits of the alarm code on the front door and then stopped. She didn't know why she stopped. The six-digit code was evident in her mind: her youngest brother's birthday. It wasn't a problem of memory, she decided. Something was wrong. The hairs on the nape of her neck were standing straight, and she felt gooseflesh on her arms, though it had to have been over eighty degrees.

The sensation brought up a memory of being at the zoo as a child, staring through thick glass at a chimpanzee, who stared back. Though she was young and it was the first time Jennifer had ever seen one, she understood that the chimp was thinking about her in probably the same way she was thinking about it.

That's what this felt like.

The sensation of being watched.

There were times when she'd felt danger where there was no danger or felt hunger right after she'd eaten, but this was different. She *knew* something was watching her right now.

The strength it took to make any sort of movement was gargantuan. The thought of moving even one muscle, even a finger to finish inputting the code, sent a chill through her and made her stomach churn. It was as if a wolf or mountain lion had spotted her, and she was trying to remain as still as possible, hoping she didn't catch its interest.

She quickly input the four additional digits with a deep breath and hurriedly tried to open the door. Instead, a long beep exuded from the box, letting her know she hadn't input the code fast enough.

"Shit!"

She quickly punched in the numbers again. This time, the box beeped, and she was able to turn the knob.

Once inside, she locked the door behind her. A quick dive into her memory of the house, and she counted five different potential entryways. Luckily, she had an alarm, but in times of stress she felt like she couldn't trust it.

The house was dark. The foyer had beige carpet and two staircases, one on either end of the room. A chandelier hung from the center of the ceiling. Though as old and unique as the house, it didn't give the place a classy or uplifting feeling. Instead, it looked outdated and worn.

She put her bag on the chair near the door. The chair was an old antique that had belonged to Huong's grandmother. In fact, many things from the grandmother were still here, including cobweb-covered wheelchairs and rusted walkers that had been crammed into the basement. It would have taken too much effort to move everything to the dump. So instead, Jennifer had left them there and hadn't entered since.

Deciding not to turn the lights on, she got halfway across the foyer before stopping. This was ridiculous. It was dark and quiet, no one was around, and she'd just gotten spooked. A creepy guy had sat across the street from her store on a bus bench and watched the store today. Probably homeless, since there was a shelter not far from her work. It was innocent, she was sure, but the way he'd stared made her uncomfortable, and she'd found herself not going near the windows.

She'd lived in this house for years by herself and never had a single break-in or even a theft out of the garage when she'd forgotten to close it. She prided herself on being tough and not easily frightened.

The windows had white drapes, and she pulled one aside and looked out. The front lawn was large, and the house had a long driveway. She saw her car parked halfway up near the garage. Across the street, Mr. and Mrs. Gutierrez were getting into their vehicle while laughing about something. The sight of known people comforted her.

The Gutierrezes' car lights flooded her foyer, and she let go of the drapes and flipped on the lights. She went upstairs to the master bedroom and the adjoining bathroom. The master bathroom had tan tiles and lights around the mirror. She looked at herself. It gave her a little surprise whenever she saw herself like this. When she wore contacts, which was rarely, she thought she looked like a different person.

As she took her contacts out, a noise startled her. A crash. Somewhere downstairs.

Her pulse pounded in her throat. She stared down into the sink and listened as intensely as a prey animal out in the jungle listened to an unfamiliar sound.

Had glass actually broken, or had she heard something else? The home had motion detectors, too. They definitely would have gone off if someone had broken in.

She had read once about an alarm installer who'd gain access to single women's homes by programming in a second alarm code only he knew and then sexually assaulting and strangling whoever was home. A large man who'd given her a creepy feeling had installed her alarm system, and she wondered if he could have been a predator.

Jennifer hurried to the top of the stairs and looked down.

"Hello?"

The home was quiet. The Gutierrezes had long since driven away, and no one else was likely to be out in the neighborhood this late at night. She hated when she was the one who had to close the store.

Slowly, each step harder to take than the previous one because of the fear weighing on her limbs, she made her way down the stairs.

20

The bottom of the stairs felt like it took an eternity to reach. Jennifer held the banister with one hand and didn't step off the last step, as though that would give her a good head start if she suddenly had to take off running upstairs.

The crash, she'd decided, sounded like it had come from the kitchen. She slipped her shoes off, revealing bare feet, and slowly made her way through the foyer, down the hallway, and past the living room.

Unlike the foyer, the kitchen had several windows. Moonlight illuminated the table in the breakfast nook.

There was no noise now. Not even the sound of a breeze rustling leaves outside. She crossed the kitchen to the set of stairs leading to the basement. The light switch was at the bottom rather than the top of the stairs. The thought of taking those steps in the dark brought up a memory from childhood. Her parents' home had a similar light because of a cheap electrician they had used. She remembered she would flip off the switch and then refuse to look behind her as she sprinted up the stairs. Absolutely sure that a hideous creature was only a step behind, its gnarled fingers catching the ends of her hair as it reached for her.

She felt like that little girl now.

Luckily, her home had a different layout than her parents'. The light from the living room illuminated the staircase, and she could see some of the basement from the top of the stairs.

Standing still a few moments, she was about to take the first step when she heard a noise downstairs. It was subtle and quiet, but it was loud enough that she knew it wasn't in her head. Was that a creak? Someone stepping on something she had left out on the floor?

She started down the steps while she took her cell phone out of her pocket. She dialed 9 and then 1 and held the phone in her palm in case she needed to hit the last number. She was halfway down when she got a sickening feeling that she shouldn't go any farther. Something was wrong.

Backing up the stairs, she dialed the last digit and held for an operator.

"911, what's your emergency?"

Loud enough so someone in the basement could hear, Jennifer said, "I need the police to come out. I think someone is in my house."

She glanced into the darkness at the bottom of the stairs. Only a glance, but it was enough. The outline of a face loomed in the dark . . . but not a face. Something over a face. The outline had the body of a man, and the deformed head of something else.

It was the most terrifying thing Jennifer had ever seen.

She shrieked and turned to dash up the stairs. But her foot slipped and she hit the stairs hard, slamming her chin into the edge of a step. A loud buzzing filled her ears.

The phone fell out of her hand and bounced down the stairs. She scrambled to her feet and ran—up the rest of the stairs, across the kitchen, down the hallway, out the front door to the sidewalk, and to her neighbors' house.

21

When the police arrived, Jennifer was sitting on the porch steps with her neighbor, Dan. His forearms rested on his knees while she sipped tea next to him, something she insisted she didn't need but was glad he'd gotten for her. Dan's wife had grumbled that Jennifer's knocking had woken up the kids, and she'd looked annoyed to see Jennifer sitting by her husband when she'd poked her head outside a minute ago.

"I'm so sorry," Jennifer said now. "I dropped my phone and couldn't go back."

"It's totally fine. Seriously. The kids'll fall back asleep in ten minutes. Great thing about being a kid, right? Nothing bothers you from sleeping."

"I just feel so stupid. I'm not even sure what I saw was a person. It was like this blurry . . . thing. It could've been in my head or just the shadows and the lights mixing and . . . I know how crazy it sounds."

"Well, no harm in the cops checking it out."

The two police officers who'd taken her information, then gone to check out the house, came back to the porch. The shorter, squatter one glanced around the lawn. The larger one, whose bulging trap muscles gave the appearance of his shoulders touching his ears, said, "We checked from top to bottom. You're all good."

"Are you sure? You checked everywhere?" Jennifer asked pleadingly.

He nodded. "The basement, the attic, the garage, and all that. No one's in there."

The other officer said, "If there was someone there, they ain't anymore. But a girl living by herself, you know, sometimes being scared plays tricks with your head if you don't have any protection."

Dan looked at her and said, "I've been telling you forever to get a gun." Then, he turned to the officer. "Don't worry, Officer, I'll get her a firearm and into the shooting range."

"That's good. I would recommend some Mace, too. Put it on your key chain and keep it on your nightstand next to you with your cell phone. But, anyway, I didn't see anything that would indicate someone was in your home this time."

Jennifer had to sign some paperwork, and the two officers reminded her about getting a gun and then left. Dan stood on his porch with his hands in his pockets.

"I hope you don't think I'm, like, taking advantage of you or something," she said.

"What? How could you possibly be taking advantage of me?"

"I dunno, just running over here and waking your kids up. I shouldn't have done that."

"Hey, if they're a little grumpy in the morning but we made sure you're safe, it's worth it."

She grinned and said, "Tell Anne sorry and that I'll bring over some cookies or something to apologize."

"I will. Call me if you need anything."

He watched her until she had gone inside her house and shut the door.

Jennifer locked the front door behind her. Never, not once, had she even thought something might happen to her here: it was her previous roommates who had insisted on alarms.

She had grown up in small towns. Places where home and car doors were left unlocked at night. Neighbors went into each other's houses when they needed to borrow something, even when no one was home.

The officers had left the lights on in the basement and most of the house, and she was glad. She would turn them off in the morning.

The master bathroom was the most dimly lit space, since two of the lights around the mirror were burned out, but it gave the room a warm glow that comforted her. She undressed, turned on the bath, and got in once it was hot and steamy.

After using a lavender body gel to help calm herself, she leaned back and closed her eyes until the water started to cool. She got out of the bath and put on shorts and an oversize T-shirt, something left over from one of her former boyfriends. Rick. He'd started leaving things like toothbrushes and clothing at her house. Slowly pushing his way in. But then he broke up with her when she informed him she was saving herself for marriage and wouldn't sleep with him. She told herself the fact that he dumped her because of it meant she had dodged a bullet.

As she ran a brush through her hair in front of the bathroom mirror, a shattering crash from the bedroom startled her so badly she dropped the brush.

A window breaking. She froze, unable to move. There were only two exits from the bedroom: the sliding glass balcony doors and the door leading to the hallway. If someone was in there, she wouldn't be able to get out without going past them.

As quietly as possible, she reached over, shut the bathroom door, and then turned the lock.

She instinctively backed away from the door and looked around. There wasn't much she could use as a weapon, but she did have a bottle of hair spray. She held it in front of her like bear spray. Then she turned off the light and got into the bathtub, pulling the shower curtain closed as quietly as possible.

Jennifer lay back in the tub and tried to hide. The tub was large, an antique, but her knees thrust up over the lip of the tub no matter how she positioned herself.

As she lay in the dark, the only sound her deep breathing, her pulse thumping in her throat, she thought she should unlock the door. If she left it locked, the intruder would undoubtedly know she was in there and break it open.

So as not to rattle the metal rings holding up the shower curtain, she slipped through a crack between the curtain and the wall and unlocked the bathroom door before sliding back into the tub.

Please . . . please . . . please . . .

The creak was light, something she wouldn't have even noticed if she hadn't been listening for it.

Someone had left the bedroom and was in the hallway.

The floor in the bedroom had been replaced and didn't creak much, but the hallway was old wood. She could hear every step the intruder took. The creaks were rhythmic and went in the opposite direction, heading to the staircase.

Had he been hiding outside on the roof and then broken the sliding glass door to get in? She couldn't imagine any other scenario where the police would miss him after searching the house. Unless he had been hiding under the house in the crawl space.

The police had returned her phone, and she'd set it on the nightstand to charge. As she snuck over to it, she heard someone taking the stairs to the main floor. The terror she felt was palpable, like some poison twisting its way through her body. Making her limbs heavy and her breathing strenuous. Her hands shook so bad she had to type in her pass code three times to unlock her phone because she kept hitting the wrong numbers.

Just as the emergency dispatch operator said, "911, what's your emergency?" the blade thrust through her back. The tip tore through flesh, sinew, and organ until it pierced her chest plate and glistened in the light.

Her last thought was how odd it was to feel her heart stop.

22

The home was on the other side of town from the Farringtons' place, almost an hour's drive. Solomon stood outside and checked the clock on his phone. The Farrington family had been killed exactly eight years ago tonight. The pathologist guessed Jennifer Garrison, who now lay in a black medical examiner's van with a green sheet over her corpse, had died at roughly the same time.

Billie spoke with detectives, then the assistant medical examiner, then the SIS techs walking out with handfuls of collected evidence. She moved masterfully between them, not wasting any time with chitchat or discussing news or gossip. A few people, after she had stopped talking with them, looked annoyed. Like they couldn't understand why someone wouldn't want to waste time at the scene of a young woman's death. When she had called Solomon and asked if he wanted to come down because a young woman had been stabbed, he didn't know it would be connected until Billie texted him a photo. A carving had been made with a knife or razor on Jennifer Garrison's belly. A skull with an upside-down cross.

Jennifer Garrison had been an average young woman working a full-time job at a clothing store while going back to school at night to become a teacher. Her neighbor said she was one of the nicest people he knew, and that she had been over earlier because she thought someone was inside her home.

Billie had called up the two cops who had cleared the house and demanded they get down here. She wanted them to see Jennifer's body.

Solomon felt a deep sadness for Jennifer Garrison. For all the things she would've done in life that wouldn't happen now. It was as if the house was haunted by memories that had never happened.

Jennifer had taken the Farringtons' place in the Reaper's pattern, and Solomon needed to know why.

Forensics was drawing, charting, videoing, and photographing, and would be for hours, but what they knew so far was that the killer had gotten in through a sliding glass door in the bedroom. Solomon managed to sneak past SIS and the detectives without anyone asking what he was doing at an active crime scene. Being inside the home gave him a small shiver. He ignored it and went upstairs.

The killer had used a glass cutter to cut a large square near the door handle, then popped the square out. It had fallen on the floor of the bedroom and shattered.

Only an amateur would push the glass out instead of trying to pull it back so they could grab it. You're new at this . . . but you'll remember next time.

Next time, he thought. The idea made him sick.

The house's alarm had gone off, but by the time the alarm company sent a message to law enforcement, Jennifer Garrison was likely already dead.

Once a murder occurred in a home, it was no longer the same house. The home would forever have the stain of that act on it. Solomon wasn't particularly superstitious, but he had seen enough to know that places could hold . . . something. Energy, memories, feelings . . . something in houses where murders had occurred made them feel different. Colder and emptier, no matter who lived there.

He moved over to the side of the bed, near the nightstand. This was where the monster had found Jennifer. He had surprised her. A thick hunting knife slid into her thoracic vertebrae with so much force the blade came an inch out of her chest in between her breasts.

He had continued to stab her after she was likely dead from the first blow. Twenty-two stab wounds in total.

Some words out of the Reaper letter ran through his head now: *There is no defense against a compulsive killer.*

But this murder hadn't been performed with precision. This was rage. And by definition, rage was uncontrollable. It was a part of the killer he hadn't meant to show Solomon.

He crossed the room and stood near the doorway. The smudge of a smooth latex glove had been found on the light-switch plate. The detectives had concluded that he'd turned off the light before killing Jennifer, but Solomon didn't think so. Something in Jennifer had triggered him, and he'd acted first. The plan, whatever it was, had been abandoned. The light switch was a distraction, as was hair found on Jennifer that a rushed field test showed as likely being dog hair. Bits of sand were found on the carpet and looked to be from outside the house, near the balcony. Evidence meant to waste resources and send them in the wrong direction.

Solomon leaned back against the wall and rubbed his temple with two fingers, which occasionally helped the migraines he frequently got. He could feel one coming on now and knew it was time to leave.

He headed outside, taking a pen out of his pocket and putting it between his teeth. On the front porch, he stood at the top step and took in the night. It was quiet and warm. Newer looking cars were parked in driveways, and lawns were neatly trimmed here. There had been a small crowd at first, but interest lasted only so long, and almost everyone had gone home.

He wondered if Jennifer ever pictured her own children running through the home.

A detective, Mark something, strolled out of the house and nodded to Solomon. They had worked together a few times when he was still at the County Attorney's Office, and Solomon knew him to be generally unpleasant.

"Helluva thing," Mark said as he brushed by Solomon, maybe nudging him a little harder than he had to. "After all these years, I still don't understand how a man can do that to someone else."

Solomon watched as the medical examiner's van pulled away. More to himself than to Mark, he said, "This isn't a man."

23

Sleep never came, so Solomon did something he had wanted to do for four years: went to an art museum.

He strolled casually through the rooms until he came to one filled with paintings. In a prominent spot on one of the walls was a replica of a familiar painting, *The Raft of the Medusa*.

In the painting, others saw the desperation in the men's faces as they realized they would die on a raft in a violent ocean. But Solomon thought about the corpses Géricault used as models to paint the men. He pictured an artist alone at night surrounded by the dead and felt an icy chill.

The actual raft had run ashore, and the starving men turned to cannibalism to survive. He wondered if starvation released some neurochemical that suppressed human beings' natural aversion to cannibalism or if the aversion itself was the unnatural part.

The anxiety that had kept him up all night gnawed at his guts now. Jennifer Garrison had been killed the way Mrs. Farrington had been killed: a blade through the heart. Why was a single victim chosen instead of a family? There *had* to be a reason.

Solomon had asked Billie to send him any personal history they had on Jennifer Garrison but so far hadn't heard anything. He was pondering this when his cell phone rang, and he saw it was Billie. He sat down on a bench in front of a sculpture of three women holding books and walking, smiles on their faces. The artist had likely used girls walking home from school as models, he thought.

"Hey," Solomon said when he answered.

"Hey. Where are you? I came by your place."

"I'm out at a museum, believe it or not."

"With the public? I'm impressed."

"Don't be. I'm about to pass out. What's up?"

"We found something I thought you should know about."

Her voice was more serious now, and it gave Solomon butterflies in his stomach.

"What is it?" he said.

"Jennifer Garrison's mother's maiden name is Farrington. Her mother is the sister of Benjamin Farrington—the father of the family . . ."

A beat of silence passed between them.

"You okay, Solomon?"

"Yeah. Yeah, I'm fine. Um, look, can we meet up? I wanna see what SIS got from the scene last night."

"Sure. Give me an hour and I'll swing by and pick you up."

"Excuse me," a young man's voice said.

A teenager stood behind Solomon wearing jeans and a hoodie.

"I'll be home in an hour," Solomon said to Billie before hanging up. He looked at the boy. "Yeah?"

"Are you Solomon?"

"I am."

He held out a sheet of paper. "Here."

"Um," he said as he took the paper, "okay. What is it?"

"I dunno. Some guy paid me fifty bucks and said to give it to you."

Solomon's heart felt like it dropped into his stomach. He opened the letter. The first line was only four words, but it pierced him so profoundly he felt like his knees would buckle.

This is Reaper speaking.

———

Billie and her deputies arrived within minutes of Solomon calling from the lobby of the museum. She sent her deputies inside and asked one to find whoever was in charge and get them to lock all the doors and announce that they'd be releasing everybody one at a time. The museum had two cameras, but they didn't face where Solomon had been handed the note. The Reaper had waited until Solomon was in a blind spot.

Several cruisers were driving in every direction away from the museum in case the boy who'd handed him the note had gotten out before Solomon had reached the entrance.

Billie leaned next to him on a stone banister outside the front entrance and folded her arms. "So a strange boy offers you a note, and you just take it without asking any questions?"

"He wasn't strange. The Reaper picked the most average-looking boy on purpose. Someone who, if he stood in a group all wearing the same clothes, I wouldn't be able to tell him apart."

"They're ready, Sheriff," a deputy said.

She straightened up and said to Solomon, "All right, you're our star witness, so let's go see how well your memory still works, old man."

———

Solomon stood in front of the museum entrance all morning, looking at each guest one by one as they left. By the time the museum had emptied, his neck and back hurt. He rolled his shoulders to relieve the ache in the center of his spine. If he stood for too long, his legs would stiffen and shoot pain from the base of his foot, up his calves and thighs, and into his hips. So he hid the pain by keeping his face passive.

The last guest went home in the afternoon. After that, only the employees were left. Solomon stared at the grass that encircled the museum.

"You okay?" Billie asked.

"He saw him. The kid saw the Reaper, and I let him walk out of here like—"

"Like a man who was caught off guard and didn't pay attention for five seconds? You're not Superman, Solomon. We can't do everything."

He shook his head. "It's not just that. The Reaper was here. Inside the museum. He was watching me, and I had no idea. I didn't notice anyone staring at me at all. He could've walked up anytime and put a bullet in my head. That's what the police don't like the public to think about. If someone is determined to kill you, they'll kill you, and there's not much anybody can do about it."

"So, are you upset that he could've killed you, or upset that he was so close to you and you didn't notice?"

Solomon didn't reply.

"It's ego, Solomon. I know what it feels like. I had a case when I was in Sex Crimes involving two gang members. You should've seen what they did to this poor girl. Tied her to a wall and threw darts at her, shaved her head to humiliate her, cut her face with razor blades so she would never forget them . . . I would've done anything for a conviction. I wanted it so bad that it kept me up at night. But guess what happened?"

"They walked."

Billie didn't answer as she glanced down at her shoes. "Some of the other members of the gang snuck into her bedroom and put a knife to her throat and let her know if she went through with testifying, they'd be back. And next time, they'd go into her parents' room, too. So she changed her story, and the case was dropped." She paused. "I cried for weeks after that. I would burst into tears at a stoplight or while eating dinner . . . I didn't think any case would affect me like that again. But I realized something: I had done everything I could. There was nothing for me to feel guilty about. I did my job, and the outcome was out of my hands. You did what you could. You can't ask yourself to do more than that."

He didn't reply for a moment and then said, "I'm going down to the station to work with your artist. Maybe we distribute a sketch of the kid and get lucky."

"Sheriff," another deputy said, hurrying out of the entrance, "we got the videos up that you wanted."

They followed him back to a small room with a security guard standing by the door in a blue-green jacket. He had his thumbs tucked into his belt and nodded hello to each of them individually as they came into the room.

"So, what time you lookin' to see on the video?"

"The entire day from the time you opened. I want to see who came in."

He raised his eyebrows. "Well, better get yourselves some coffee, then."

———

Solomon and Billie had hours of video to go through. The system was closed circuit, not digital. The equipment was so rudimentary that they couldn't fast-forward the videos. The security guard checked in on them occasionally and saw their frustration. On his way out, he mumbled to no one in particular, "Tell the county to give us more money, and we'll get fast-forward."

Solomon sat in an uncomfortable chair with his feet up on a desk. The room was darkened, and they had the video playing on a monitor in front of them. The machine was something from twenty years ago. Still, the graininess of the video and the slightly dulled colors reminded him of television sitcoms in the eighties, when he was a boy. Television was what he'd turned to when he wanted to escape into something pleasantly comforting.

One deputy sat in the corner, soundly snoring, and Billie rested her head on her arm against another desk. Solomon had told her to go home several times, but she insisted she wouldn't leave him here alone to do this. That he was her responsibility.

He watched the faces of the people coming and going and, with each one, tried to pick up something. A smirk. A serious expression. A glance at the cameras. Anything that would differentiate them from the crowd so Solomon could follow up on them. There was nothing. Every person could've been replaced with every other person. Somewhere in that crowd was the *thing* he was looking for, and it dug deep into him that he couldn't tell them from anyone else.

Solomon stretched his neck from side to side. Then, finally, he paused the video and thanked the stars it at least had that ability so he could go to the bathroom.

Slowly making his way down the hall, he observed the works of art on display to either side of him. Paintings of men in colorful uniforms pinned with medals, women in large, puffy dresses with odd-looking hats that made them look like peacocks. A couple of landscape paintings and a blue sky with white clouds above a still sea. Solomon stopped at that one and stared at it. He had never seen the ocean in person, and anything depicting it interested him.

After using the bathroom, he went to the front entrance. A deputy sat there in a chair sipping coffee. Solomon nodded to him on the way out.

The air had a pine scent from the surrounding woods, with the tree line a couple hundred feet away. The thick patch of forest led to the mountains along the Sand Hollow Front and then stretched out farther than a person could see.

He took out the pen from his pocket and put it in between his teeth, biting down into a groove that he had already made in the plastic.

A breeze blew, brushing his hair across his forehead. He chewed on the pen while he pulled out a copy of the letter. The original had been rushed to the Utah State Crime Lab for analysis. The note was hand-written in the same beautifully elegant script they'd seen before. He sat down on the front steps and read the letter twice before lowering it and looking out at the forest. There were woods behind his house when he was young, and he remembered nights staring out at them, certain that there were monsters behind every tree.

The doors opened behind him, and Billie stood there. Her look of surprise worried him enough that he said, "What happened?"

"We need to go. Now."

———

Billie parked on the curb in front of Solomon's apartment building. The truck hadn't even come to a stop when he got out and hurried to the front entrance. He input the code on the door and held it open for Billie.

They shared the elevator with a woman carrying a small dog in a purse. The dog growled at him, probably smelling Russ's fur on his clothes. The woman smiled at Solomon before the elevator dinged and she got off.

When the elevator stopped on his floor, he saw two deputies standing in the hallway speaking in hushed tones.

The door behind them was open, and he could hear other voices coming from inside. He felt ill as he reached Kelly's apartment. He stood near the door and leaned on his cane.

———

Other than the voices coming from the living room, it was silent.

He crossed the living room and stared at the shaggy red rug that had been thrown over the bare floor.

The bathroom and kitchen were empty. He went to the first bedroom, where Billie was already standing at the door.

It was a teenager's bedroom. Kelly's room.

Blood stained a white throw rug near the bed. The sheets were black, so the dark stains and spatters were barely visible. Some of the blood had spattered against the wall in tiny droplets. From the direction of the spatter, Solomon could tell someone had hit another person with a fist or blunt object going from left to right. Left-handed.

"Who's primary?" Solomon shouted.

"I am," a squat man with golden hair said.

"Who called it in?"

"Your neighbor across the hall. He mentioned your name, and when I saw that, I thought I should let the sheriff know."

"Mentioned my name for what?"

He cleared his throat. "When he told us he heard screaming, he mentioned that there was a man down the hall who spent a lot of time with the underage girl in the apartment the screams were coming from."

Solomon didn't respond.

"Gil," a deputy said to the man who'd been speaking, "the parents are here."

Gil glanced at Solomon in a way that made sure Solomon knew what he thought of him and this mess he'd created before going out to the living room to explain to Kelly's parents that she was gone.

24

When Billie stepped outside, Solomon was sitting on the porch steps of the apartment building while deputies and forensic techs came in and out.

Billie sat next to him.

"The parents' alibi is solid," she said. "Dinner and a movie. He . . . must've waited for them to leave. Who knows how long he was watching the place."

"He took her because of me," Solomon said, staring at a dirty oil stain on the street in front of him.

She glanced through the door and saw two of her deputies speaking with a detective in a gray suit. All of them had coffees in their hands.

"Solomon, there was a lot of blood. I'm not sure she could surv—"

"The last thing we did was argue. She asked if she could live with me and I said no."

"You couldn't possibly have known something would happen to her."

"She might've been safe in my apartment."

"Then he would've gotten her when she left for school. You can't protect someone all the time. This isn't your fault."

He blew out a deep breath and looked up at a deputy going into the building. "What happened at the museum threw me. Once I knew he was watching me, I should've known he'd be watching the people around me, too. I should've known I might be putting her in danger."

Another deputy came by on a cell phone and stepped between them without acknowledging that people were there.

"Solomon, this is not your fault."

He rose. "Sure as hell feels like it."

25

Billie got home before the sun was up. She threw her keys into a bowl on the dining table and then went to the bathroom. She brushed her teeth, changed into a Joan Jett T-shirt with shorts, and then went to the upstairs bedroom. Fatigue weighed down every muscle in her body.

The bedroom was sparse: a bed and a few works of art, neon 1980s prints on the walls. She had always thought that if there was clutter around a person, their mind would be cluttered, too.

The bed was soft and warm, and she was glad Dax wasn't sleeping over tonight; she felt like being alone.

As she drifted off, she saw Allyx Murray on the ground, half her head pressed into the dirt. Wounds on her back opened up her chest, draining her of blood. Her eyes glossy like marbles. Billie had stood next to the body and stared down at those eyes. Once full of life. Now nothing more than meat.

The dull milky eyes darted up and took her in as the corpse's mouth opened and dark black blood seeped out past the teeth. The corpse screamed.

Billie jumped up in bed. She was sweating and had to forcefully suck air so she could breathe. She hadn't even realized she'd fallen asleep.

The room was quiet as the air conditioner clicked on. A comforting familiarity.

She swung her legs over the bed and only then realized that she'd been woken by her phone vibrating on the nightstand.

It was Solomon.

"Hey," she said.

"Hey. You okay?"

"Yes, why?"

"You sound outta breath."

"Just tired. What's up?"

"I'm down at the lab. We got preliminary. Only one blood type at the scene, Kelly's. She didn't scratch or injure him at all, like I'd hoped."

A pause.

"What is it, Solomon?"

"I think we need to do something drastic."

"Like what?"

"We need to leak to the press that we have his DNA."

"You want to lie to the public?"

"I know, I know, it's a shitty move. But we have to push him to act. He doesn't think we're close to him. If we can get him to panic, he'll make mistakes."

"He might also tie up loose ends like Kelly and disappear again."

"I have to do something. I can't sit in my apartment and wait to get a call that they've found her body."

She looked down at the stains on a rug near her bed. "What if we save that as a last resort? We haven't even talked to all the neighbors yet. I'd be surprised if someone didn't see a man pulling a girl into a car."

There was a pause in the conversation, and then he said, "Billie, if she—"

"I know. But if she's still alive, we're not going to let that happen."

26

Solomon hadn't even met many neighbors in his own building, so the building across the street was utterly unknown to him.

Billie wore jeans and a T-shirt with her badge wallet around her neck on a lanyard. He wore a sports coat and instantly felt the sweat rolling down his back and neck. When he took it off, revealing the Rage Against the Machine shirt underneath, Billie chuckled.

"What?" he said with a grin.

"Really?"

"Hey, I'm cool enough to like Rage."

"You're a nerd. Own it."

He shrugged. "Nerds end up ruling the world." They crossed a busy intersection when the light turned. "What about you? Were you the cheerleader dating the hot football star in high school?"

"Oh my hell, no. I was the chubby kid cutting classes with the kids who were always in detention."

"What would you do instead?"

"Smoke pot and listen to metal."

"Oh, snap. You were a stoner?"

She smiled. "I guess I was."

"I liked the stoners. They were always too high to be mean to me."

The building across the street was a four-story brick building with brown trim around the windows. Everyone on every floor had a window facing Solomon's building, and there was a good possibility somebody would have seen someone coming out with a struggling teenager . . . or a body.

The deputies had already spoken to everyone they could. Still, Billie had a list of the residents who hadn't been home when they had come here for interviews, so they would hit all the apartments the deputies had missed.

They had to wait a few minutes for someone to come out of the front entrance, since it was key-code locked, but once inside, Solomon was reminded of his own building and wondered if it had been constructed by the same people.

He glanced around and saw there wasn't an elevator. He sighed, and Billie noticed before saying, "I'll get the top floors. You get the bottom."

———

There were eight apartments on each floor, and they had twelve apartments to check across four floors. But it turned out to be futile. No one had seen anything, no one had heard anything, and several people said they wanted nothing to do with the police and shut their doors.

It was an hour later when they met back up. Solomon knocked on the final door on the second floor, and a blonde woman with short hair and a thin black blouse answered. She smiled at Solomon, and he smiled back.

"Hi," she said only to him.

"Hi."

Billie glanced between them. "Excuse me, Ms. . . . ."

"My name's Sceri."

"Well, Sceri, we're with the Tooele County Sheriff's Office. We're speaking to everyone in the neighborhood about something that happened yesterday afternoon."

"That girl getting kidnapped?"

Billie glanced at Solomon before saying, "News travels fast."

"Not really, I just have a nosy neighbor who knows everything that happens around here."

Solomon said, "What did you hear about it?"

"Not much. That some girl was kidnapped across the street and the police were here at all hours."

Billie looked past the woman into her apartment. Candles and incense were lit, and soft yoga music played. She seemed too casual about the murders. She spoke about them like she was recalling a television program she had watched.

"But you didn't see anything yesterday?"

She sighed and folded her arms before leaning on the doorframe. "No, not really. Not yesterday anyway."

Solomon said, "What do you mean *not yesterday*?"

"The day before yesterday there was this creepy guy hanging around. I actually was going to call the cops but didn't think they'd care. Like they'd think I'm in hysterics or something."

"What did you see?"

"Just this guy in the street. He was standing there for a really long time. I mean like eight or nine hours. I went out and came back and he was just standing there against the wall. Like he was waiting for somebody."

"Where did you see him exactly?" Billie asked.

"Just out in front of my building. I think he was watching the building across the street."

"When during the day was this?" Solomon asked.

"I don't know. I left in the morning and came back in the afternoon and he was still there."

"Caucasian or another race?" Solomon said, taking out his phone and opening a note-taking app.

"He was a white guy."

"What did he look like?"

"Oh, I don't know. I only glanced at him, and he was wearing a hat with the hoodie from his jacket over it. It was hard to see his face."

Billie said, "Did you see anyone else around?"

She shook her head. "No, nobody was out."

Solomon said, "Did he get a good look at you?"

She shrugged. "Maybe."

"Do you think you could recognize him if you saw him again?"

"Oh, no, I don't think so. That's kinda why I never bothered calling the police. I really can't help much."

Solomon leaned on his cane. "Where were you looking before you looked up at him?"

"Looking? I don't know. Down at the sidewalk, I guess."

"Did he say anything to make you look?"

She thought a moment. "No, I don't think so. I just kinda looked up and saw him there."

"If you had to write a description of him, like in a letter to a friend, what's the first thing you would say about him?"

"I really don't know."

"Try," Billie said.

A sigh escaped her, and she looked a bit annoyed. Billie guessed she had grown up in a big city. People raised in big cities treated crime as an everyday occurrence rather than the aberration it was seen as in smaller towns. "I don't know . . . I guess his hands."

"What about his hands?"

"He wore these like really expensive-looking leather gloves. Didn't really fit his outfit."

"Black gloves?"

"Yeah."

"Round face, square face, long face . . . ?"

"Umm . . . I think kind of a round face. But I didn't get more than a glance at it, so I really can't say."

Solomon said, "What color was his hoodie?"

123

"I don't know, navy blue, maybe. Really, it was just a glance."

Billie said, "But it was enough to make you consider calling the police, so it was clearly more than just a glance."

"If you say so."

"What stands out when you think about him? Anything unique? Tattoos, scars, braces, glasses . . ."

"No. Nothing. Just thought it was weird that he was in the same spot all day staring at a building. But I guess he could've left when I was gone and come back later."

Billie said, "Was he holding anything?"

"No."

"Did he say anything to you?"

"No, I just smiled and said hello. More because I thought it would be weird to walk by without saying anything. He didn't say anything back. Just kinda looked at me and then looked away. Guys, he was really average looking, and if my neighbor hadn't told me what happened, I wouldn't have even remembered I saw him. I don't think I can help you."

They asked a few more questions and got her information. Her name was Sceri Gale, and she worked at a yoga studio a few blocks away. Several times, Billie caught her looking at Solomon just a bit too long.

"Well," Solomon finally said, "thanks for your time. We'll leave you alone."

"Sure. Hope you find him."

"Yeah," Solomon said, looking over to another apartment where a woman stepped out, looked at them, and then went back inside and shut the door. "I hope we do, too."

27

Solomon couldn't sleep, so he paced the Sheriff's Office hallways. They had released to the press that they not only had DNA evidence but a witness who'd seen the Reaper the night of the murders. Billie had a few contacts in the media and had reached out to sources she trusted, knowing they would craft the story the way they were asked to frame it, as a favor.

They also sent two deputies to pick up Sceri Gale and take her to a safe house. If the Reaper thought she could identify him, Solomon had no doubt he would try to silence her.

He rounded a corner and came to a long hallway with offices on either side. Two detectives were leaving, and they nodded to him. Then, when they thought they were out of earshot, they said, "That's the guy who believes in vampires."

The rumor had circulated, probably started by Knox, that Solomon's book had concluded vampires were responsible for unsolved serial murders. Only people who hadn't actually read the book believed that, of course. But, he told himself as consolation, a category zero killer and a vampire weren't all that different. In many ways, they were both the undead. Whatever it was that made someone human, they didn't have.

Solomon found a wooden bench and sat down. The bench faced a window that looked out over the courtyard. A small garden was planted there among a few outdoor tables. There were no doors, and it didn't seem like anybody could get to the garden.

He thought back to the kid who'd given him the note. He wore a baseball cap, so Solomon couldn't say for sure what type of hairstyle he had, but he was pale, muscular—his biceps bulged his shirtsleeves—and young. And he'd quickly disappeared after handing off the note. Solomon was sure he had run to the front entrance to get there before Solomon could.

A kid. Probably who Sceri Gale saw that day staring at Solomon's building.

If their killer was a young man, at least they could say it wasn't the same person from eight years ago. Not the one who wrote the poetic letter lamenting his dark drive. But why would a kid want to copy the Reaper? There were so many more widely known serial murderers who would've gotten him more attention. Or maybe the kid in the museum really had been handed a note and had nothing to do with it, and the young man Sceri Gale saw was there for an unrelated reason?

His phone vibrated. It was Billie.

"Burning the midnight oil?" he said as a greeting.

"Just checking in."

"Why, Billie Gray, are you worried about me?"

"I thought it best I make sure you don't die on me."

"I appreciate that. I'd prefer not to die as well." He lay down on the bench. It was hard and uncomfortable, but his back ached, and relieving the pressure felt like a drug coursing through his muscles. Making them loose and relaxed.

"Can I ask you something?" he said.

"Ask away."

"Why are you so concerned with this?"

"What do you mean?"

"Something about this case buried itself inside of you. I was wondering what it was."

She hesitated.

"I don't know. Do you know what it is about it that buried itself inside of you?"

"Not really."

"I don't think we can know. Murder's just something we respond to, however we respond to it."

"That's the nature of the beast. Murder is inherently chaotic, but there are some arguments that it's evolutionarily necessary."

"Necessary?"

"The great apes use four limbs for movement, we use two. Why? What caused us to stand upright when moving on four limbs is more effective?"

"So we could run?"

"That's one theory. The other is so that we could murder. It's difficult to kill with your bare hands, so weapons are better mechanisms. We stood upright and changed the entire trajectory of the species so that we could murder more efficiently."

"You're just a hit at parties, I imagine, Solomon."

"Life is dark. Show me it isn't and I'll quit dwelling on it."

He heard a faucet run and then turn off.

He thought back to eight years ago when he had met with the mother of one of the final victims. She had wept in his office and said, "Please promise me you won't let him do this to anyone else's daughter."

Solomon promised and had forgotten it. The woman died of heart disease two years ago. Solomon only knew about it because the husband had reached out to him with an email and asked that he fulfill his promise to her. It was one of the last things she mentioned before passing.

"Everyone in this field really does have that one case, don't they?" he said.

"Yeah, they do."

His phone dinged with an email. He looked at the notification on his screen and saw it was from a sender he didn't recognize.

"Lemme call you back," he said before hanging up.

He opened the email.

The first line read, This is Reaper speaking.

28

It was one in the morning when Melinda Toby woke up to the sound of the front door opening. She had tried to sleep for several hours, but it wouldn't come. Not while Braden was gone. Though only sixteen, he no longer told her where he was going or what he was doing or who he was doing it with.

She put on slippers and her robe and went downstairs. Noises were coming from the kitchen. She didn't turn on any lights but stood at the entryway and watched her son in the dim pantry light. Even in the semidark, she could see the thick veins in his forearms. He always squeezed those stupid grip pumps to increase his forearm strength, and she never understood why.

He guzzled soda out of a two-liter bottle and ate cookies and melted chocolate spread on white bread. When he was little, she had tried to get him to eat fruits and vegetables, and he chose instead to starve himself to the point that she had to take him to the emergency room to get an IV and feeding tube. After that, she had never rechallenged him on what to eat.

She flipped on the light. He didn't look up from the food he was making on the counter.

"It's one in the morning, Braden. Where were you?"

"Out," he said, his attention not wavering from the chocolate hazelnut spread he was pouring on the bread like syrup.

"I know you were out. I'm asking where. You said you would be home by ten."

He smashed the spread with a second slice of bread and bit into it, chocolate oozing from his mouth and lips onto the counter. Melinda thought he looked disgusting, like some animal, but she kept it to herself and watched him take another bite, shoving nearly half the sandwich into his mouth.

"I got a call from Aunt Amanda today," she said casually, trying to put herself at ease, telling herself what she felt were the normal feelings of a mother toward a rebellious teenage son.

"Oh yeah?" he said without looking at her.

"Yeah," she said with a tinge of excitement that he was actually responding to her. Most of the time, if he responded at all, it was with grunts or nods.

Their orange tabby, Pickles, jumped onto the counter. The cat got near his food, and Braden roughly pushed him away.

"Braden, don't be rough with the cat."

Pickles came back slowly, the scent of the mountain of sugar irresistible, and this time Braden grinned. She hated his grins.

Braden scooped up the cat. His muscles rippled. The wrestling team, something she had massively encouraged when he showed interest, hoping it would occupy his time and thoughts, had turned out to have been a mistake. His thoughts were the same, but now he was stronger and had less fear of confrontation.

He held Pickles with one hand and picked up the kitchen knife with the other. A nine-inch steel butcher's knife meant to cut large slabs of meat and bones. He put the tip near the cat's belly.

"What are you doing? Put him down this instant!"

"What would you do, Mom, if I cut Pickles open right here in front of you? Would you scream? Would you start crying and never stop?"

Pickles tried to wiggle free, and Braden held the cat tighter.

"Braden," she said as sternly as possible, swallowing down the dark fear that was crawling over her entire body, "I'm only going to say this once. Get that knife away from him."

"Or what?" he said with a mischievous smile. "What are you gonna do if I spill his guts all over your pretty little counter?"

"I will march upstairs and take every one of those stupid knives you've been collecting and throw them in the dumpster. Then I'm going to take your keys and sell your truck tomorrow."

There was a slight change in his face. Not much, but enough that she knew she'd struck the nerve she'd wanted to hit. The only possessions he owned that he cared about were the knives he had been collecting since he was fourteen and an old truck he'd helped pay for with his own money from summer jobs.

"You'd never touch my knives."

It was the first time in years Melinda had heard uncertainty in her son's voice. "Try me," she said without averting her gaze. The truth was, she had no idea what she would do if he slit open the belly of an innocent animal that he knew his mother loved. What could she do?

After a few seconds where the tension hung in the air like cold fog, Braden lowered the knife and set it on the counter. He nuzzled Pickles softly and then said, "You take things too seriously, Mom. I was joking."

He picked up his mess of a sandwich that he had piled onto his plate and left the room. Melinda stood rigid until he left. When he was gone, she ran to Pickles and held him tightly. Tears flowed, and she dashed to the bathroom and locked the door. She sat on the toilet with the cat in her arms and wept.

29

The Tooele County Sheriff's Office had the youngest chief forensic technologist in the state, a twenty-four-year-old woman from Delhi named Binita, who wore thick glasses and barely spoke to anyone else in the office. Billie stood by the door of her office as Solomon paced somewhere outside.

Binita had several posters up: one of Elon Musk, one of Nikola Tesla, and one of Justin Bieber. She printed out a copy of the email like Billie had asked and handed it to her. Billie leaned against the wall as she reread it.

> This is Reaper speaking. Do you really have DNA, and was there really a witness? Respond to this email telling me the truth in the next day, or I'll detonate a bomb on a school bus.

The Reaper letter from eight years ago didn't sound anything like this. This letter, short as it was, had a tinge of panic in it. It wasn't measured, and the language wasn't as sophisticated. Whoever wrote this was spooked, and the Reaper didn't get spooked.

Solomon came in a minute later with three Diet Cokes and handed her one and put one on Binita's desk. He looked disheveled and had scruff on his face. His face was pale, and his lips chapped. He sat down in a chair next to Binita and put his cane in front of him with his hands folded over it. He didn't browse his phone or start chitchatting just to have something to do. He simply stared quietly at his cane, lost in his own thoughts. Billie had never seen anyone else with the ability to simply sit quietly and do nothing for long periods.

"Wow," Binita said.

"What?" Billie said, handing the letter to Solomon, who glanced at it and set it down on the desk.

"So, people don't realize how easy it is to track email. I got the IP address in like a minute. Guy's in Stansbury Park in a house near where Cottonwood Mall used to be."

"That's it?" Billie said. "That easy?"

She shook her head while opening the can of soda. "No. You can bounce signals around so nobody knows where the initial communication originated. This guy is probably doing the same thing, so I would be surprised if this was his real address. But it's a place to start at least."

Billie looked at Solomon and said, "You want to check it out now?"

"Yes. And I feel like getting a Coke Slurpee on the way, so win-win."

———

The home they were parked in front of was a two-story redbrick with a green lawn and a wooden fence around the yard. The two windows at the front of the house were shaped like ovals, which gave it the appearance of a face looking out at the street.

The music blared in the truck, and several times Billie grimaced as the front man of the band roared in his native language. The drums sounded like they were on the edge of breaking.

"What is this?" she shouted.

"Brazilian speed metal. Band called Eaters of the Dead. Or something like that."

"Can we turn it down?"

He reached to the stereo and turned the volume down. "Okay, but you're missing out. This music is meant to be enjoyed at top volume."

"Enjoyed? I've had teeth drillings at the dentist that sounded more pleasant."

"To each their own. It helps me think."

Solomon glanced in the side-view mirror. The deputies in Kevlar the sheriff had brought along shared two cars. Though they didn't expect to find anything here, Billie felt it was better safe than sorry. But she also didn't want a SWAT team raiding some poor family's house in the middle of the night and someone accidentally getting shot.

Billie said, "You didn't say a word the entire drive down here," as she passed him an unopened can of energy drink.

He popped it open and took a sip, and spit it up as he coughed. It felt like he'd swallowed toxic waste. "What is this, jet fuel?"

"Never said it tasted good."

"It's going to make your heart explode."

"And what's your drink?"

"Honestly? Prune juice."

She watched him for a second and then laughed.

"What? The bedouins on the Arabian Peninsula always carried prunes with them because they have every nutrient a human being needs."

"So," she said, still chuckling, "you're telling me you spend your days sitting around sipping prune juice and listening to death metal?"

"Hell no. That crap is nasty. I can only choke it down with whiskey. Who's that?"

They both set eyes on a man who'd pulled to a stop in the driveway in a black sedan. He got out of the driver's side and went to the trunk. Billie immediately said into the radio, "Blue Team, stand down. I don't want fingers anywhere near those triggers until we have confirmation of aggression."

A series of "ten fours" came through, and Solomon was surprised by how disappointed they all sounded. He had always figured the type of person who wants to get into a shootout should not be the type of person who's given a gun.

The home belonged to a man named McKay Tanner, who was married with one child. He worked a job as a data processor at a place called Donher Genetics and had no criminal history. Not surprising if he was the Reaper and could contain his impulses enough to avoid interacting with law enforcement.

The man went into the house and closed the door.

"I got visual," one of the detectives said through the radio. "He's in the kitchen now."

Solomon raised the binoculars that he'd taken from Billie's glove box to his eyes. The home appeared too balanced not to have had at least some help from an interior decorator. The color schemes were too proportional. Human beings didn't think in organized proportions like that, and it had to have been done purposefully, with a lot of thought. Other than that, it didn't appear any different from any other home. Solomon didn't know what he expected: pentagrams and skulls would be the last thing a killer like this would let other people see.

"Did you not get much sleep?"

"Could say that." He lowered the binoculars. He wasn't about to share with her that he'd been having nightmares. First, a quick flash of light, and then Kelly on her back, screaming as the warmth of blood flowed out of her body.

"It's not your fault, Solomon."

He was surprised by her perception. "You can say it all you want; doesn't make it true."

A deputy in plain clothes walked by the home with his hands in the pockets of a thick jacket. When he was around the corner, he radioed in that he hadn't seen any movement inside the home.

"Do you know what my father would say about you?" Billie said after acknowledging what the deputy had radioed. "He told me about this prosecutor that was 'both the smartest and the stupidest son of a bitch' he'd ever met. But he said you were more enthusiastic than anyone in that office." She hesitated a moment.

"What is it?" Solomon asked.

"What is what?"

"He clearly said something else you don't want to tell me. What was it?"

"He also told me it was going to end in tragedy one day and that you knew it."

Solomon leaned back on the seat and didn't respond. "When we going in?"

"You in a rush?"

"Yes. We have no idea how much longer he's going to keep her alive, if she is still alive." He tapped his finger against his thigh a second and then said, "I'm going in by myself."

"What?"

Before she could say anything else, Solomon had opened the door, gotten out, and was headed toward the home.

30

Solomon tried to make as little noise as possible with his cane. He glanced into one of the homes he passed, the one next door to the home the email had come from, and saw the light on in the kitchen. The curtains opened a little as someone stared out at him. He smiled and waved, hoping to calm any fears of why people were running around in the dark.

Billie came out after him, quiet-shouting into the radio for every officer to stand down immediately. When she caught up to him, she grabbed his arm and snapped, "What the hell are you doing?"

"Going in."

"That's not your job."

"It's not illegal to knock and say hello to people, is it? Because frankly, that's not the America I grew up in."

"Solomon—"

"Just chill out. I know what I'm doing. Promise. It's way less risk for everyone if I just talk to him for thirty seconds and see if he's our man."

"You know I can't let you do that, right?"

"Thirty seconds. Promise. If it's going sideways at all, just shut it down and we'll walk away. If this isn't him, if this is just a house he targeted to make it look like the email came from here, then if we raid this house and somebody innocent gets hurt, are you okay with that?

Because I'm not. Not when thirty seconds of talking could prevent it. This is the best way, trust me."

He could tell she didn't buy it, but she let his arm go anyway and said, "Fine. But I'm coming with you."

The two of them walked to the front door of the house. Solomon rang the doorbell. A woman answered in a pink pullover and tiny shorts. She was smiling and then lost the smile when she saw the two of them.

"Um, hi."

Solomon said, "Hi, sorry to interrupt. We were just hoping to speak with your husband."

"And who are you exactly?"

"It's best we talk to him. We saw him pull up, so if we could have five minutes of his time, we'll be out of your hair."

Before she could respond, a man came up behind her. His shirt was untucked and his tie was off, his shoes kicked by the door. He looked worried and said, "I'm sorry, who are you?"

"McKay Tanner?" Billie said.

"Yes."

Billie flashed her badge and said, "Mind if we chat out here for a minute? We're with the Sheriff's Office. Won't take long."

"What's this about?"

"Let's have you step outside, and then we'll tell you everything. You and your wife, please. And is there anybody else in the home?"

He was silent a second as he and his wife exchanged a glance. "Just my son, Benjamin."

"We'll need him to come out, too."

"I'm not going anywhere until I see proof you are who you say you are. People can buy fake badges."

Billie took out her laminated ID card and held it up so he could take a closer look. It was clear he wouldn't have been able to tell a real ID from a fake one, but he seemed pacified enough.

"I'll, um, go get him."

"Actually," Solomon quickly said, "we need both of you to stay where we can see you."

He looked at his wife again. "Why? What the hell is going on?"

They heard footfalls on the stairs, and a boy came bounding down in shorts and a striped shirt.

"Dad? What's going on?"

"Ben," Solomon said, "we need you to come down here and stand with your parents, please."

The boy did as he was asked. McKay stood in front of him as though protecting him, and Solomon took a quick peek at the home's interior. Couches and chairs, photos on the walls, sports on the television in the living room. About as average a home as he had ever seen.

He wondered if it were possible the monster he had been dreaming about for eight years actually lived here, pretending he was human. Going to baseball games and having barbecues, spending time with friends, and shouting at sports. All a facade. All a costume he put on to ensure no one saw what was underneath. The real him. The twisted mess with blank eyes that passively took in the world, seeing no difference between the living and the dead.

"I'm going to be perfectly honest with you, McKay, we have a search warrant to come into your home. I don't want to do that. It's really invasive to have twenty police officers tearing apart your belongings. I would rather we settle this face-to-face right now."

The mother put her hands on the boy's shoulders as though that would protect him from what was coming and said, "McKay, what's going on?"

"I don't know," he replied before turning to Solomon. "What do you want?"

"We need the computers in your house. All of them. How many are there?"

He swallowed. "Three. My laptop, Ben's laptop, and my office computer. Why do you need those?"

"You're sure there's no other computers? If the police go searching through here, they're not going to find another one? Because if so, you should tell us now."

He shook his head. "No, there's no other computers."

"Okay. I believe you."

Billie spoke into her radio, asking for assistance. Within moments, several deputies in green Kevlar vests appeared, their rifles lowered but their trigger fingers on the guards. McKay lost all the color in his face, and his mouth dropped open. Solomon had been fooled by these types of men before, but he would be shocked if McKay's innocence was an act this time. It looked as genuine as anything he'd ever seen.

"McKay, I'd like you to take these gentlemen and show them where the three computers are, as well as any cell phones. I'm going to stay here with your wife and son and make sure nothing happens to them. Okay? I give you my word, nothing will happen to them."

"O . . . kay."

"Good. Deputies, if you would, please."

Billie looked to her men and nodded before two of them went inside with McKay. Another two began searching the house, ensuring there wasn't anyone who would surprise them with a shotgun blast to the back.

"And see if there's any more laptops or phones."

The family looked terrified, but this was nothing compared to how they would've felt if the police had broken down their door with a battering ram. Throwing them to the floor with knees in their backs as they tore apart their house room by room.

Billie spoke with the wife to calm her anxiety and even made her smile with a joke about teenagers. Solomon kept his eyes on the interior of the house, slowly moving from one side to the other. Finally, he took a step past the mother and stood in the entryway. He could smell dinner cooking, and a commercial was playing on the television now.

On the mantel were photographs and one little statuette. A boy's body with a jack-o'-lantern for a head. The teeth were sharp but crooked, and the boy held a bag of Halloween candy. Its eyes were angled downward, and the smile on its face appeared sinister.

"Sheriff?" a deputy said. "Got the computers and all their cell phones. I'll run them down. Just need your signature on the COC form."

Billie signed the chain of custody log and handed it back to the deputy, who left the home with another deputy while carrying the computers. McKay stood with his family. He put his arm around his wife. His eyes were wide with fear.

Billie said, "Mr. Tanner, would you mind talking in private with us, please?"

"All right."

They went out to the front porch, and she shut the door behind them. Solomon sat on a swinging chair on the porch, and she stood in front of McKay. He was fidgeting and checked his watch.

"You have a beautiful family," she said.

"Thanks. Look, what's this really about? I think I have a right to know."

"It's only fair, considering how cooperative you've been. There was an email sent from your IP address that we're trying to track down the origin of. Do you know anything about it?"

He shook his head. "Email sent to who?"

"To me," Solomon said.

"I've never met you in my life."

Billie said, "Mr. Tanner, the email was sent from your home, and I'm guessing from one of those computers or your phones. We'll know soon enough."

"Holy shit, do I need a lawyer? Am I accused of committing a crime?"

"All we know right now is that the email was sent from your IP address. That's it. Any help you can give us would let us quickly cross you off our list and move on."

He shook his head. "I'd love to help, but it wasn't sent from here. It's just me, my wife, and my son. None of us have any reason to email you."

Solomon looked over at the boy and his mother standing in the window. "Do you mind if we speak to your son?"

31

Benjamin Tanner was short and muscular. He stood on the porch with his arms folded and couldn't look them in the eyes. His father stood behind him, and Solomon said, "Can we talk with him alone?"

McKay hesitated, and Billie quickly added, "No one is under arrest, Mr. Tanner. We won't say anything inappropriate. I give you my word."

"I'd prefer to stay." McKay looked at his son and said, "Did you send this man an email?"

He shrugged. "I don't know. Who are you?"

Solomon wished he could've had a chance to probe the boy's thinking before his father had just come out and asked the question. "Solomon Shepard. I'm a former deputy county attorney."

"I've never heard of you."

"Maybe. We're gonna find which computer the email was sent from, and I have a feeling it's going to be yours, isn't it, Ben?"

"What? I don't know what you're talking about," he said, glancing between his father and Solomon. "Why would I send you an email? What did it say?"

"You sure you don't know?"

"No, I don't know. I don't even know what's going on."

McKay looked at his boy and said, "There was an email sent to the police from our house. I didn't do it, and I'm sure your mother didn't do it, so they're asking you."

"Why would I send an email to someone I don't know?"

"I have no idea, son. Did you send it?"

"No," he said emphatically. He was terrified.

"It's okay, Ben. If you sent it as a prank or something—"

"I didn't!"

Solomon noticed the boy's knees and saw injuries that looked like rug burn or road rash. "Cut up your knees pretty bad."

"From the mat. I'm on the wrestling team and didn't have my kneepads."

"Huh. You hang out with the team outside of school?"

"Yeah, we're all friends. Why?"

"Were any of these friends over at your house yesterday?"

He looked at his father, who nodded.

Ben said, "Yeah, one of them was over here."

"Who?"

"Braden."

Billie opened the note-taking app on her phone. "Braden what?"

"His last name's Toby. He lives up the block near the elementary school."

Solomon said, "Did he have access to your laptop?"

"I don't know."

"Is it password protected?"

"Yeah."

The boy was holding something back.

"He knows your password, doesn't he?"

Ben didn't say anything for a moment. "I don't know."

"Tell us the truth, Ben, because after we leave here, you don't want to be seen as helping Braden. Trust me."

His father said, "Did you see him use it at all?"

Ben shook his head.

Billie added, "Were you with him the entire time he was in your home?"

"Um . . . no. No, 'cause my mom needed help in the basement, and Braden hung out while I helped her."

"In your room?"

He nodded.

"Does he know your password or not? You don't want to lie to the sheriff."

He swallowed and kept glancing to his father. "Yeah . . . yeah, it's just my birthday."

"Which house did you say was his?"

Benjamin pointed it out. It was an average-size home with a fence and a small yard. White with a pointed roof like a steeple. The house was completely dark, and there were no cars in the driveway, no flower beds, no toys out, not even a mailbox. Like no one lived there.

"Who lives with him?"

"Just his mom."

"Do you have a picture of Braden?"

"No."

Solomon had started to move off the porch and head in the direction of the house when Billie stepped in front of him. She gently put her hand on his forearm and whispered, "Let me handle it. That's what we're paid for."

Solomon looked at the house again and nodded.

The truck felt stuffy even with the windows down. Solomon checked the temperature on his phone: ninety-six. He went to turn on some music, and Billie said, "For the love of all that's holy, no more Japanese or Brazilian death metal."

"I was going to play some Norwegian for a change. And don't be a hater."

"Do you even know what that means?"

"Probably not."

He looked out at the home. Billie had wisely said her deputies would get Braden out of the house and take him down cleanly and safely. So they'd stood by as Benjamin called Braden and asked him to come over because he'd gotten a new video game console he wanted to show him. The lights inside the Tobys' home had turned on a few minutes later, but no one had come out.

"If it is him, it'd make him one of the youngest serial murderers in history," Billie said.

"One of, not *the*."

"Who does that honor go to?"

"Amarjeet Sada. He was eight years old and would strangle other children in his village and hide the bodies. When he was interrogated, he laughed about the murders and asked for more biscuits."

"Wow. Where is he now?"

"No one knows. He was too young to imprison for murder in India, so they kept him in an asylum until he was eighteen and then released him."

She shook her head but didn't take her eyes off the house. "What would cause an eight-year-old to do that?"

"The psychologist they brought in said he found a brain abnormality. So it could be that."

"You don't sound convinced."

"An organic origin could explain his enjoyment of the suffering of others, but most killers with organic brain disorders or injuries are disorganized killers. They don't take steps to not get caught because they don't think what they're doing is wrong. They'll leave bodies out in the open or kill in front of others. Amarjeet didn't do that. He took time to hide the bodies where people weren't likely to find them. That doesn't say *brain abnormality* to me."

"What does it say?"

"I don't know." He thought a moment. "Do you know where the idea of demons comes from?"

"Who would possibly know that except you."

He grinned. "They're one of the first things human beings ever made art about. We found demons on cave paintings in the South of France dating back almost forty thousand years. The ancients believed that if there was enough tragedy, enough suffering, demons could be imprinted onto a place . . . or a person."

"So you think this boy is a demon? Not just some screwed-up kid who idolizes a serial killer he thinks is a rock star?"

"I didn't say I believed it. I said the ancients believed it."

"What do you believe?"

"I believe there's things in this world that have been here a lot longer than us."

The front porch light came on. A young man in jeans and a T-shirt with a baseball cap came out.

"Is that the one who gave you the note?"

"Maybe. I can't tell. It's too dark."

She got on the radio and said, "Take him."

Deputies swarmed around the boy from where they'd been stationed out of sight. Braden stood motionless. They barked orders. The boy kept his head low. Then, slowly, he looked up at the flashlights and firearms pointed at him. His hands were at his sides, and the deputies were shouting for him to get down on the ground.

In a flash, he turned and dashed back into the house.

32

"Shit!"

Billie jumped out of the car as her deputies raced in after the boy. She looped around the house in a full sprint to the backyard in time to see Braden hop the fence and disappear.

There was little moonlight and only a handful of streetlights. The beams of flashlights cut through the darkness as deputies ran out the back, but the boy was fast and had a head start. A woman was screaming from inside the home.

Billie ran down the block and came around the corner. The neighborhood was quiet and still and only had two streetlamps before a dead end blocked off by homes and then a ravine behind them. Braden couldn't have run right through. He would have to hide in one of the homes or come through here to get to the next neighborhood.

"Anyone have visual?" she said into her radio.

"Negative."

"Consider him armed and extremely dangerous. Don't take any chances."

"Roger that."

She walked in the middle of the road, glancing into homes as she did so. Never, not once, had she fired her gun on the job, and she'd only had to pull it out on a handful of occasions. The thought of having to use it now on a teenager made her stomach tighten into a fist.

"Braden?" she shouted. "Braden, are you out here? I don't want to hurt you. I want to talk to you. That's all. Just talk."

No reply. She unsnapped the strap on her holster and stopped. The crunch of leaves—or maybe twigs or gravel—came from somewhere to the right of her. She heard crickets now and felt the trickle of sweat on her neck.

"Braden? I don't want to hurt you, son. Just come out."

Another sound. This one behind her. She turned, her heart pounding, and withdrew her weapon. She fell into the Weaver stance and scanned left, then right. It took a moment to register that the noise was a rock someone had thrown.

As she looked down at the rock, Braden tackled her from behind like a linebacker. His veiny hands went around her throat from behind. His weight felt like a boulder on top of her as she fought to turn around.

The gun had been knocked out of her hand. She grabbed at his hands on her neck, which were hard as stone and sweaty. Drool slopped from his mouth as he squeezed her windpipe, growling like an animal. She saw stars and felt herself losing consciousness.

Her gun was out of reach. Tucking her chin down, she managed to get the soft part of the skin between his thumb and pointer finger in her mouth. She bit down so hard she tasted coppery blood. His grip loosened enough that she managed to crawl out from under him and grab her weapon. The second she had it in her hand, Braden let go. He held his hands up and got off her, getting onto his knees. Giving her no excuse to shoot him.

Coughing and sucking breath as though she had been drowning, Billie held the firearm on him from her position on the ground. Pointed at his chest. The boy was looking down and she couldn't see his eyes, but she could see the lower part of his face. He was smiling.

"Do it," he whispered.

She felt the smoothness of the trigger, the weight of the gun, and time seemed to slow. How many people had he killed? How much suffering had this one boy brought into the world? Would he truly be missed?

"Do it. I want you to do it."

Boots stomped the pavement. Her deputies swarmed Braden and had cuffs on him in less than ten seconds. Solomon came around the corner a moment later. She holstered her weapon, and he helped her to her feet.

"Your body looked like it was bracing for kickback," he said. "Tell me you weren't a second away from doing what I think you were going to do."

"I don't know what you're talking about."

As Braden was lifted by several deputies, he looked at Billie, and winked.

33

Solomon stood outside one of the interview rooms at the sheriff's station. Two male detectives sat at a table with Braden in the next room on the other side of the one-way glass. The boy had a youthful face, handsome and with a glint of intelligence in his eyes. He was heavily muscled—had to be from steroid use since he was far too young to have developed that much muscle naturally—and a prominent vein ran from his neck down past his collar and thumped along with the beat of his heart.

He hadn't spoken since his arrest.

Billie sat on a couch in the hallway, sipping water. She probably wouldn't admit it, but Solomon knew she was shaken. So he went over and sat next to her but left the intercom on so they could hear what was going on in the interview room.

"This isn't a joke, it's serious," one of the detectives said. "It would be better for everyone if you helped us out. You help us, and I give you my word, we'll help you. You're only sixteen, a juvenile. That means there's a lot we can do for you that we couldn't do for an adult. But we can't help unless you tell us what happened."

Braden didn't move, didn't even seem to blink. Solomon could tell the boy was a million miles away and not listening to a word the detective said.

"Nothing's going to happen tonight," Solomon said. "His mother's on the way down and will probably ask for a lawyer. You should go home and get some sleep."

She stared at him with a look that said, *Are you kidding me?* and he shrugged and said, "Just a suggestion."

The bottle of water crackled as she finished the last swallow. "I've had people attack me before, but nothing like this. He was so angry. I've never seen anger like that up close."

"Hey, you survived. You beat him, and now he's sitting in that room, and it's only a matter of time before everything comes out. You won. I know it came at a cost, but you saved lives tonight."

She ran her fingers across the deep purple bruises on her neck. The paramedics had asked her to go to the ER to get thoroughly checked out, and she promised she would later. Solomon didn't hear the rattle in her voice that a cracked windpipe would cause. He would stay with her as long as he could, just in case.

After a good hour of attempting to get Braden to talk, the two detectives came out of the interview room. Both of them had their jackets off and rings of sweat under their arms.

"Nothing," one of them said. "Little dipshit won't say a word."

Solomon stared at the boy through the glass. He sat still as a block of stone.

"What's the temp in here?"

"The temperature?" one of the detectives asked.

"Yeah."

He shrugged. "I don't know. Gotta be eighty."

"Turn on the heat."

"What? Why?"

"Turn up the heat as far as it can go. And then close as many windows as you can so we can get this place as hot as possible."

The detective looked at Billie, who nodded her approval. Then he mumbled something and wandered off. A deputy in uniform, an older male with white hair, poked his head around the corner and said, "The mother's here."

Billie replied, "Stall her. Give her some coffee and tell her we'll bring her right back."

She rose and stood next to Solomon. "Let's hope he sweats easy."

———

The heat quickly grew noticeably worse. Finally, when it was over a hundred, both detectives and Billie and Solomon fanned themselves with small electric fans they'd scrounged up from people's offices. Braden sat quietly. His cuffs rattled as he pulled out a few strands of hair from his head and then aligned them on the table in front of him in what looked like a circle, but what Solomon could tell was his attempt at a skull.

The bald patches on his scalp and eyebrows revealed he had trichotillomania: the uncontrollable urge to pull out hair.

"You got another towel? A clean one?" Solomon said to one of the detectives, who sat dabbing the sweat off his neck with a white hand towel. He had taken off his tie and rolled up his sleeves, and his forearms were thick and pale.

"Yeah."

"Hand it to him along with a can of soda. Ask a few mundane questions but don't focus on the towel at all. Don't even look at it. Then when he doesn't respond, tell him you're gonna get his mom and be right back."

The detective looked like he was about to say something, probably something along the lines of telling Solomon where he could shove his towel and soda, but Billie said, "Just do it, Joey."

Joey left for a bit and came back with the towel and soda. He went into the room. Braden barely seemed to notice. His eyes were locked on to the strands of hair on the table.

"Sorry," Joey said as he set the towel and orange soda on the table near Braden. "Air conditioner's busted."

Joey sat down and said, "You're too young to experience this, but once you hit a certain age, everything's either too hot or too cold."

He tapped the desk a few times, hoping for some sort of response, but got none.

"Well, anyway, Braden, your mom is here. I'll get her, and I'll give you two some privacy."

He left the room, and Braden sat staring at the door.

Come on, Solomon thought. *Come on . . .*

Braden reached up and opened the tab on the soda. He took a long drink and then set it down before picking up the towel. He wiped the sweat off his face and tossed the towel back on the table.

"Detective, please get in there and get our towel."

Billie looked at him and grinned.

34

Melinda Toby sat on the couch at the sheriff's station and tried to calm her shaking hands. Everything had happened so fast that she still hadn't processed it. All she remembered was Braden opening the door and leaving and then running back into the house. Before she could ask him what was going on, men dressed in dark uniforms stormed the house with guns drawn. She screamed as one of them grabbed her and threw her to the floor, twisting her arms behind her back and shouting at her not to move.

A woman came into the waiting area and brought her an ice-filled drink. She was pretty with pink tips to her platinum blonde hair and colorful tattoos on her forearms. The police shield around her neck identified her as the sheriff.

"Thank you," Melinda said, letting the coolness of the cup dissipate into her hands.

The sheriff sat in a chair near the couch. "Iced chamomile. My mom used to give me chamomile when I had nightmares. She said that nightmares were scared of chamomile."

A weak grin came to Melinda as she took a sip. Some of the tea slopped out of the cup because her hands were shaking so badly.

"I'm sorry, I spilled. I'll find some paper towels."

"No," the sheriff said as she held out her hand, gesturing for Melinda to stay seated, "don't bother. It's not a big deal."

Melinda crossed her legs. "No one will talk to me. Will you please tell me what's going on?"

The sheriff inhaled a deep breath and looked to the floor, rubbing her fingertip against her thumb slowly as if she were thinking about what to say. "Do you mind if I call you Melinda?"

"Not at all."

"Good. I've always liked that name. I have a cousin somewhere named Melinda, but we don't talk. I think she's slipped up and lost her house again. Drugs are a chaotic thing."

"I'm sorry to hear that. Were you at risk of ending up the same?"

"No. I had sports and painting, music. I kept myself busy. What about you? Any black sheep siblings, or were you the black sheep?"

"I have a half brother . . . somewhere. He was a child from my mother's first marriage before she met my father."

"Doesn't sound like you two are close."

Melinda nodded and looked down at her hands. "It's about the same situation as with your cousin. They say money's the root of all evil, but I don't think so. I think drugs are the root of all evil."

"I've seen enough that I think I would tend to agree."

The two looked at each other, and Melinda thought that the sheriff would be gorgeous with makeup and wondered why she didn't wear any.

"Will you tell me what's going on, Sheriff?"

"Billie is fine. And yes, of course. I'll give you my card before you leave, and if you have any questions, you can call me."

"Thank you," Melinda said, looking down into her cup. "I don't . . . I don't really have anybody to help me with all this . . . whatever this is. It's just me and Braden. So what are they accusing him of doing?"

"Melinda, your son is suspected of doing some terrible things. I don't mean to be insensitive about it, but does he suffer from any mental disorders that you know of?"

Melinda swallowed and looked down into her tea. She closed her eyes. When she opened them again, a glimmer of hope that she would wake up in bed from a dream was snuffed out, and it gave her a heavy sadness that didn't feel like it would be lifted again.

"What terrible things?"

Billie held her gaze. "What's your son like, Melinda?"

"What's he *like*?"

"Yes. Is he quiet? Loud? Does he like being the center of attention, or would he rather—"

"You want to know if he's violent, don't you?"

She nodded. "Yes. I do."

The cold of the cup had faded, and she set it down on the floor in front of the couch. The floor was dirty, and it brought up an obsessive urge to clean. Her father said she'd gotten it from her mother, who grew up in a tiny apartment with eight other siblings. If she didn't clean the house, it wouldn't get cleaned, so she had developed a compulsion, and Melinda remembered her cleaning day and night before her death.

"I didn't know his father very well. I didn't go out much in high school, so when one of the cute boys invited me to a party, I thought . . ." Tears came to her eyes, and she didn't even feel them at first. "He . . . um . . ."

Billie put her hand over Melinda's. "I understand. You don't need to tell me any more if it makes you uncomfortable."

She nodded. "Thank you. It's just not something I think about."

Billie gave her hand a light squeeze, then let go. "Men are definitely the crueler gender."

"Women can be just as cruel, but for different reasons." She thought a moment, staring at a spot on the floor. "I was sixteen and pregnant without a dime to my name, living in my father's basement."

"That couldn't have been easy."

"No, it wasn't. And my father was an alcoholic, so in addition to the baby, I had to keep taking care of my father. I sometimes feel like I didn't have a childhood at all."

Billie leaned forward with her elbows on her knees. "What was Braden like as a child?"

"He was . . . different. But I'd never been around young children, so I didn't know."

"Different how?"

"He didn't talk until he was seven years old. The doctors told me nothing was wrong with him. That he was perfectly capable of talking, he just refused. And it seemed like the more speech therapists and classes I got him in, the more he fought me. It was like . . . he enjoyed making me worry."

"What did you think was wrong with him?"

"I didn't know. I thought all kids were that way. But as he got older, and he finally started talking . . . it got worse. He never laughed. Never. But sometimes I would catch him looking at someone with a smile that . . ."

She trailed off and didn't finish her sentence. It felt like everything wanted to come out, to spill right on the floor and hopefully alleviate some of the heavy grayness that followed her around like a cloud. But she didn't know who to trust. The sheriff seemed genuine, but she was here to get information that would help put Braden in prison for the rest of his life. Melinda told herself she had to remember that.

After a time, Billie said, "You knew early on, didn't you? That something was wrong with him?"

Tears forced their way out, though Melinda fought them. Billie got her some tissues, and she took two and dabbed at her eyes. "He wasn't a bad child, not until much later. He just . . . had to do things his own way." She chuckled mirthlessly at a memory: Braden refusing to get potty-trained until Melinda left him alone to do it. He did it because, he had said later, nobody told him to.

"I thought his independence was a good thing. Shows how great of a mother I am."

"Whatever is or isn't wrong with Braden, it's not your fault."

"Whenever something's wrong with a child, everyone blames the mother." She dried the last of her tears. "Do I need a lawyer for him?"

Billie licked a portion of her lower lip. "Yes, he should have a lawyer."

Melinda nodded. "I'll get him one. Can I see him?"

"Sure. I'll take you back."

35

Solomon had been left alone in the hall outside the interview room. He couldn't take his eyes off the boy. Braden didn't mumble or talk to himself or rock back and forth. Solomon didn't see any facial tics, any sudden laughter or despair, any sort of one-way conversation that could be indicative of schizophrenia or schizoaffective disorder. When looking at Braden Toby, as hard as he tried not to, he saw only a child.

No one else was around. The deputy that was supposed to be sitting outside the interview room had gone to smoke, since Solomon was already here.

Solomon rolled up his sleeves. He unbuttoned the top two buttons on his shirt, revealing the golden cross that hung around his neck. A trinket given to him by his mother before her suicide that hadn't come off since. Even though he no longer was a man of faith. Maybe that had been his mother's plan all along: knowing he was going to leave spirituality behind, she gave him a final gift and asked him to carry it with him for protection. A way to have religion in his life without having it in his life.

Solomon glanced around to make sure no one was nearby and then went inside the room. Braden didn't seem to notice that someone else had entered until Solomon was seated across from him.

"Did you like my letter?"

He didn't sound like a teenager, much more like a man. The steroids had lowered his voice.

His muscles bulged underneath his shirt, and veins wrapped around his forearms and ran up into his biceps. He looked like he could break Solomon in half without even trying.

"Do you lift weights because you enjoy it or because it makes you a more efficient killer?" Solomon said.

"You didn't answer my question."

Solomon watched Braden's dark eyes and angular face, his mouth, and the way his lips were slightly wet from his tongue running across them. The way his nostrils flared. The small bald patches on his head and eyebrows where he had ripped out his hair.

"Yes, I liked your letter."

Braden said, "Good. Then ask me anything you want. It's truth time."

Solomon tapped his cane against the floor softly enough that it didn't make any sound. "It's eloquent, isn't it? The letter from the real Reaper? For a while, I thought I might be looking for someone with a literature background. The reference to *Beowulf* isn't something many people would get. Though I guess I should be flattered he assumed we would know."

Despite the muscle, deep voice, and mature demeanor, Braden Toby was still a high school student, and his face reflected it. Solomon thought back to himself in high school and remembered thinking he knew everything, only to get older and find out he knew nothing.

"Where is she, Braden? She's all I care about right now. I'm not looking for a confession or to build a case against you or anything like that. I just want Kelly back safe with her mom." He hesitated. "If she's already dead, I'd like to at least return her body to her family for burial."

Braden blinked slowly and said, "It sucks to want something really bad, doesn't it? I know what that feels like."

The anger that bubbled inside of Solomon seemed like it could come bursting out in a string of profanities, but all he did was look down to the rubber tip of his cane and push it gently against the linoleum floor.

"At least tell me if she's alive."

No response.

"How did you even know I knew her?"

Braden shrugged, and the grin never left his face.

Solomon turned back to his cane. A war raged inside him right now. This child had probably been through so much trauma to cause him to turn out this way, on top of whatever genetic factors and brain injuries had contributed, that he was deserving of pity. But Solomon also knew the world would be a better place without the boy in it.

He pushed on his cane and used it to stand. He was nearly to the door when Braden said, "I liked your book."

Solomon turned to him.

"I liked the categories for people like me. It was interesting."

"People like you?"

"People who don't let anybody tell them what's good and evil."

Solomon sat back down. "Then who decides what's good and evil?"

"I do. You do. We choose what's evil and what's not. Anything's allowed." He touched the tip of each finger to his thumb, running up and down the fingers quickly like a wave. His nails had been bitten down so much each finger had remnants of dried blood. The bald patches on his head went all the way down the back. Solomon could see why witnesses had seen him with a hat on and why he had worn one when handing his note to Solomon at the museum. He'd simply be too distinct and identifiable without one.

Braden stared at the hair arranged on the table in front of him. "Do you know the morality we have now, Christian morality, was created by slaves? It was the morality of the slaves in Rome. The Romans had a better morality. Do whatever you want since the gods do whatever they want. But the slaves took what they were forced to be, humble and meek and all that bullshit, and they said it's morality. Society's morality is the morality of slaves. I'm not a slave."

"Rome collapsed under its immorality, and the slaves took over the world. The Romans' morality wasn't superior, it just seemed like it was."

Braden popped another wad of hair out of his head and aligned it on the table in a curve. Then he tore out another one and played with it for a while. "You know how you have thirteen categories of killers? What category am I?"

His voice had a glimmer of hope in it, and it churned Solomon's stomach. The boy wanted infamy; he wanted to cause fear and be admired for it. He wanted respect and didn't even realize that by copying the crimes of someone else, he had given that very thing up.

"I don't know yet."

Braden set down the hair he was playing with and slid it over to the other strands he had pulled out, and started forming a circle with them. "I thought you were wrong that Jeffrey Dahmer was a thirteen."

"Really?" Solomon said. "Why's that?"

"I think he felt bad for all that shit he did. He was lonely. That's why he drilled holes in their heads and poured acid in. He thought he could make zombies that would never leave him. He did what he did out of loneliness. I felt bad for him."

"Are you sure you're capable of feeling bad for people?"

"Are you?"

They didn't speak as Braden took a sip of the orange drink and then said, "Have you ever heard of Jean Ahadi? He wasn't in your book."

"I haven't."

"He was a general in the Congo. Killed like six thousand people. He used to dip bread in a bowl of their blood and eat it."

Solomon rested both hands on the handle of his cane. "You seem pretty knowledgeable about the subject of killing."

Braden grinned as he continued playing with the hair on the table, forming it in the shape of a skull. "I read a lot."

The door opened, and the deputy meant to guard Braden poked his head in. "Sorry, Counselor, but I got orders from the sheriff that no one can be in here with him. His mom's told us she's getting a lawyer for him."

"Thanks. We were done anyway."

He rose and glanced at Braden, who didn't lift his eyes from the hair on the table. "Tell me where she is, Braden. Last chance to help yourself."

When no response came, Solomon swallowed his anger and turned toward the door.

As Solomon left, Braden said, "If you knew about everything I've done in my life, you'd make a new category for me, too."

36

Two weeks after Braden's arrest, Melinda awoke with a headache. She made some coffee before finding the bottle of fish food in a cupboard. Braden had sat quietly in the police interview room, and when she asked what had happened, he'd only said to make sure his fish was fed.

She went upstairs to his room. It was bare. The fishbowl sat on a desk he occasionally used but never for schoolwork. School didn't interest him, but he read for hours on end. One time, when she was cleaning up his room, she saw that his mattress bulged. When she lifted it, expecting a stash of dirty magazines, she instead found books. Books on serial killers, weapons, torture, and anatomy. She'd brushed it off as intellectual curiosity. But now that the sheriff had explained to her what he would be charged with, she understood what she had been looking at.

After feeding the fish, she took a quick shower and put on her scrubs and some makeup. Her shift started in twenty minutes, and she knew she would be late but didn't mind today.

The sun was coming through the bathroom windows, and it would be another hot day. She turned on the radio to have a voice in the house, and it was blaring a talk show, someone ranting about some issue she knew nothing about. She turned the radio off and stared at herself in the mirror.

After trying to eat something for breakfast and being unable to, she got her keys and walked through the connecting door to the garage.

When she opened the garage door, she saw it.

Red.

Spattered everywhere. Over her lawn, over the front porch, over her windows. And scrawled across her front door were the words BURN IN HELL.

How, she wondered, had they done all this without her noticing anything? She didn't sleep much anymore, and she figured she must've been awake when they did this.

She tried scrubbing the paint with bleach, which helped a little, but there was so much of it she knew she couldn't get it off in time for work, so it had to be left for later. But at least she had gotten the word MURDERER off her driveway.

The hospital wasn't far, but she took the long way so she could try to get in the right mindset. She found herself crying in the bathroom for long periods sometimes and made an effort now to prepare for the day better.

When she did pull in, nervousness gnawed at her as she scanned for news crews. They'd been trying to interview her for days and she had successfully dodged them so far, but she didn't know how much longer that would last.

When it was clear nobody from the news was around, she got out and went inside.

Hiva, a Filipina girl a year out of nursing school, manned the nurses' station. She didn't look up from her paperwork as she said, "Rough night?"

"How can you tell?"

"You're only late when you have a rough night. Have you ever even used a vacation day?"

"Oh, I need to keep my mind occupied right now. It's fine."

The truth was, she had no debt and substantial savings from frugal living. The reason she didn't take vacations was that she had no one to go with; Braden never wanted to travel, and her boyfriend of the past six months was a busy CTO at a technology company and couldn't take time off. The thought of going alone to an unfamiliar place didn't appeal to her: she had done that too much already.

The head nurse, a bigger man named Charles who liked to have a stethoscope around his neck at all times, came out of his office when he heard Melinda's voice. "Can I see you a second?"

She went into the office and stood in front of the desk. Charles shut the door behind her and said, "Have a seat."

As far back as she could remember, Charles had never shut the door for one of their conversations.

The two sat across from each other. Charles moved some papers aside, then cleared his throat.

"I'm going to get to the point, Melinda. We're having some patients who have a problem with you treating them."

"What patients?"

"Doesn't matter. What matters is that it's more than one."

"If someone has a problem with how I do things, I think I have the right to—"

"It's not the way you do things, not at all. You're a fantastic nurse, and everybody here knows it." He cleared his throat again. "But the complaints have made some of us uncomfortable because of everything that's going on."

She sat in stunned silence. What did that have to do with her job?

"I don't know what you want me to say to that. I have no defense. My son is accused of doing horrible things."

He nodded. "I understand. But we have to think about the patients first. I talked to Bruce this morning, and he felt it would be best if . . ." He cleared his throat again and didn't speak.

"No," she said, alarmed. "No, you can't fire me. I'm the most experienced person you have on that floor."

"I know, and that's what makes this so much harder. Because I know it's not your fault. But whenever they talk about your son, they mention you. And there's been several mentions in the press about the hospital, and reporters have been showing up and pretending to be patients to get me or Bruce talking about it and all sorts of crazy things. It's gotten out of hand."

"So your solution is to fire me? What have I done to deserve this?"

"Nothing. Absolutely nothing. You're completely innocent. But that's life, isn't it? Bad things happen to everybody."

Melinda felt tears coming, and she put her hand to her forehead and lowered her gaze so Charles wouldn't see her cry.

"I don't know what to do," she said as emotion choked her. "I need this job. I need to be here right now and have my mind taken off of everything. I visited him last night, Charles. I saw my son in a jumpsuit in a place with bars and armed guards. Do you have any idea what that feels like?"

He hesitated a bit and wiped at his desk, though there was no dust. "No, I don't. And I'm sorry I have to do this . . . but I have to."

She swallowed and rose. "Then to hell with you and to hell with this place!"

Melinda stormed out of the hospital, even though several nurses asked her if she was all right. She ignored them and hurried out. When she got to the front entrance, she ran to her car and didn't cry until she was alone with the doors closed.

———

The law offices were large and plush and in the most expensive-looking building in downtown Salt Lake. Melinda sat on a lavish leather couch and checked her phone. It was two in the afternoon. The slow time at work. Right now, she should be hovering over the nurses' desk, sharing war stories of the day and snacking on whatever treats someone had brought in. She'd always felt alone, but never more so than now.

Two people, a young couple, sat across from her in the waiting area. They would glance at her and then whisper to each other. She pretended she didn't notice.

"Ms. Toby?" the receptionist said from her massive red cherrywood desk. "Mr. Yang is ready for you now. I'll take you back."

The offices took up an entire floor, and she saw men and women sitting in front of screens, drafting documents whose titles she didn't understand. One office they passed had a man pouring some whiskey from a minibar into a tumbler. Another had a woman who stared angrily at them as they walked by. As though she was ready to bite the head off of anyone who looked her way.

Dennis Yang was the best defense attorney referral she could get. Her neighbor up the street was a lawyer, and she had recommended him for criminal matters. Melinda wondered how much a lawyer with an office like this would charge.

Dennis Yang wore a tan suit and sat at his desk. His white shirt was immaculately pressed and clean, and his gold and black tie had a thick windsor knot. A gold Rolex was on his wrist, and it shimmered in the sun as he rose and held out his hand.

"Ms. Toby, so nice to meet you."

She shook, and he offered her a seat in front of his desk. The chairs were leather and thick. Uncomfortable but immaculate and impressive.

"Thank you for meeting with me today on such short notice," she said. "I'm here for my son, Braden Toby."

He nodded. "Yes, my paralegal prepared a brief description. My understanding is he's in police custody and hasn't spoken to them."

"I don't know for certain, but I don't think he's talked to them."

"Good. Regardless of whether our firm represents him or not, it's very important you let him know not to speak to anybody about this case. Even other juveniles at the detention facility. Sometimes they'll garner confessions from other children and tell the authorities in exchange for special favors."

"Oh, okay. I'll let him know."

He pulled over a legal pad and pen. "How old is he?"

"Sixteen. Turns seventeen in three months."

"Where is his father in all this?"

"I don't know. I haven't spoken to him in sixteen years."

"Has Braden spoken to you about the details of this case at all?"

She shook her head. "No. I didn't know anything about it until the police told me the night he got arrested."

"Tell me about how they arrested him."

"I don't really know much. One second, Braden was leaving; the next, he ran into the house, and several police officers with guns came running after him. One of them threw me down and hurt my back. I have an appointment with a physical therapist later this week because it's not getting better."

"I should tell you, Ms. Toby, that should you hire our firm, Braden would be my client, not you. Even though you are paying the bill. That means that attorney-client privilege does not apply to you, and anything you tell me, a court can force me to reveal. I won't reveal it, and we'll pretend this conversation never happened, but I want you to be aware that my loyalties will lie with Braden. I will do whatever I can to protect him, and that may involve attacking others. Even yourself."

"Yes, I understand. That's what I want. Someone who will fight for him." Emotion suddenly tightened her throat, and she had to swallow so she wouldn't burst into tears. "He's a unique child. I don't believe it's his fault . . . do you have kids?"

"Yes, I do. But they're grown up and out of the house."

"I bet they're good kids. When they were young, you were full of hope of all the possibilities open to them. I didn't have that. You can't know what it feels like to watch your child growing into something . . . awful." She looked down to the floor. "Sometimes, his cruelty shocks me."

Dennis Yang inhaled deeply and thought a moment. "People can choose who to become, but there are people who are simply born with disadvantages that maybe the rest of us don't have, and it leads them to proclivities we don't understand. But of course, we need other people. So even if they have these proclivities, they have to learn to live in society. And, pardon my saying so, but if they don't have the right guides, these people can turn to . . . troubling behavior. But that doesn't mean they were born bad or that they can't change."

Her hands felt dry. When she was stressed, really stressed, eczema broke out on her fingers, and she constantly had to apply lotion, though she'd forgotten to today. It seemed so unimportant now.

"Can you help him, Mr. Yang?"

He leaned forward on the desk and tapped the pen in his hand lightly against the legal pad. "I'm not going to lie to you, Ms. Toby, and I expect the same courtesy from you and Braden. I am the best attorney in the state for matters like this, and our firm has resources that many firms don't have. Connections to police administrations, judges, prosecutors, mediators, and even legislators and a senator. Many of them are lawyers who either worked here or want to work here, so we may get special favors occasionally. If anyone can help your son, it's our firm."

"Do you think you can get him out?"

"I don't know. We have to look at the strength of the State's case. The fact that he is still a juvenile is good, but I have a feeling that won't last. For a case this publicized and with this many victims, political pressure to try him as an adult will be formidable."

"What does that mean?"

"It means he could be facing the death penalty."

"Oh, my heavens! Oh, no." The tears came now, and she didn't hold them back. Dennis Yang sat there calmly, a person used to people crying in front of him.

"We're not at the place yet where we need to talk about that. There's a long road between right now and then. So let's focus on the here and now."

"Yes, of course," she said, wiping tears away.

"Our normal fee for a case of this magnitude is a hundred and fifty thousand, paid upfront as a retainer and billed at four hundred per hour."

She wiped the last of her tears away. "I can pull it out of my retirement account. And my father left me some money. I'll make sure you're paid."

"Good." He brought the legal pad near him again. "I'll need some more information from you, and then I'll go visit Braden."

37

Solomon looked down from his balcony at the reporters gathered in the street. He was amazed how long they could be there for; he had always assumed they were so busy they had to jump from story to story, but they had camped out in front and tried to get quotes from him every time he left the building.

They harassed Kelly's mother and stepfather, too.

The thought pierced him with a dread he didn't think he could feel. If she was dead, it was his fault . . . and he would never forgive himself.

A knock at the door roused him from his thoughts, and when he answered, he saw Billie with a bag of bagels and two bottles of water. She shoved one of the waters into his hand and came inside the apartment. He got the impression she was bringing things over all the time because she was worried he wasn't eating.

"Anything?" he said.

She put the bagels on the counter and took one out, placing it on a napkin for him with a small container of cream cheese. "Afraid not. He refuses to speak with anyone. And we just received an appearance of counsel notice."

He started spreading the cream cheese on the bagel with a plastic knife. "Who?"

She took a sip of the coffee. "Dennis Yang."

Memories that hadn't been brought up in a long time popped into his head; he felt his breath quicken and had to consciously slow down his breathing. Dennis Yang had represented the defendant who had attacked and almost killed Solomon in court. Solomon remembered lying on the floor, bleeding to death, as the bailiffs tackled the defendant. Dennis had stood at the defense table, too shocked to move or say anything.

"He's the best," Solomon said. "One seventy IQ, Harvard Law grad, and political connections up the wazoo. That's who I'd hire if it were my son."

Billie nodded and looked out through his balcony doors. "My father said you two had a bit of a rivalry."

"I don't know, maybe. There's people who you're polite to, but there's just something about them that rubs you the wrong way."

"I think you might have a frenemy."

The bagel was warm and soft. Solomon took another bite and put it back down on the counter. Billie remained standing, and so did he, though he leaned on his cane. "I was thinking . . . maybe I should prosecute this."

"Why?"

"It's my fault she's dead. What am I supposed to do with that? Just keep living my life like nothing happened? I don't want to risk a prosecutor who doesn't give a shit about this case taking it and cutting a deal with Braden."

"Not my place to tell you what to do. But I would support you either way."

"I need to think about it a little more."

She nodded once and moved toward the door. "Oh," she said, turning around at the door, "by the way. Your towel came back from the lab. It's a 98.3 percent certainty that the sweat we found on Allyx Murray is from Braden Toby. The first case of its kind. I think it'll determine whether sweat is used in court going forward or not. Hope whoever prosecutes it doesn't screw it up."

When he went to shut the door after she had left, he looked over to Kelly's apartment, half expecting her to be sitting in the hallway with earbuds in her ears.

Shit.

38

Dennis Yang parked his Maserati in the jail parking lot and looked out over the yard. The inmates were out in their orange jumpsuits. The female population was separated from the male population by two chain-link fences. The two genders were lined up, talking and flirting and joking. Making the painful time grind by a little more pleasantly.

The juvenile detention wing was in a large building behind the jail. He took the paved walkway around to the flat, square building and heard a young woman screaming. Two guards had her pinned down as she fought and spit and swore. The guards had her arms twisted so far behind her back they looked like they might snap.

The two guards lifted the prisoner by her arms and dragged her back inside. Dennis shook his head. Barbarism on both sides.

The juvenile facility was crowded and filled with vulgar shouting and the occasional bout of laughter.

Parents lined up to visit their kids, many holding babies or trying to wrangle toddlers.

Dennis flashed his state Bar card at one of the guards he knew, and he escorted him through the metal detectors and let him pass through, even though he set it off.

"How are we today, Mr. Yang?"

"Good, Philip. How are you?"

"Oh, not bad. We got a new puppy, and I ain't sleeping much, but other than that, it's smooth sailing."

"Well, that's why I never wanted dogs. They're like children with four legs instead of two."

He chuckled. "Guessin' you ain't got kids, then?"

"Two, but they were raised by their mother. Preferred it that way."

"Well, to each his own. They are a pain in the ass, though. I'll give ya that. So, anyway, who you here for?"

"Braden Toby."

The guard whistled. "You heard anything about him?"

"A little."

"Copied the Reaper from eight years ago. Did a damn good job, too, from what I heard."

Their footsteps echoed down the long corridor. Dennis glanced at the man's shoes and saw a hole, and it disgusted him to see the sock underneath.

Dennis said, "He's locked away in here, so he couldn't have done that great a job."

"Fair enough."

They made their way through a pair of metal doors, and the noise intensified. That was probably the one thing that Dennis could never get used to, even after forty years of law practice. The sheer noise of incarceration. Like sound was locked up with the inmates and had nowhere to go.

A room used for attorneys and therapists to meet with the children was unlocked. The lights were already on, and Philip told him to holler when he was ready to go. Dennis thanked him and sat down at a gray table with a single chair across from him. He'd always found it beneficial to be friendly to the staff of the courts and jails. Never knew when he'd have to pull a favor. Though he would, under any other circumstances, not have anything to do with someone like Philip. The man was weak and powerless, and therefore couldn't do anything for Dennis, with the exception of occasionally letting him visit late at night or get a visiting room to himself.

The door reopened, and Philip brought in Braden Toby. Most juveniles weren't handcuffed, but Braden was. Philip took the cuffs off and said "Behave" to Braden before leaving.

"Please, Mr. Toby, have a seat."

Braden sat down. His mother had told Dennis he pulled out his own hair, but Dennis wasn't prepared for the amount of hair that was missing. Large swaths of scalp were bald. Parts of his eyebrows had been tugged out as well, and dried blood had caked over the bald spots. Before Dennis could say anything about it, Braden yanked on one of his eyebrows and ripped a chunk out, arranging the hairs on the table in front of him. Blood dribbled into his eye, but he made no move to wipe it away.

"May I call you Braden?"

Braden ripped out another few hairs from the eyebrow and continued to form them into a semicircle in front of him as though no one else was in the room.

"Mr. Toby?" He leaned forward. "Braden," he said a bit more sternly. "I need you to look at me."

Braden's eyes seemed to flicker as they looked up at him. He ran a finger over the hairs on the table to get them symmetrical and then leaned back in the chair. The muscles in his forearms rippled, and Dennis could see the V shape his upper body took, his back muscles making it nearly impossible for his arms to touch his sides. If someone hadn't told him Braden Toby was sixteen, he never would've guessed. The boy looked more like a college football player.

"My name is Dennis Yang, and I'm an attorney. I've been hired by your mother to represent you. I'm going to tell you exactly what I told her: you're not to talk to anybody about this case from now on. You speak only to me. The other detainees may pretend to be your friend, but—"

"They're scared of me."

The voice didn't fit the young face. It had something to it. Some streak of adulthood that a child of sixteen wasn't meant to have.

"That's fine, but I still don't want you talking to them." Dennis folded his arms on the table in front of him. Many juveniles had trouble staring adults in the eyes—particularly if they perceived the adults as having authority over them—but Braden stared directly into his pupils.

"I want you to know that anything you tell me is protected by the attorney-client privilege. That means no one can ever get me to divulge anything you say. Not even a judge. So you can be perfectly honest with me and tell me everything. But I don't want you to confess to doing the crime. So let's pretend we're speaking in hypotheticals. That's a protection in case I have to put you on the stand to say you didn't do this. Do you understand?"

Braden watched him a moment, and the hardened expression softened, and he blinked for what Dennis thought was the first time since coming into the room. "Have you read Solomon Shepard's book?"

Dennis leaned back. The voice was calmer now, the edge in it gone. Now it was the voice of a sixteen-year-old boy. Dennis wondered if what he'd heard before had been in his head.

"Why do you ask?"

"It's a good book. He talks about something called a category zero. It's the perfect human killer. Someone who's born to kill. And they're the ones that don't get caught, so we know almost nothing about them." He lightly touched the hair arranged in front of him. "I would really like to know if he thinks I'm a category zero."

He nodded as though the boy had said the most casual thing in the world. "Maybe. Why does it matter?"

"Ted Bundy's a category nine, BTK's a category ten. Dahmer a thirteen. There's only a few category zeroes in history. You can't have any other reason for killing, and you can't have brain damage or a mental illness because that means something else was responsible for killing. Category zeroes have to be perfectly normal and happy, but kill anyway."

Dennis recalled Solomon's book in detail. He was someone Dennis had gone up against frequently in court. So he'd read his book and deeply analyzed it. He liked to think of himself akin to General Patton reading Erwin Rommel's book before the African campaign. But he did not particularly want to discuss *this* topic with *this* particular client.

"I'm pretty sure I'm a category zero," Braden said.

"*Pretty* sure?"

Braden shrugged.

Dennis's phone buzzed, and he reached into his pocket and silenced it. "You don't speak like any sixteen-year-old I've ever met."

The boy leaned forward. "When they find out everything I've done, you're going to be famous."

It wasn't often Dennis was surprised by a client, and in fact, it had been so long he couldn't remember the last time it had happened. But he felt it now, a mild shock at some sort of energy coming from the boy he hadn't expected. Older energy, not the energy of youth.

Dennis believed that a defense attorney either defended everyone or they should just retire, because the Constitution was all that mattered and if the attorney couldn't defend *everyone*, they didn't understand that anymore and needed to leave the profession.

Dennis would defend this boy. But he decided he didn't like the young man.

39

Solomon got out of the Uber and stood on the sidewalk. The Justice Center, objectively, was ugly. A square box with square windows. But when he'd graduated law school and come here to apply for his first job as an attorney, the building had seemed as imposing as a mountain. He remembered standing out here like this then, too. He saw nothing but thick glass and brick, a building meant to withstand time. Now he saw the cracks in the bricks, the smears on the glass, the litter surrounding the building. It looked like every other part of the city now.

He went inside and was greeted by a guard. There hadn't been a guard here when Solomon worked in the office.

The guard scanned a card, and the elevator doors opened. Solomon got on, and the guard pushed the fifth-floor button.

Knox had always struck him as paranoid, but even for him, this was a bit much. Solomon knew Knox wasn't important enough to warrant this kind of security.

When Knox was a section lead, he slowly started promoting people in the office that he knew would be loyal to him. He was a terrible attorney and an even worse trial lawyer, but Solomon had been impressed how, almost instinctually, the man knew how to turn an organization to his side with virtually no one noticing.

After seeing how masterfully he packed the essential positions with people he could control, Solomon knew then that Knox would be the county attorney, and maybe even mayor, governor, or beyond one day. And he couldn't think of a worse person to have those positions than someone who cared only about himself.

A new receptionist led him back. The offices hadn't changed much, other than the order of where the prosecutors were. Solomon had no doubt the offices closest to Knox's were for the prosecutors who had proved their loyalty to him.

The receptionist knocked on the office door, poked her head in, and said something, then shut the door and turned to Solomon. "He'll be a second."

Solomon sat in a waiting area with a water cooler and old magazines at least a few months past their stories being relevant. The carpet was a hard, stain-resistant brand that looked twenty years out of date. A painting up on the wall showed a sunset behind some mountains. It reminded him of the last time he had seen it.

It was when he was leaving for court the day he was almost killed.

The trial was a simple stalking case where the defendant, Timothy Derrick Watts, had been terrorizing his ex-girlfriend. Showing up at her work, at her friends' homes, at the gym. When she woke up and saw him in her bedroom one night, she took out a stalking injunction, and that's when the terror had really started.

The woman was almost killed and had to change her identity and move to a different state. Once, Solomon had called to check up on her, and she wept on the phone and said she missed her family but knew it was too dangerous to ever see them.

Solomon was going to hit Watts as hard as he could, one to fifteen years at the Utah State Prison, with a letter to the parole board every year to keep the man inside for as long as possible.

It was during closing arguments, after it was clear that the trial was going to end in a conviction, that Watts took out the shiv he'd been sculpting in his jail cell while awaiting trial.

Watts jumped up when Solomon was turned entirely toward the jury and thrust the razor-sharp hunk of metal and plastic into his spine. Then he jerked it out of his flesh and stabbed him again. He got in six thrusts before Solomon managed to push him off. The bailiffs tased and tackled Watts, who was laughing. It was the laughing Solomon remembered most. A sound that often interrupted his dreams.

The next thing he knew, he was staring up at the ceiling with people shouting around him. He felt the stickiness of the blood that soaked his back. Paramedics and EMTs arrived, and he remembered a flurry of faces, sensations, and sounds as blood pooled around him. The paramedic had blue pants and a white uniform top, and the shirt was stained with blood.

Someone rolled Solomon over to get him on a stretcher. When they did that, Solomon realized he wasn't able to help them by pushing himself up. He couldn't move his legs.

"Excuse me, Mr. Shepard?"

He looked up to see the receptionist and didn't know how long she'd been there.

"Yeah, sorry. Daydreaming," he said with an awkward grin.

"That's all right. He's ready for you now."

He followed her back as she held the door open for him. Knox sat in a gray suit with his orange hair feathered on his head. His demeanor was simultaneously loud and severe. The only time Solomon had ever seen the man laugh was when one of his prosecutors fell and fractured his elbow.

"Solomon Shepard . . . last man standing. So to speak."

Solomon sat down across from him and leaned the cane between his legs as he put his hands on the silver lion's head knob at the top.

"Why the lion?" Knox asked.

He shrugged. "They didn't have any clowns. You know how fond I am of clowns, don't you, Knox?"

Through a highly unethical act on the part of a therapist they both knew whom Knox visited, Solomon had learned Knox was deathly afraid of clowns. From then on, Solomon brought up clowns whenever he could around Knox, without telling him why.

Knox leaned back in his seat and steepled his fingers. His lips quivered oddly, and Solomon thought he was trying to repress either a string of uncontrollable profanity or a laugh.

"I guess congratulations are in order for winning the election," Solomon quickly said before Knox could explode. Normally, Solomon wouldn't mind, but he needed something from Knox and had to play nice right now.

Knox nodded, not taking his eyes off him. "Yes, it is a shame you weren't here to celebrate the victory."

"Yeah. It's weird, though, because I knew your predecessor really well, Knox. Gary and I went way back. And not once did he ever tell me retirement was on the horizon. Then one day outta the blue, I read in the paper that the county attorney is retiring and has named you his replacement. Weird, isn't it?"

"It was an odd turn of events," he said with a sigh, as though discussing something irrelevant and uninteresting. "You look too thin. You should get married. A wife's good cooking can help pack some meat on those bones. Are you able to exercise at all?"

Solomon's eyes kept going to the miniature figurine of a man holding up a starter pistol on Knox's desk. He wondered if he could get away with flinging it at Knox's head before security got up here.

"What do you want, Solomon? I'm a busy man."

"You know what I want."

"I really don't."

Solomon took the chewed-up pen out of his pocket but kept it low as he twirled it in his fingers. "I want to prosecute the boy."

Knox laughed. "Do you remember that one of the last things you did in this office was try to hurt my chances of becoming county attorney? When I confronted you, something was said about my mother, but I don't remember what. Do you?"

"I don't."

He had called her Shrek because of her enormous height and short temper.

"I'm willing to put everything aside for this, Knox. But, let's not forget the shade went both ways. You did dirt to me, too. I lost one promotion that I know of, and the raise that came with it, directly because of you."

Knox waved his hand dismissively. "You wouldn't have gotten that spot anyway. Know what your problem is, Solomon? You don't really understand people. Not in a meaningful way. You think human beings are rational and that you can predict their behavior. That when we're irrational, it's an aberration. That's not the way the world works. It's not how people are. Rationality is an aberration. Irrationality is the essence of men. Because of that, you have to assume everyone's your enemy. When you do that, you will never be surprised, and you will never be disappointed. You'll go a lot further in life than a limp and a rent-controlled apartment. If you'll excuse my saying so."

Solomon felt the smoothness of the handle in his hand and ran his fingers over the lion's mane, which was faded from constant rubbing. "That's a lonely life, Knox."

He grinned a toothy grin. "Maybe, but people will break more than your heart if you trust the wrong ones."

Before Solomon could reply, Knox's receptionist buzzed him and said he had a call waiting. An obvious excuse in case he wanted to get out of the meeting fast.

"Your fake-ass call is waiting for you," Solomon said, "so I'll make my pitch brief. You're a crap trial lawyer, and you know it. Juries hate your guts, and judges don't trust you. But we both know that's not your forte. The law is just a vehicle for you into whatever it is you really want, so it doesn't matter that you couldn't win an argument with a four-year-old. You're good at your skill set. So you're going to want someone who actually has a chance at getting a conviction. That's just a fact.

"Another fact is that I'm a better homicide prosecutor than anyone you got. You know why I know that? Because you stacked this office full of people loyal to you rather than the ones with talent that really deserved it. And the media is watching your every move, so you need a win. Reelection isn't too far away, and people will remember what happens here. So no one here can prosecute Braden Toby, but you also can't bring in someone from another jurisdiction. People will be asking why you need them and questioning your competence."

"I'm not seeing a point—"

"But if I take the case, you could paint it to the press that you're so concerned for the public's well-being that you pulled your best homicide prosecutor out of retirement for this case. You can act as much the hero part as you want. And then, if I win, you get all the credit. If I lose, you blame it on me."

Solomon used his cane to stand. "You're going to realize that I'm right, and this is the best course of action for you, so I'm going to start on Monday. Also, my office is going to stay at the sheriff's station. No reason we should see each other every day. And I want a per diem for lunches and drinks. Lots of drinks. With little umbrellas if possible."

Solomon tipped over the statuette of the man with the starter pistol and left the office.

40

Billie came into the station early and was surprised to see Solomon already there. He had his jacket off and wore suspenders instead of a belt. A pen was being roughly chewed between his teeth, and he was staring at a piece of paper and mumbling to himself as though attempting to memorize what was on it.

"You all right?" she said, leaning against his office door.

"Yeah, I'm good. Oh, I'm prosecuting the Toby case, so I'll need to stay in this office a bit longer."

"You what? Are you joking?"

"Knox gave me permission on Friday. Well, not so much gave it as sat there quietly and didn't fight it. Anyway, I'm sure he's cool with it."

"Solomon, that's great, but you sure you want to undertake something like this because of guilt?"

He lowered the sheet of paper. "One of the best young people I've ever met might be dead because of me. I have to do something. I can't just sit at home and watch the news on this. I can't."

"The weight of the world is not on your shoulders, Solomon. You can't solve all the world's problems by yourself."

He tapped the pen against his teeth. "That's not what you told me when you showed up at my door and dropped this on me."

"Dropped it on you? I asked for your help, and you gave it willingly. I didn't put a gun to your head."

He lowered the pen. "I don't want to fight."

"Neither do I."

"Actually, I have a favor to ask."

"What?"

"I'll tell you on the way."

———

The drive was scenic, with mountains and empty valleys, and warmly pleasant. Billie played a country music station and refused to change it to metal.

"Can I ask you something?" he said. "Why'd you really drop out of grad school? It's not because you could be more proactive as a cop. Teachers can be just as proactive and make huge impacts. Why the switch?"

"Why do people do that?"

"Do what?"

"They say, 'Can I ask you something?' but then they don't wait for a response before they start talking."

Solomon chuckled.

In the sunlight, the Tobys' neighborhood appeared much different. Billie remembered it as ominous and dark and little else. But now she saw toys left out and children playing on lush, green front yards.

"So what are we doing again?" Billie said as they got out of the truck in the driveway. They headed to the front door of the modest home.

"I need a witness to these conversations since I'm a prosecutor for the State, and I can't drive, and Uber would've been like forty bucks."

"Good to be needed, I guess."

They knocked on the front door.

Before Solomon could knock again, Melinda Toby pulled up to her house and parked behind them. It was then, turning toward her, that Billie noticed the faint hint of red paint spatters over the driveway and walkway. She knew it had been done purposefully because she could make out part of a word in one of the stains, what she guessed said *Devil*.

"Hello, Ms. Toby," Billie said.

"Sheriff," she said with relief in her voice. "I'm so glad it's you. I've been getting reporters all day and night. One even tried to break in to interview me."

"I'll have some extra patrols come by the neighborhood if it helps."

"Oh, thank you! You just made my day."

Melinda moved between them and stuck her key in the lock. "Come in. I'll get us some iced tea."

The home was small but clean. Gray carpets and yellow linoleum in the kitchen. Dull white walls and gray furniture. Billie thought this was how mortuaries decorated.

"You know, I was thinking," Melinda said from the kitchen, "you were so nice I thought I would do some baking and bring it by the station. I've got a recipe for German chocolate cake that is heavenly."

Billie sat in the middle of the couch, and Solomon sat on the end. Melinda brought out cookies on a plate and three glasses of iced tea. Solomon took a cookie and leaned back on the couch as he bit into it. While he chewed, he looked around at the home. Stopping for a short while on a wall decoration that consisted of an old framed 1940s poster for a ski lodge.

"How is he?" Melinda said, the smile long gone from her face now.

Billie said, "I wouldn't know, Ms. Toby. I don't get updates unless something's wrong. But the fact that I haven't gotten any updates means that I'm sure he's perfectly fine."

She nodded. "He may look like he's made of steel, but he's a child. I know sometimes people who work with teenagers forget they're just kids."

She smiled again—but this time stared off into space, and the smile slowly faded from her lips. A memory had come to her that made her clearly uncomfortable, and her countenance became one of fear.

Solomon leaned forward with a soft expression and said, "Ms. Toby, all three of us want the same thing. We all want to know the best thing for Braden and the victims' families moving forward. The most important question to ask is whether he's a child or not. And the easiest way to answer that is to work together."

"I agree."

"Then first things first: you've hired an attorney for Braden but not for yourself. Are you all right talking to us without one?"

"Of course."

"Good. Then next question—what the hell is that?"

He pointed to a plastic fish on the wall wearing a sombrero and a big smile on its face.

"It was my father's. He was a police officer in San Francisco, where we lived before moving here, and that was one of the gifts he received when he retired. I hated the damn thing, but he always loved it. He thought it was unique. I felt too bad throwing it away after he passed, so there it sits. It's an eyesore, I know."

"No," Solomon said, clearly regretting bringing it up, "it's not that bad. Your father was right: it is unique."

She glanced at the silver handle of his cane. Solomon noticed and said, "Back injury."

"I'm guessing you weren't born with it?"

"You would guess right."

"Well, it looks very distinguished, if you ask me."

Billie interrupted. "Ms. Toby, do you mind if we go take a quick peek at Braden's room? I know it's already been searched, but Mr. Shepard hasn't seen it in person and has a superstitious belief in going places rather than looking at pictures."

"Oh, well, no, I don't mind. I've left it the same way he did. He doesn't like me touching his things."

Melinda rose and led them up the stairs while telling them the home's history. How it was built by some man for his ailing daughter and the daughter ended up dying inside one of the bedrooms.

She was about to go into the room first when Solomon said, "I truly don't mean this in a disrespectful way, but would you mind if we looked by ourselves?"

"Um, no. No, I suppose not. I'll just, um, I'll just be in the kitchen straightening up."

When she was back downstairs, Billie looked at him and said, "She's odd."

"She did just find out her son is a serial killer. She's entitled to be a little odd, I think." He pushed the door open all the way.

Billie first noticed the posters. Namely that there was only one: Charles Manson's mug shot. Beneath it on a desk was a small fishbowl that held a blue fish with pointy fins. The rest of the room was neat and tidy, almost empty. The windows had no drapes and the room was filled with light. She had not expected a room like this. She'd pictured old posters of heavy metal bands up on the walls, drugs on a desk, empty fast-food containers piled on a dirty carpet, and windows painted black so no one could see in . . . anything other than a clean, light-filled room no different from any other room with the exception of the single poster.

"Look at this," Solomon said.

She turned to see a small bookshelf near the closet. It held books about torture, collected photography series of war wounds, and another one about birth defects. Several books on satanism, the Nazis, and the occult.

He opened the closet door. Braden's clothes were neatly hung, and underneath them on the floor were several pairs of shoes.

Solomon said, "With the exception of Count Dracula's library, you'd never guess anything was going on with this kid." He took out his pen and began chewing on it. "The fantasy has to develop first, and that can take years. If he's already killing at sixteen, I can't imagine how early he started fantasizing about it."

Billie lifted a backpack that hung on a hook. Inside, she found several drawings on a white pad. The drawings were detailed but there was no color. Instead, everything was filled in with pencil. Mutilated corpses, rageful ghosts exploding out of people's bodies, a girl with flowers in her hair and a skull for a face.

"Stunning," Solomon said. "Wonder why SIS didn't take it?"

"I don't know. Maybe it wasn't up there when we were here. And what do you mean *stunning*? You actually like these?"

"I mean, I wouldn't hang it up in a children's dentist's office, but they're actually well done."

"Opinions vary, I suppose," she said as she dropped the pad onto the bed like it was toxic waste.

"Hello, hello," Solomon said, glancing into the backpack.

"Wait, put these on," Billie said, handing him some latex gloves from a small package in her jacket pocket.

After putting the gloves on, he pulled out a stack of papers in envelopes from the backpack.

"What is it?" she said.

He opened the first few letters. "They're letters to the Reaper. Unaddressed."

"Think there's any possibility he knows who it is?"

Solomon shook his head. "No stamps, no return address. I think our boy was just expressing himself to express himself. Listen to this. 'You inspired me when I was six years old. I saw a show about you when I stayed up too late and my mom was asleep. I loved the way you teased the police. You'll see me soon in the news, too. Maybe if you like what you see you can find me? If you're already in jail for something else, let me know, and I can send you some things you might like.'"

"Well, that would've been an interesting relationship."

"Yeah, Abbott and Costello from hell."

She took a few of the letters and flipped through them. "I'll have SIS go through the letters, see if we can find anything useful."

Solomon took photos of each letter on his phone.

"For a little late night reading," he said.

41

The first court hearing was scheduled for the middle of the week in juvenile court. Almost immediately, Solomon filed a writ asking the court to release the case to the Tooele County District Court so that Braden Toby could be tried as an adult for thirty-one felony crimes.

Solomon waited outside the courtroom in the hallway on a bench. Usually, he would've been waved through by the guards with a greeting, but he didn't know any of them now. They searched him and then wanded him and made him show identification.

The judge assigned was Isaac Boyce. Solomon had never appeared in front of him. He was an older judge who had been appointed to the juvenile court after Solomon had already retired.

He felt the heaviness of his cane and let it slide down his palm and tap the linoleum floor before bouncing up again.

"Solomon, I didn't expect to see you here," Dennis Yang said as he sat next to him on the bench.

"No one's more surprised than me."

"You look tired. Not much sleep?"

"Not lately. How about you? I figured you'd moved on to only representing the rich."

"The rich are boring. All their cases are either greed or lust, which I suppose are the same thing. We have to keep ourselves entertained in our careers as we get older, don't we?"

"Entertainment . . . not sure I can come up with a more inappropriate word to describe all this."

"It's all entertainment, Solomon. Don't you know that by now?"

The doors opened, and the bailiff said, "Open for business, fellas."

"Age before beauty," Solomon said, gesturing to the courtroom.

Dennis went inside, and Solomon followed.

The courtroom was decorated with a large copy of the Constitution behind the judge's bench and had only two windows. The artificial lights made the beige carpet's stains thrust out like lesions on skin.

"You ever been in front of Judge Boyce?" Dennis said, setting his briefcase down on the respondent's table.

In juvenile court, everything in the criminal system was given a different name. Defendants were respondents, and the State was the plaintiff. Respondents weren't sentenced; their matter was adjudicated, and they were given "tasks" to complete as part of the case. Several decades ago, a study had found that labeling children as criminals changed their self-image. Children filled the role of the titles shoved on them.

"I haven't had the pleasure, no."

"Oh, *pleasure* isn't the word. He was a schoolteacher in a former life and would dish out corporal punishment with a thick paddle. When the child abuse laws changed, he left teaching and returned to his original law career."

"I'll try not to get paddled, then."

A clerk came out, a middle-aged woman with brown hair and a lot of jewelry. Her nails were painted blue, and she was carrying a box of files. She set them down, then sat in a little nook built out for her near the judge's bench. She nodded once to the bailiff, who bellowed, "All rise, Third District Juvenile Court is now in session. The Honorable Isaac Boyce presiding."

Each attorney stood next to his respective table as the judge sat down. The judge was a thin man with a head entirely too large for his body, giving him a lollipop appearance. If he leaned too far forward or backward, the momentum from his head might take him all the way down.

The double doors behind them opened, and Solomon saw Billie come in wearing a pantsuit.

She smiled at him.

"Counselors, state your appearances, please."

"Solomon Shepard for the plaintiff."

"Dennis Yang for the respondent."

The judge glanced up with small eyes, then took his gaze back down to the files in front of him.

"I don't believe you've appeared in front of me before, Mr. Shepard."

"I have not, Your Honor."

"Then I want to make a few things clear at the outset. First, I expect all motions to be filed by midnight of the due date. One second more, and simply do not submit them because they will not be read. I also anticipate a suit or pressed jacket at all hearings—with a clean tie. And your shoes should be shined if possible."

"Um." Solomon chuckled. "You're joking, right?" he said, suddenly unsure.

The judge stared at him harshly, then took a breath and leaned forward. "And I expect you to always stand when addressing this court. I assume that won't be a problem of too much difficulty?"

Solomon was suddenly conscious of his cane and felt a slight blush in his cheeks.

"Mr. Yang," the judge said in what Solomon swore was a happier tone. "How are we, sir?"

"Still above ground, Judge. Life, it seems, has a sense of humor."

The judge laughed, an awkward sound and cadence. A man trying to laugh who didn't know how.

"How are your Jazz doing this year?" Boyce said.

"Donovan Mitchell's a prodigy. Next Michael Jordan, you watch."

The judge nodded with a half smile and glanced at Solomon. It was a subtle, quick motion, but Solomon got the gist of it: *Yes, I like him better than you, and don't you dare bring it up.*

"Now," the judge said, putting on some glasses and reading over them precisely as a schoolteacher would, "we have Mr. Braden Cunningham Toby today. Bailiff, would you please?"

The bailiff knocked on a thick wooden door, and another bailiff brought in Braden. He was wearing an orange Juvenile Detention Center jumpsuit with thick white socks and sandals. Sandals instead of shoes so laces couldn't be used to commit suicide or strangle someone else.

Braden looked right at Solomon and blew him a kiss. Solomon felt the anger wanting to come out of him but simply bit down and felt his jaw muscles flex. He took out his pen and chewed for a second, then looked back to Billie, who mouthed something about *Braden can go self-fornicate.*

Solomon noticed that Dennis and Braden didn't acknowledge each other.

"Are you," the judge said in the same tone he'd taken with Solomon, "Braden Cunningham Toby?"

"Yeah."

"Excellent. Now, if you have any questions, young man, please direct them to your excellent counsel, Mr. Yang."

The judge explained the different hearings, the motions that could be filed, and the primary arguments he might hear from the attorneys.

"Do you have any questions about any of that, Mr. Toby?" the judge finally said.

Dennis leaned over and whispered, "No, Your Honor."

"No, Your Honor."

The judge gave a slight smirk at the courtesy of adding *Your Honor* when respondents were not expected to address the judge properly during their first hearing. Most of these children had never been taught etiquette or social norms. They were too busy making sure their siblings had enough to eat or making sure their alcoholic mother didn't accidentally drink herself to death, or taking the attention away from abusive fathers so that they would beat them instead of their younger siblings.

"Counsel, I assume you have seen Mr. Yang's request for this court to retain the matter in response to your motion to certify this case an aggravated offense and transfer it to the district court?"

"I have."

"Counsel, please stand."

Solomon felt that slight heat in his cheeks again. He rose and said, "I have, Your Honor."

"I assume you object to it and do not stipulate?"

"I do not."

"Then I think we can schedule the hearing now. Heidi, what do we have available soon?"

"August fifth to the tenth."

"Five days enough for the hearing, gentlemen?"

Dennis didn't stand. "That's fine, Judge," he said.

"That should work."

"Then this court is adjourned until August the fifth. Please submit a brief of all potential arguments, gentlemen, and have it in by Friday, August the first, at midnight. This court is in recess."

When the judge said, "Thank you for your time," he looked only at Dennis.

Dennis came up to Solomon at the plaintiff's table and said, "Let's talk before the hearing. I don't see any reason why we can't resolve this matter."

"I'll give you five reasons."

Dennis grinned. "I see now why you came back. You've taken this personally. I've been doing this longer than you, young man, and I can tell you one thing: you do not take these matters personally. They must be treated like puzzles and nothing more." He glanced over to Braden, who was being taken back to the detention facility.

"If you don't treat them that way, you're going to regret it. I promise you."

42

Melinda sat across from the manager, a portly man in a vomit-colored tie and a white shirt with faint stains on it. He looked over her CV, and she noticed that his eyes weren't moving in a way that would indicate he was actually reading her credentials.

The job was at a care facility where she would be one of the junior nurses. The pay was half what she'd been making at her previous job, and it was a bit of a drive from her house, but she'd had three interviews already, and when they recognized her face, they suddenly lost interest or told her they would give her a call back when they could.

This man had recognized her right when he saw her. Funny that they had all read her name and didn't recognize it, but they did her face.

"We have a lot of qualified candidates, and we'll have to see—"

"Wait," she said, closing her eyes a moment, "just wait. I know what you're going to say because the last three interviews I've had said the same thing. I know I've been on the news lately, and I know why and I'm perfectly aware of all that. But what my son did or didn't do does not affect how I would work here. I'm a good nurse. I deserve more than this."

He folded his hands and stared at her. "Ms. Toby, we're a small institution that survives on word of mouth. If it got out that you work here, some people might not want to drop their family members off. How many? I don't know, but even a handful could have serious consequences for us. It's absolutely nothing personal, and I bet you're a fantastic nurse, but—"

"Please don't do this. Please. I need to work."

"I'm sorry, but I can't help you."

Melinda rose and ignored him on her way out as he asked if she wanted her CV back. When she got to her car, she saw several people looking through an office window. Drawn in soap on her windshield was an image of a woman giving birth to a devil with long horns and fangs. Someone must've recognized her name, too, and let everybody else know who was coming in for an interview. Making her feel unwelcome would ensure she didn't want to work here.

On the way home, she came to a stoplight. Crossing the street were a woman and her son. The young boy was holding her hand and trying to balance a large ice cream cone with his free hand.

Braden had never liked cuddling or hand-holding. Even as an infant, he wouldn't cry for any reason, so she never rocked him or spent time holding him for comfort. When she did hold him, he squirmed and kicked and screamed, until one day she realized that it was because he didn't like being touched. She had stopped showing him affection by the time he was three. It wasn't worth the fight.

As the light turned, she decided not to think about such things. Everything about him was tainted now. It felt as if her entire life had changed in an instant. Every memory, every sensation, every conversation. She had once caught him masturbating to a photo of a tied-up woman in a detective fiction magazine. Was that a sign she should've noticed? Was it something buried inside him pointing to deeper troubles, or did all boys do things like that? She was both his mother and his father, and she realized she hadn't known how to raise a man. A sense of guilt filled her to the point tears welled in her eyes.

The car behind her honked after the light had turned green. She wiped her tears away and pulled forward.

43

Solomon had read through the court psychiatrist's evaluation of Braden Toby twice already, but he still sat on the court steps the day of the hearing and reread it. The psychiatrist was someone he'd worked with before, a Lebanese American woman named Ruth Fuller. She was brilliant but controversial because of some of her staunch beliefs that weren't entirely based on data or evidence. But Solomon liked her. She didn't care what anybody thought about her.

One thing that struck him about the report was the history section. He'd learned several things about Braden Toby he didn't know before.

The boy had an affinity as a child for smearing his fecal matter over the walls of the home and his room. The first time it happened, his mother thought it was an aberration. When it happened the second, then third and fourth times, she realized something was wrong with him.

What must have that been like, he wondered, for Melinda Toby? To see what her son was becoming and know she was helpless to stop it?

His phone buzzed, and he took it out of his pocket. It was a calendar reminder, and all it said was "Pay Kelly for July deliveries."

A grin came to his face as he thought about her haggling with him to get a few extra bucks. It was one of the most enjoyable parts of their relationship, and looking back, he wondered if she knew it and did it more for him than for herself.

He lowered his phone and stared out at nothing.

Her parents would be right to hate him.

A shadow appeared in front of him. The sun was in his eyes when he looked up, and he had to squint. It was Billie in a black skirt and blouse.

"You look good. Like a sexy librarian or something."

"Sexy?"

"You know what I mean." He used his cane to stand and said, "Everyone throws up at their first trial, but I never did. I was proud of that." He grinned awkwardly. "I threw up this morning."

She straightened his tie. "You'll be fine. Come on, I'll walk you in."

———

The courtroom seemed warmer today, and though he wasn't sweating yet, Solomon knew he would, so he took his jacket off. Dennis Yang came in and sat at the respondent's table and nodded hello to Billie, who sat in the bench seats. He wore white pants and a cream sports coat with an off-white shirt. It created the appearance of a humble man with humble clothes, but it was an illusion. Solomon had seen him out on the town before, and he dressed in Armani suits and wore gold watches. Lawyering, for a lot of people, was just theater.

"You look too thin," Dennis said to Solomon. "You should come over and let my wife cook for you. She's a great cook."

"Yeah? How is she, by the way?"

"Good. She retired a few years ago and spends her time in the garden and with her lady friends."

"Speaking of lady friends, I saw you at Club Silver back in the day. I remember it clearly because you were with someone like twenty, and I thought, 'That couldn't be his wife. Must be his daughter.' Blonde, red dress, black pumps . . . ring a bell?"

Dennis grimaced, and it put a smile on Solomon's face.

The clerk came out and set a box of files underneath the bench, and then the bailiff called out that court was back in session. Judge Boyce walked out quickly. He wore thin little glasses today, and as much as Solomon tried not to imagine it, he kept thinking the judge looked like an executioner presiding over mock trials during the French Revolution and sentencing everyone to death. A monstrous living lollipop with too much power.

"How are we, Counsel?"

"Good, Your Honor."

"Mr. Yang?"

"Doing well, thank you, Judge."

"Mr. Shepard, you will wear a jacket in my courtroom."

Solomon held his gaze a moment, then put on his jacket. He kept thinking over and over, *Pick your battles.*

The judge took a quick glance around the courtroom. The only people here were Billie and Braden's mother. Melinda sat quietly near one of the windows, and the way the sunlight hit her face made her look like her mind was a million miles away. Solomon felt for her as much as anyone in this case.

"Let's bring out Mr. Toby."

Braden was brought out in cuffs again. His gaze went to his mother, but there was no smile or grin or attempt to speak with her. There was no recognition in his eyes, as though he were looking at a stranger. His mother burst into tears and had to leave the courtroom.

The judge waited until the doors closed before speaking again.

"We're here for the matter of Braden Cunningham Toby, case number 224267. Counsels will state their appearances."

"Solomon Shepard for the plaintiff."

"Dennis Yang for the respondent."

"And we are here today to address the plaintiff's motion to certify the violations under their petition as aggravated offenses, under Utah

Code 78A-6-703, and transfer this matter to the district court. Mr. Shepard, please proceed."

"Thank you, Your Honor," he said as he stood. His cane suddenly felt heavier. "Your Honor, the standard we adhere to for juveniles in no way—"

"What are you doing, Mr. Shepard?"

"Um," he said, glancing at Dennis. "Giving opening statements."

"It's customary in my courtroom to waive opening statements, Counsel. I know what the issues are and don't need you pointing them out for me."

"Are you sure? I've been told I have a pleasant voice."

The attempt at levity didn't play well. Judge Boyce gave him a hard stare. Then, slowly, like a villain in a movie, he slid the glasses off his face and set them down on the bench. His eyebrows turned inward and flared up. He looked so absolutely ridiculous with his body proportions and the amount of anger he was displaying that Solomon couldn't help but think of a lollipop with a mad face painted on it.

He didn't suppress it in time and chuckled.

"Is something funny, Counsel?" Boyce said sternly.

"No, Your Honor, it was only an attempt at humor."

"Counsel, I can't believe I have to do this, but I'll give you a lecture your parents should have given you decades ago. There is an appropriate time and place for everything. This is not the time and place for humor. Humor is for barrooms and bathrooms. Is that understood?"

"Did you say bath—yes, Your Honor. I understand."

The judge kept his eyes on Solomon a bit longer, then put his glasses back on and said, "The plaintiff will call its first witness."

44

The run to the bathroom to cry had taken everything out of Melinda.

She leaned against the sink and tried to save what little was left of her makeup. A woman came into the restroom and gave her an odd glare before going into a stall. Melinda sniffed and wiped the last of the tears away before leaving the restroom.

When she came out into the hall, two women were standing there. She thought they needed to get past her to get into the restroom and said, "Sorry," as she stepped aside.

The two women stepped with her. She looked up and saw the anger on one of their faces. No, not anger. Not really. Hatred. A pure, unfiltered hatred.

Melinda guessed they were related to victims.

"Otto and Allyx were our parents," the one in the white shirt said.

"I'm sorry," she said, trying to get past them again. Instead, the woman stepped in front of her, preventing her from leaving.

"Are you?" the woman on the right, wearing a tan halter top, said. "Are you sorry, you piece of human garbage?"

The woman in the white shirt gently put her hand on her sister's shoulder. "It's okay. Let me talk to her. Just sit down for a minute. You've been on your feet for two days."

The woman in the halter top left and the other one stared down at the floor with her arms crossed. Then she looked up, and she and

Melinda held each other's gaze. Melinda didn't know whether to push her way past, run, or go back into the restroom. So she did nothing.

"I'm sorry. Rebecca's . . . she's not herself. She and my mother were really close." The woman touched her necklace. "I know you're not responsible. Rebecca knows it, too. But this pain is so deep it's unbearable. You feel like if you don't get it out, you're going to explode. And we don't have her killer to explode on. Rebecca just . . . you were the closest thing."

Melinda swallowed. "I understand."

"Good." The woman unfolded her arms and put her hands in her back pockets in a more casual gesture. Melinda noticed a locket on the necklace and was sure it held a photo of her parents she carried with her now.

"If there's anything I can do . . ." Melinda trailed off. "I'm sorry. Never mind. I am the last person you should be around."

Melinda moved to leave, and the woman grabbed her arm.

"There is something you can do."

"What?"

"I want you to talk to your son and convince him to plead guilty."

The words didn't register right away, but when they did, Melinda was stunned she had really asked that. "I can't do that."

"Yes, you can."

"I'm not his lawyer. I don't know anything about what he should be pleading guilty to."

"Rebecca wants to see him locked away, I want to see him locked away, but I don't want to go through court. I've been through this process before, for something a long time ago that happened in college. And it was the worst experience of my life. I don't want my parents' memory to be attacked like that. I don't want reporters at my house and at Rebecca's work anymore. So I'm trying to convince her to leave the country with me for a while. There's a little place in Puerto Rico I know about. I think a couple months away would do wonders for her. But she won't leave as long as this case is going on."

Melinda opened her mouth to say something, but no words came. She didn't know what to say to this woman who was in so much pain it made Melinda want to cry. "I'm sorry. I can't help you."

She quickly hurried down the hallway back to the courtroom. The woman called to her, but Melinda ignored it and ran through the double doors.

The judge gave her a quick glance, and she sat down on the nearest bench. A moment later, the two daughters came in and sat down across the room. Rebecca looked rageful, her eyes never wavering from Braden.

The sheriff came over and sat next to Melinda. The judge was reading some document in silence while the lawyers looked to be preparing notes.

"Are you doing okay?" Billie whispered.

She nodded. "Yes, thank you. But why are you so nice to me? Most people see me coming and cross the street now."

"I know you did nothing to deserve this, and I also know the entire world blames you."

Melinda looked at Braden. "He looks much thinner," she whispered. "And he has a black eye and some cuts."

"Juvenile detention is not a pleasant place."

"If this is juvenile detention, what's adult prison going to do to him? He's only sixteen."

"I know. They have protective custody for prisoners like him."

Melinda inhaled deeply and looked at the wrinkles in her hands. So many of them weren't there last year. Her watch had a blue face and she murmured, seemingly to herself, "I remember when my eyes were this blue."

Melinda wrung her hands, trying to get some blood back in her fingers, and wished she had some water. Her mouth and throat felt like she'd been chewing on dry sand. "You believe he should be tried as a minor, right?"

Billie shrugged with a slight shake of her head. "I have no idea. Sometimes what's right and what's wrong isn't so obvious."

Melinda stared at her son's back. Then, as though he felt her staring at him, he turned and looked at her, and slowly smiled.

45

Solomon waited patiently while the judge reread the motions. The courtroom had a damp heat to it now, and he wondered if the air-conditioning was on the fritz like it always used to be four years ago. His face was hot, his palms sweating. Never, not once, did he remember being this nervous in a courtroom. Even as a law student, clerking for a judge, when he had to address the Court, he did it with confidence. Now his hands shook at the thought.

"Go ahead, Counsel."

"The plaintiff would call Sheriff Elizabeth Gray to the stand."

Billie went to the witness stand. Solomon noticed Dennis checking out her backside. Braden was not. He had arranged hairs in a pattern on the table. It took Solomon a moment to recognize it as an upside-down cross.

Solomon took to the lectern and said, "State your name for the record, please."

"Elizabeth Julia Gray."

"What do you do, Ms. Gray?"

"I'm the sheriff for Tooele County."

The judge sighed. "Counsel, those qualifications are for juries. I know everybody's qualifications. Skip ahead, please. I'd like to get home before Christmas."

"Why? Do you need to say 'Bah, humbug' to some poor family?"

Instantly, Solomon regretted saying it. He waited for the tirade from the judge, but none came. The judge was writing something down and apparently hadn't heard what he said.

Solomon cleared his throat. "You familiar with this case, Sheriff?"

"Yes, my father, the previous sheriff, was one of the primary investigators on the original Reaper case for the county, so I took a personal interest in this case as an investigator."

"Why?"

"I initially thought it could be the same person from the previous case. But of course, Mr. Toby would have been eight years old at the time."

"Tell us, briefly, the pertinent facts to give the judge some background. You don't need to go into details. That's for the trial."

She nodded. "I understand. Essentially, Mr. Toby was attempting to copy a serial murderer named the Reaper. Mr. Toby is alleged to have murdered a couple, the Murrays, at their home here in the city in the same area where the Reaper had killed his first known victims. He then killed Mr. Robert Larson, an Uber driver who took him back to the city center, where we assume his truck was parked. We then believe that he broke into the home of Jennifer Garrison on a separate occasion and murdered her with a hunting knife. In this part of his own cycle, the Reaper had killed a family, the Farringtons. Ms. Garrison was the niece of Mr. Farrington."

"Tell us about how you apprehended Mr. Toby."

Dennis Yang stood up and said, "Your Honor, the only relevant question in this proceeding is whether my client should be tried as a minor or an adult. As such, his mental state at the time of these crimes is pertinent to this hearing. Whether or not he committed these crimes is not the question before the court. And unless it's related to answering the question about his mental state, none of his actions pre- or post-arrest are relevant."

"I agree," Judge Boyce said.

"Your Honor, I'm trying to give you some background. Reading briefs on what happened is not the same as a victim's daughter taking the stand and telling you how different her life is because of what this boy did."

"You cannot play on my emotions as though I've never done this before, Mr. Shepard. I care about, and *only* about, whether this young man legally had the mental capacity to commit aggravated murder such to the degree that he should not be treated as a child." He leaned forward a little more. "And if you ever say something like 'Bah, humbug' to me again, I'm going to lock you up for contempt. Understood?"

Solomon glanced at Dennis, who had a wide grin on his face. "Understood."

"Good. Now let's get to the meat of the matter."

Solomon turned back to Billie. "You've interacted with the respondent, in this case, Sheriff?"

"I have."

"What we're trying to ascertain is whether there was any type of diminished capacity. Whether of organic origins, mental illness, psychosis, or simply due to Mr. Toby's age. We want to know if he understood the full consequences of his actions in a way a reasonable adult would."

"I understand."

"Tell us about your interactions with him."

She looked at Braden, who was staring at her.

"Well, I've investigated over thirty murders in my career and interviewed many types of defendants—"

"Respondents," the judge interjected.

"Yes, I'm sorry. Respondents. I've dealt with minors accused of murder before, and Mr. Toby did not have the behavior you would expect. Depending on their age, I suppose, most minors break down and cry when they realize the consequences facing them. Often, they show remorse and cry for their parents . . . many of them, at least on an emotional level, don't understand why the victims are not coming back. Mr. Toby did not display any of that. Instead, he seemed almost to be . . . enjoying the shock he'd elicited from us."

"Objection."

"Sustained."

Solomon leaned on the lectern. "Did he write any letters to the victims' families apologizing for what he'd done?"

"He did not. I don't believe he cared about the impact on the families."

"Objection," Dennis said, on his feet now. "Judge, I recognize that the rules of evidence are lax in a hearing of this sort, but we must maintain a modicum of rationality. Everything the sheriff said is meant to elicit a sympathetic response from you and paint my client as cold and calculating. However, the sheriff is not a mental health professional and could not possibly say whether my client cared about the impact of these murders on the families. Therefore, I would ask that the entirety of her testimony be stricken."

"A witness is allowed to testify on what they saw and heard," Solomon said. "She's investigated over thirty murders. She should be able to testify as to her general impressions of the respondent's demeanor in her interactions with him."

The judge thought a moment. "General impressions would be such things as 'He was agitated' or 'He appeared unkempt and nervous.' What she has testified to are mental states. I agree with the respondent's counsel in this matter. I will move to strike all of the sheriff's testimony and disregard it in adjudicating this matter."

"Your Honor, this is not my first rodeo. I know she can't get up there and talk about mental states, but she can tell whether the respondent was enjoying himself or not."

"I've made my ruling. Now, do you have any pertinent questions for this witness?"

He ran his tongue along his cheek so that he wouldn't say what he wanted to say. "No."

"Mr. Yang, any questions?"

"Just a few, Your Honor."

Dennis took to the lectern as Solomon sat down. Dennis didn't like standing behind it and instead leaned on it casually. "Ms. Gray, how are you today?"

"I'm fine, thank you."

"Good. Just a few questions, if I may. First, do you have any grudges against teenage boys that might cloud your thinking?"

She shook her head. "No, of course not."

"Had you ever met my client before you interacted with him in this case?"

"No."

"You never spoke on the phone or corresponded with him . . . inter-acted with him on social media or some such avenue?"

"No, I didn't know him in any capacity."

"And yet you felt comfortable making judgments about what he enjoyed or didn't enjoy. But you've never seen my client enjoy something before, have you?"

"No, I have not."

"And you couldn't say with certainty how he acts when he enjoys something or when he is pained by something?"

"As a law enforcement veteran, I can tell when someone is enjoying the pain they've caused."

"Possibly, but we're not talking about someone. We're talking about a sixteen-year-old boy. How many sixteen-year-old boys have you arrested for aggravated homicide?"

"Other than the respondent, none."

"Do you have a sixteen-year-old son?"

"No."

"Any sixteen-year-old nephews?"

"No."

"Do you interact with any sixteen-year-old boys daily?"

"No, I do not," she said, a hint of frustration in her voice.

"So, we might as well replace a sixteen-year-old boy with a were-wolf, and you would know just about as much about both, correct? Maybe even more about werewolves."

"Objection, Counsel is testifying."

"Sustained."

Dennis took a couple of steps toward the stand. "I see you had a year of graduate school in biology, Sheriff. Is that right?"

"Yes."

"Any education in early childhood development?"

"No."

"Psychology?"

"No."

"Sociology?"

"No, Counsel. Nothing like that."

"Nothing like mental health, correct?"

"Correct."

"Your specialty—proposed specialty, I should say, since you dropped out—in graduate school was morphology. The study of how animals change physical form through evolution, correct?"

"That is correct."

"So to be clear, you don't know any boys his age, you don't have any relatives his age, you've never arrested someone his age for this crime, and you have no background in family or childhood studies or any of the mental health fields, and you met my client on the night he was arrested for murder, the worst night of his life. Yet, you feel comfortable making judgments about what he must be like under normal and abnormal circumstances. Does that about sum it up, Ms. Gray?"

She hesitated and glanced at Solomon. "Counsel, I'm here to testify about what I heard and saw. I saw the enjoyment on his face. I saw that he liked the pain he was causing. If I'm not allowed to say that, so be it. But that's what I saw."

"What's he thinking now?"

"Excuse me?"

"You know more about him now than you did on the night of the arrest, when he was allegedly enjoying himself. If you can ascertain what he's feeling, tell us what he's feeling now."

"I wouldn't know."

"Take a guess."

"Objection," Solomon said. "Badgering."

"Overruled. You opened this door yourself, Mr. Shepard. Answer the question, Sheriff."

She sighed. "I don't know what he's feeling now. Probably some sort of pleasure at the discomfort he's causing."

"Braden," Dennis said, "are you getting pleasure from this?"

Before Solomon could object, Braden said, "No."

Dennis held up a hand to Solomon, indicating it was too late and to save his objection. "Ms. Gray, you were untruthful before about not having any experience with sixteen-year-old boys, weren't you?"

"I don't know what you mean."

"In high school, you filed a report with the school police officer alleging that your boyfriend at the time drugged and sexually assaulted you, correct?"

Billie's face went white as a sheet. Solomon jumped to his feet, using the table instead of his cane, and said, "Your Honor! That is completely irrelevant to this hearing and meant only to shock and confuse the witness into—"

The judge held up his hand in a placating manner. "Easy, Mr. Shepard. Mr. Yang, that question was grossly inappropriate and irrelevant. I will strike it immediately and disregard it. And I would like you to apologize to Ms. Gray."

"Of course, Judge. I simply wanted to show that when the sheriff stated she has no reason to have a grudge against teenage boys, she was either mistaken or untruthful. Either way, I apologize, Ms. Gray. I can occasionally get carried away in defense of the helpless. No further questions, Your Honor."

"Thank you," the judge said, writing something down on the yellow legal pad in front of him. "Any redirect from the plaintiff?"

"No, Your Honor."

"You may step down, Sheriff." He looked at the clock. "I have an appointment in twenty minutes, so let's resume tomorrow with the next witness. Court is adjourned."

"All rise," the bailiff said loudly.

Solomon gathered his papers as the judge left. Dennis said something to Braden, and then the boy was led away by the bailiffs.

"That was a low blow," Solomon said.

Dennis shrugged. "My client is on trial for his life. I've always said that prosecutors should spend a couple of years doing defense work to taste the pressure. If I lose, my client's life is ruined permanently. If you lose, well, there'll always be other cases. It's not the same type of pressure."

"If I lose, your client is going to kill more innocent people. You're defending one life, and I'm defending dozens. So you're right, it's not the same type of pressure."

Dennis grinned. "Don't forget about his mother. In addition to Braden, she and everyone else in her family will be devastated. We both help, and we both hurt. Remember that before you get on a high horse about being the good guy." He glanced over to make sure Braden was gone, and then he left the courtroom.

Solomon sighed as he gathered up the rest of his papers and a few books he'd brought to give the appearance of being prepared. Billie was waiting for him by the entrance of the courtroom. He walked out with her.

"That wasn't the most pleasant time I've had in court," she said.

"I'm so sorry, Billie. I didn't think he would cross the line like that."

"It's not your fault. But at least he's made clear now he's not interested in a deal."

"No, he's not. He wants Braden out, and he's willing to hurt people to make it happen."

46

As Solomon and Billie got onto the elevator, a man in a shiny suit with a purple tie put his arm in between the doors and snuck on. Solomon recognized him. Richard Mackenzie. A former crime beat reporter with the local paper and now a local celebrity podcaster. He preferred the moniker "Mac" and liked to say it was what his squad in the military called him, though Solomon knew he had never served in the military.

His black, curly hair sat atop a round face with mischievous eyes that held an intelligence he didn't like to display.

"There he is. Solomon Shepard. How's it going, brother?"

"Mac. You still got that orange tan, I see."

"Hey, we gotta stay nice and vitamin D'd up in these winter climates, right? I heard you were back, but I didn't believe it."

"Lemme guess, you want a quote?"

He chuckled. "No, brother, no quote. Things have changed. My podcast is the number one true crime podcast in the state. I got sponsors to deal with, a television show in production, and interviews I gotta edit. Way too busy for just a quote from some midlevel prosecutor."

"Sounds like you got everything you ever wanted."

The doors to the elevator dinged and opened, and Billie stepped off. Solomon followed her, and Mac hurriedly got in front of him and walked backward.

"I didn't mean it personally, and you know that. How 'bout to make it up to you, I have you on the podcast?"

Solomon chuckled. "That was well played, Mac. First, insult me, hope it hurts, then offer me the interview to ease my hurt feelings. You still got that sharp, rat-like mind, don't you?"

He laughed. "You know me too well. But come on, it's just one interview. I'm bumping the county attorney for you. Doesn't that scream how important I think you are?"

Solomon stopped. "You'd bump Knox for me?"

"Yeah."

"Would you tell him it's for me?"

"I don't see why that matters, but sure."

Solomon glanced at Billie, who grinned and shook her head. "You boys just don't know how to play nice, do you?"

Mac said, "So is that a yes?"

"Yeah, Mac, fine. I'll come."

"Right on." Mac took out his phone and AirDropped his address onto Solomon's phone with a wave of the device. It was something Solomon had never seen before, and it reminded him of Arthur C. Clarke's musing that advanced technology is indistinguishable from magic.

"Eight o'clock on Thursday. Don't be late," he said, walking away and pointing with both hands.

Billie strolled next to Solomon as they went out to the parking garage. Several people were smoking in the cramped space outside the doorway, and the lack of air circulation gave the stale air a bitter smell. Mixed with exhaust, when the court was busy, like it was now, the smoke created a noxious fume that made it difficult to breathe. They hurried past to the rows of cars.

"You can't trust him. You know that, right? He wants you on his podcast to sandbag you," Billie said.

"Yeah, but thinking about Knox's face when he finds out he was bumped for me will make up for it."

Their shoes were loud on the pavement while they walked. A couple of women near a car comforted a man who sat in the driver's seat and wept. Solomon heard him say something like "I wish it was me instead" as they walked past.

"Well," she said, glancing down at her shoes, "whatever happens, you're doing a great job."

"I'm not, but thanks anyway."

She took her keys out, turned off the alarm, and unlocked the doors. "Need a ride?"

"I'm good, thanks. Want to walk for a bit and clear my head."

She got into her truck. He watched her pull out, and she waved to him, and he waved back. When he was alone, he glanced at the elevator leading back up to the courtrooms, then took the ramp out onto the streets.

Though a low crime area in general, Tooele had pockets where even the police feared going at night. This stretch of neighborhood in front of the courthouse used to be one of those areas. There had been shootings and stabbings nearly every weekend. Teenagers dragged State and looked to flirt with cars filled with others around their age, and the concentration of people led to flared tempers.

The city eventually had to ban the practice of dragging State because the murder rate for the county had doubled in three years, and pressure was being put on politicians to do something. Utah was a state that relied on winter tourism. People from all over the world would come here to ski since the state had some of the most exclusive resorts in the world.

Those resorts wouldn't want to stay in a state if it became known as a murder capital, and the government would do whatever they suggested so the tourists wouldn't leave for Aspen instead.

Solomon had always thought if you wanted to understand how something worked, just follow where the money goes.

He strolled down the sidewalk in the afternoon sun and walked until evening when the sun was setting. The parking lot of a Taco Time was as good as any other place to rest. He stood with both hands on his cane and watched as the sun was pulled down below the mountains and the streetlights came on. Billie texted him and asked what he was doing, and he told her.

Solomon ordered a burrito and sat at one of the outside tables. He watched the cars and the people going by, making up stories for them like he used to do as a child. A ninety-three-year-old uncle had once told him he did the same thing, and Solomon thought it strange that humans became child-like again near death.

A man's voice broke the calm when he shouted at his girlfriend or wife. Solomon looked over to the sidewalk and saw a large male in a white undershirt holding a girl in sweats. The girl was crying and trying to pull away. The man was screaming at her while holding her elbow with hands so large they wrapped all the way around her arm. Unfortunately, the streetlights were burned out over in that section of the block, and he couldn't make out their faces very well.

Solomon looked around, and there was no one else nearby other than him.

Shit.

"Hey, let her go. Hey!"

The man looked up at him, though Solomon still couldn't get a clear view of his face. He gripped his cane tighter and wished he'd bought a heavier one.

Just as he thought the man was about to break into a sprint for him, a police cruiser rolled into the parking lot. Two police officers got out and went into the Taco Time. The man let go of the woman and disappeared into the darkness.

The woman stood there awhile, then was swallowed up by the darkness, too.

Solomon sat back down, his heart in his throat. He watched the burrito wrapper flutter in an exhaust-tinted breeze and thought about Maria, Kelly's mother. He wondered if Travis had been laying off her, and how long it would last, if so. Eventually, there would be more beatings, more apologies, then worse beatings and more apologies and gifts. Then, at some point, she would either break away and free herself . . . or die.

The thought soured his appetite and made him think of this case. What was he even doing in that courtroom? He had no right to be back. What he had told Knox was true: he was the best homicide prosecutor in the state . . . *back then*. Now, he was a man who lived alone in an apartment with a cat and sometimes had panic attacks so bad he couldn't go outside.

He would tell Knox that he couldn't hack it and was quitting. But, of course, anything that was done after would be tainted by his involvement. Any resolution that wasn't a slap on the wrist would be appealed by Dennis Yang, arguing that Solomon had tainted the entire case for the State and that dismissal was the only just outcome. If Solomon stayed on the case, he was going to lose. If he left, the next attorney was going to lose.

The fact was, that boy would be back out on the streets in a couple of years to kill again. Again and again and again. Until the police killed him or got lucky, and one of the victims got to a gun in time.

Solomon took out his phone to leave a message for Knox, telling him that he was quitting. Before he could dial, he saw Billie's truck come to a stop in front of the Taco Time. He set the phone down and gave her a weak grin as she sat across from him at the table.

"Come for the tacos?" Solomon said.

"You looked sad when I left. Thought you might need a friend right now. Besides, I had nothing but a binge of *American Hauntings* waiting for me at home."

"What's your favorite season?"

"One. Yours?"

"Three. That hotel."

"Really? That was so dark. Why that one?"

"It was based on a real hotel in Los Angeles. They had dozens of mysterious murders and suicides. Richard Ramirez, the Nightstalker, lived there during his killing spree. After him, Dean Harold stayed there in the exact same room Ramirez did. Harold went on ride-alongs with the cops and had them tell him about where the prostitutes were and how often the cops patrolled the area so he could kill them more efficiently."

"How many murders did he confess to?"

"Varied, depending on what day they asked him. He was only convicted of one in Austria. He began writing in prison and impressed the literati enough that they lobbied to release him as a rehabilitated killer. When he got out, he killed nine more women."

"Sounds charming. What ended up happening to him?"

"He hung himself in his cell. But the weird thing was that one of the guards reported that there were two voices in the cell right before it happened."

She raised her eyebrows. "That's probably not a story you should share with many people."

"Eh. Everybody already thinks I'm morbid." He took a small bite of his burrito. "Have Kelly's parents been calling you for updates?"

"No, actually. They haven't called at all."

"Not once?"

"No. It's unusual for parents of a missing child."

"Huh."

The thought made Solomon think about Dean Harold and his plays. Solomon had read some of the plays after Harold was already incarcerated for murder, and he'd had to stop reading. There were times when the darkness was too much, and he couldn't absorb any more.

"Do you know the difference between darkness and light, Billie? Darkness sticks to you. I feel like I've seen so much of it that I was ready to retire before I was stabbed. I'd thought about it and decided to do it a few weeks before. I knew I'd already burned out and lost it, and I still came back every day back then thinking I could prosecute like I used to. I couldn't. And I especially can't now, all this time later. I'm not that man anymore."

"No, you're a new man. It's okay to change, Solomon. You don't need to stay the same to do good work." She grabbed his soda and took a drink. "Can you even imagine living with the memory of telling Knox that you can't do this? Of giving up? Not to mention it might not even matter. Braden Toby might still go free even with someone else prosecuting."

He shook his head. "I know. I really screwed the pooch on this."

"Hey . . . you did not screw the pooch. This isn't on you; this is on Braden Toby. You're doing what you can within the system. It just so happens that system is Judge Boyce, who cares more about impressing the top lawyers in the state and making good connections than doing what's right. If we'd gotten another judge, the outcome would've been different."

"Yeah, that was a terrible draw for us."

"I've rarely seen a judge so clearly biased. I wonder if you prosecuted one of his family members or something?"

Solomon thought a moment, gazing off at the darkness where the man and woman had stood shouting a minute ago. Then he stood up. "Gotta check on something."

"Now?"

"Yeah."

"Here, I'll drive you."

"No, I got a couple different places to go. I'll see you tomorrow in court."

Solomon called an Uber as he started heading back toward the sheriff's station.

47

The following day, Judge Boyce had taken off his robe and was sitting down at his desk when Solomon burst into his office. Right behind him, the judge's clerk was trying to hold him back.

His clerk said, "I'm so sorry, Judge. He burst in."

The judge leaned back in his chair and said, "That's all right, Heidi. I'll take it from here."

"Are you sure? I can call up Eddie."

"No, I don't think Mr. Shepard is any sort of threat, but thank you." The judge turned to Solomon and held out his hand, indicating he should sit down. Solomon did so. He glanced back and saw Heidi shut the door.

Judge Boyce took a can of V8 juice out of a small fridge and offered one to Solomon, who declined.

The two men sat quietly a moment while the judge popped open his drink and took a sip.

"You know, Counsel, this is a clear ex parte conversation without Mr. Yang here. I could sanction you and report you to the Bar."

"I really thought you were just some jackass on a power trip who didn't like me but would set that aside and be fair anyway. Then you kept going, and I had to think, wow, for someone that I've never done anything to, he *really* doesn't like me. So I thought maybe that's what it was. Maybe I did something to him. And I figured it out by chance."

Solomon opened his satchel and grabbed a few pages held together with a paper clip. He flung them on the desk. The judge glanced down as he took another sip of drink but didn't move to pick them up.

"What is that?"

"That, Your Honor, is a sealed record for a criminal case from eighteen years ago. I had to pull a few favors at the court administrator's office to get it. See, most people don't know, even most judges, that when a criminal case is sealed, the files aren't destroyed right away. The courts didn't start using electronic files until well into 2012, so anything before that still has a paper file. The paper file has to be scanned into an electronic file, and you know how backed up everybody is. It'll take decades to scan everything. So sealed cases still exist; they're just not available to the public . . . unless, of course, you know people with the key to the storage rooms."

The judge didn't move for a while, and then his jaw muscles flexed. He stared at Solomon with a venom that said if it were possible, he would do more than sanction him or hold him in contempt.

"It's inconsequential," the judge finally said.

"Opposing counsel was your lawyer in a criminal case, and you didn't feel you should divulge that to me? I read the reports. You tried to pick up a prostitute, and Yang got it sealed for you. That should've disqualified you from the bench."

"Nonsense."

"At the least, you had a duty to inform me of the conflict, and you didn't."

Boyce put his drink down and leaned forward. "What I have or have not done in my past, or who represented me, has nothing to do with the legal arguments in my court."

"You couldn't have a clearer conflict, but you still took the case and didn't notify me. That's an ethics violation. What I should do is fill out a report with the JEC today and file a motion to have you recused from this case."

Anger filled his eyes in a way Solomon hadn't seen before, and he worried that the judge might have a physical episode and Solomon would have to give CPR.

"You do whatever you have to do, Counsel."

"I'm not going to report you. Frankly, I don't care. I think you should be able to serve on the bench. We all make mistakes. But you can't be on this case. Recuse yourself. Today." He rose before the judge could say anything else. "If the first words in court aren't, 'I have a conflict and must recuse myself,' I'm putting on the record what I found and filing a motion to recuse you and notifying the JEC about your conduct. Lotta media attention on this case. And 'Judge Picks Up Working Girl and Keeps It Quiet' sure sounds like a good headline."

He got to the door before the judge growled, "If you're going to attack the king, you better not miss. That's a big risk you took."

Solomon turned. "Yeah, but the fact that you called yourself *the king* shows me I did the right thing. You know, I've heard the Maldives are an amazing place to retire to. Why put yourself through this every day? You've earned the right to spend your golden years someplace nice."

He opened the door and stepped out, getting a dirty look from the clerk as he went to the courtroom.

———

"All rise," the bailiff said. "Third District Court is back in session. The Honorable Isaac Boyce presiding."

Honorable, Solomon thought. *Yeah.*

The judge walked in. He sat down at the bench and leaned back, staring at both attorneys. Then he leaned forward to get himself close to the microphone and said, "I have discovered a potential conflict that may prevent me from being objective and will have to consider the consequences before continuing. I will let you know my decision tomorrow. Court is adjourned."

Dennis was on his feet. "Your Honor, may we discuss this in chambers, please?"

"No, we may not."

"But Judge, I think we deserve—"

"You will have my decision tomorrow, Mr. Yang. Thank you both for your time."

He hit the gavel in finality, then hurried out of the courtroom without looking at anyone. The bailiff shrugged at the clerk, who appeared confused. She glanced around, unsure what to do, then gathered up her files and ran out the door the judge had gone through.

"What the hell just happened?" Dennis said to Solomon.

"I expect that shit from him, but not from you, Dennis. You should've told me you were his lawyer."

"I don't know what you're talking about, Counsel. But if I did, I would say I told you that we do what we have to do to win for our side."

"You still have to sleep at night. How do you sleep?" Solomon watched as Braden was taken away by the bailiffs. "Find out where the girl is and I'll cut him a deal . . . if she's still alive."

"I don't know why you keep bringing that up. He had nothing to do with that."

"Just take it to him. Tell him he'll have a shot at having a life at some point if he tells us where she is."

Solomon turned to leave, then stopped. "You know, I was thinking this morning, if you're willing to do this, what else are you willing to do?"

"What do you mean?"

"After your client stabbed me, a mistrial was declared, and Watts got a new trial. We were almost done with his case, and everyone in that courtroom knew he would get convicted. He couldn't have done something to get a mistrial at a more opportune time. Almost like someone who knows criminal procedure told him to do something crazy."

Dennis picked up his briefcase. "You need to get out more, Solomon. You're starting to see conspiracies everywhere."

"Yeah, I'm sure that must be it."

He watched Dennis leave, then looked over to where Braden Toby had been sitting. Even though he'd only been there a short time, Solomon could see hairs lined up on the table.

He got his satchel and left the courtroom.

48

Though Tooele seemed like a city that wouldn't have a homeless problem—anyplace with long winters usually didn't—the city services had recently been overwhelmed with the number of homeless flocking there. Without enough beds at the shelters, parks filled up with tents and sleeping bags. Sections of the industrial district were littered with garbage, and people had to step over hypodermic needles and feces. Solomon hadn't been there in a long time and was shocked at how different it looked.

A few men stood on a corner and smoked. Solomon got out of the Uber and asked the driver to wait a few minutes for him. The driver said he couldn't because he had another ride lined up, though Solomon was sure he didn't at this hour.

The three men eyed him as he approached. One said something Solomon couldn't hear, and the three of them chuckled.

"Can I ask you guys something?" Solomon said. "I'm looking for where the youth stays."

"The *youth*?" a guy with a tattoo on his neck said mockingly.

"I know they don't sleep in the general shelters, they go somewhere else. You guys know where?"

"Get outta here, man. Before someone beats your ass with that cane."

"How about fifty bucks?"

It was a risk to offer them money since they could easily beat him and take his wallet, but all he had on him was a fifty. He took out his wallet and opened it, ensuring they saw that only one bill was in there. He held it out to them. The one with the neck tattoo looked to the bill, then to him before taking it.

"There's a bridge off 300 West. They sleep there when the shelter's full."

"Bridge off 300 West. Cool. Thanks."

The address wasn't far, and Solomon walked there. This district had nothing but warehouses or businesses that had moved into warehouses and tried to make them look like office space. Other than a few low-income apartment buildings, nobody lived around here, and it gave the place a haunted feel.

Under a massive overpass meant for four lanes of traffic off the freeway, he saw groups of tents packed in tightly. Kids in their teens sat around in a circle and drank. One of them had an acoustic guitar and wore thick glasses.

Solomon approached them, and the difference in the vibe between them and the men he had just encountered was pronounced. The men had instantly grown aggressive, and only when they saw a benefit to being calm did they stop. The teens immediately looked at him with fear, and Solomon felt for them. To live in a world where every person was a potential threat must've been exhausting.

"Excuse me, I'm looking for someone. Kelly Greer. She's sixteen, black hair, really snarky look on her face all the time."

The kid with the guitar smiled, and Solomon thought he seemed relieved.

"Who are you?" one of the girls said.

"I'm her neighbor, Solomon. Is she here?"

"No. Never met her."

The way the girl said it and the reaction of the kids told him she was lying. He leaned on his cane and watched the girl, who couldn't look him in the eyes.

"Hundred bucks if you can tell me where she is."

The boy with the guitar and the girl looked at each other, and the boy said, "She's at Dominic's house."

"Matt!" the girl snapped, outraged that he would betray her trust for a hundred bucks.

"We barely know her," Matt said.

"Who's Dominic?"

"Some rich dude up in the Aves. He lets us stay there sometimes."

"Where does he live?"

"Another hundred bucks."

"Two hundred bucks just for answering two questions?"

"You wanna find her or not?"

The young man had a smirk as he strummed his guitar once.

"Yeah." Solomon sighed. "Fine, two hundred."

"Where's the money?"

"I have to go to an ATM."

"Yeah, well, we ain't goin' anywhere."

49

Billie met Dax at a Chinese restaurant that was open until midnight. He sat in a booth furiously texting with both thumbs. A full beer and an empty bottle were on the table in front of him. She sat across from him, ordered a glass of wine, and leaned her head back on the booth seat.

"You look tired," he said, not glancing up from his phone.

"Been a long few weeks."

"Hey, you remember Lynn? We went to high school? She's gonna be in town tomorrow. You wanna grab lunch with her?"

"Meeting your old girlfriends isn't exactly on the top of my to-do list."

"It was a long time ago. No one remembers who dated who."

"Weren't you going to get married?"

He shrugged. "Who remembers? Anyway, I'll just go with her. If you wanna come, lemme know."

"What is that?"

"What?"

"What you just did? You made a pity offer, then said you were going anyway. If you want to go to lunch with another woman, you don't need my permission, and you don't need to try to trick me."

"I wasn't tricking you. I thought you may wanna come."

"You knew I wouldn't."

He lowered his phone. "How the hell am I supposed to know that? We barely see each other anymore. I only wanted to spend some time with you."

She closed her eyes and shook her head. "You're right. I'm sorry. I'm under a lot of stress."

"So? Quit."

"I can't quit."

"Yeah, you can. You won't, though. You were the one that told me cops don't last long because they get burned out. Maybe you're burned out. Come work with me."

"A pyramid scheme doesn't really sound like the best place for me, but thanks."

He chuckled. "You know it's not a pyramid scheme. The Ohnoloy drink is going to be the next orange juice. Watch."

She rubbed her face with her hands and thought about how boring their last few conversations had been. A streak of guilt ran through her when she realized how much more interested she was in going home and reviewing the Braden Toby case files.

Her phone buzzed, and it was Solomon.

"One sec," she said. "Hello?"

"I think Kelly's still alive. Some teens around the shelter have seen her."

"Where are you?"

"At the shelter. I just had a thought that she might've run away."

"Solomon, there was a lot of blood in her room."

"I know. I don't know what happened, but if there's even a possibility she's still alive, I have to do something about it. I just called an Uber and am headed over to some guy's house they said she's staying at."

"Cancel it. I'll be there in twenty." She hung up and said, "Have to go."

"You just got here."

"It's important."

"And I'm not?"

"I'm sorry, but having a seafood enchilada is not as important as finding out whether a sixteen-year-old girl I thought was dead is all right."

He clicked his tongue against his teeth and said, "All right, fine. Have fun."

"I can't believe you're mad about this. She's a kid."

"What the hell did you become the boss for if you can't send someone to do this shit for you?" When she didn't respond, he gave a mirthless chuckle. "You don't *want* to send anyone else, do you? Guess I'm just too boring for you, aren't I?"

"That's not it at all."

"I think that's exactly it."

"I don't have time for this right now," she said as she stood up.

He grabbed her wrist. "If you leave, I won't be answering again when you call."

"Let go of my arm, Dax," she said, staring him in the eyes.

"I'm serious."

"So am I. You're hurting me. Let go of my arm right now."

He let go. She turned and left the restaurant without looking back.

———

When they were in her truck, Billie noticed Solomon tapping his cane against the floor. He seemed agitated, on edge. The nervous energy he gave off was strong enough that she felt it, too. At one point, he rolled down the window, then rolled it back up a second later, only to roll it down again.

"Don't get your hopes up," she said. "They could've just wanted the money and have no idea who you're talking about."

"Maybe. I don't think so, though."

"You were pretty sure Braden Toby took her. What makes you so sure he didn't now?"

"I understand her stepfather not calling you, I doubt he cares, but that's odd for her mother not to check up on our progress. Maybe Kelly reached out to her to say that she's all right?"

"Wouldn't she try to reach out to you?"

"Maybe she felt like she already had. Before she disappeared, she asked if she could live with me, and I rejected her."

The address was in a more upscale area of the city. The homes were older but large, and packed in tightly so that hardly anyone had a front or backyard, though the view of the city at night was stunning. Sparkling gems spread out over a dark valley.

When they parked, Solomon got out first and stared at the home. It was gaudy. Pillars with gold trim and a horseshoe driveway. The kind of place meant to shove the amount it cost into other people's faces.

They knocked on the large double doors, and no one answered for a long time. Then, finally, when someone did open the door, it was a woman in her twenties wearing a skimpy outfit that revealed her muscular abdomen. Her nails were long and painted red with white sparkles.

Billie said, "Do you live here?"

"Um, sort of."

"Well, we're looking for a Kelly Greer. We were told she's staying here."

"Oh, I don't know. But, um, lemme grab D."

She shut the door, but Solomon put his cane in between it and the frame and slowly pushed it open again so he could see inside. The walls were as tacky as the exterior. Paintings of ancestors he was sure were not the owner's, generals in long-forgotten wars, busts of people who looked distinguished but probably never existed.

A man in sweats and sunglasses answered the door. Older with white hair cut short.

"Yeah?" he said.

"Solomon Shepard. I'm looking for a girl named Kelly Greer. Sixteen, black hair, half white, half Hispanic, has a scar going down her cheek. Is she here?"

"I don't know. She might be."

Billie said, "Do you have a lot of sixteen-year-olds living with you that you don't know about?"

"I let whoever crash here when they need. Who the hell are you anyway?"

"I'm her neighbor. She's missing."

He shrugged. "Look around if you want. Cammy, show him around."

The girl who'd answered the door said, "Let's check the movie room."

The home was much larger than it appeared on the outside. One room led to another, which led to another, and the entertainment room was down a set of three staircases in an underground basement decked out in white carpet and a massive projection screen. A pool table and weight set were near the back, and a full bar was at the front. The screen took up an entire wall in front of a dozen theater seats and a popcorn maker. Girls were passed out everywhere, and a guy with no shirt on sat in one of the seats, watching a movie with his feet up on the seat in front of him.

"Tony, have you seen a girl named Kelly?"

"Kelly?" he said without looking back.

"Yeah, Mexican chick. Teenager."

"Oh, yeah, her. Yeah, she was here."

Solomon said, "Where is she now?" with hope in his voice he tried to hide.

He shrugged. "I don't know."

Solomon moved in front of him and blocked his view of the screen.

"Hey, I'm watchin' that."

"It's really important I find her. When was the last time you saw her?"

"I don't know," he said, trying to watch the screen around him. "Like a couple days ago."

"Does she sleep here?"

"Sometimes."

"Where does she go when she's not here?"

"I don't know, man. I don't know her that good."

Solomon reached up with his cane to the projector on the ceiling and twisted it to the right, so the image was cast on a corner.

"Hey!" the young man said. He tried to stand, and Solomon pushed him back down with his cane and held the tip against his chest. Billie came over and made sure he saw the badge clipped to her waistband.

"Think real hard," Solomon said. "Where could she be right now?"

"I don't know what that girl's into, but I keep to my own, you know. Don't cause trouble, and trouble won't come to you."

"I can appreciate that, but she's already in trouble. I want to help her get out of it."

He didn't answer.

"The fact that you won't answer me tells me I'm not gonna like what you're about to say."

He shrugged and tried to watch the distorted image in the corner. "Dom sets dates up for the girls."

"Dates?" Billie said.

"Yeah, you know. Dates. Nothing's free. They stay here, but they gotta go on dates sometimes with dudes Dom sets up."

"So he's a pimp."

"I don't know. I just wanna watch my movie, man."

Billie looked to the girl, Cammy, and said, "What happens on these dates?"

"It's not like that. Dom makes it clear there's no sex unless the girls want it. Most of the time, it's taking old guys out to, like, the symphony or dinner or whatever. Wherever they need a date."

"Is Kelly on a date right now?"

"Probably. I don't know."

"Well," Solomon said, fixing the projector and sitting down, "we'll be here while you go find out. You got any popcorn?"

50

Solomon awoke to the sound of the alarm on his phone and fell out of bed, trying to turn it off.

Last night had been a waste. Waiting until the early morning at Dominic's house, hoping Kelly would show up, and having his heart pound every time the front door opened. Billie fell asleep in one of the theater seats about halfway through *Die Hard*.

Russ jumped up onto the sink, his tail waving back and forth like a snake. Solomon rubbed his head, and the cat's eyes started drifting closed.

"You get up, eat, sleep, use the litter box, eat, sleep, chase ghosts and laser pointers, and eat again. Is that the secret to happiness? Don't think about anything, just live in the present?"

Solomon watched him for a few seconds, genuinely jealous that he could so quickly fall asleep, and then got dressed and left.

————

The sun was barely up by the time he got to the courthouse. The doors weren't opened yet, and he waited in line with the few people there. One man, smoking a cigarette and picking at a scab on his forearm, asked him what he was there for, and Solomon said, "Murder."

The man said, "Right on," but didn't speak to him again.

Solomon sat on a bench outside Judge Boyce's courtroom after they were let inside the building. His stomach was in knots. The motion had been made to recuse the judge. Still, he could picture Boyce stewing all night in a seething hatred, then changing his mind and making Solomon take this to the Judicial Ethics Committee. It would then be a long, drawn-out battle trying to prove that he had acted inappropriately. Even if they found that he had, most judges received fines or brief suspensions. It was nearly impossible to take down a judge who'd been given life tenure. Judges were the last form of tyranny left in America.

Billie sat down next to him in a business suit with her badge around her neck.

"You got an interview or something?" he said.

She smiled. "Thought I'd look nice for our new judge."

"Hopefully, a new judge. Boyce is too crazy to predict what he'll do."

She put both hands on the bench and straightened her arms, leaning forward a little. "How'd you sleep?"

"Got like two hours. I stayed up all night in the theater room chatting with a really high Tony, who is actually pretty cool, by the way. He's getting his degree in film studies, and he's the only other person I've met that has a VHS collection of eighties horror." He looked at the courtroom as someone tried the doors and they were locked. "What about you? Did you manage to get a few hours?"

"No. My mother had some issues last night, so I had to be over there helping my father."

He tapped the tip of his cane against a crack in the linoleum in front of him. "That sounds more serious than taking care of her when she has a cold."

She looked over to some people waiting in front of the courtroom doors while the bailiff fumbled with keys. "I owe her enough to not stick her someplace to be taken care of by strangers."

"Even if they can do a better job?"

"We're doing fine."

Solomon hadn't meant to hurt her, but she needed to hear it. He'd seen it before: devoted children thinking it was their obligation to take care of ailing parents who required constant supervision. Wearing down both the child and the parent and ruining the small amount of time they had left with each other. He didn't want that for her.

The sound of high heels echoed in the corridor, and Dr. Ruth Fuller approached in a burgundy suit. She gave a polite smile before saying, "Sheriff, good to see you again."

"You too. Love the suit."

"Gotta play the part." She looked at Solomon. "You ready?"

"Not really."

The doors to another courtroom opened, and people started going in. The bailiff unlocked Judge Boyce's courtroom, and Solomon got a shot of adrenaline that made him quiver. He didn't know if he would have the strength for the fight he would have to go through if Boyce refused to step down.

He used his cane to stand. "Better face the music, I guess."

51

Solomon was seated first, and Dennis Yang came in a moment later. He wore a white suit with a yellow tie and didn't say hello. The judge's bench still had Judge Boyce's nameplate, and it gave Solomon a sinking feeling.

Braden was brought out. The boy's eyes were odd. He didn't take in the environment like other people did, with at least mild curiosity. For him, it seemed like nothing outside of himself was even there.

"All rise," the bailiff said after the clerk had come out and set up. "Third District Court is now back in session. The Honorable—"

Solomon closed his eyes and thought if he heard Judge Boyce's name, he might pass out right there.

"Lisa Covey presiding."

The judge was a slim woman with curly black hair and a pleasant smile. She sat down and said, "Please be seated. How is everyone doing?"

"Good, Judge," Dennis said.

"Fine, thank you, Your Honor."

"Mr. Toby, how are we today?"

He stared at her and didn't answer. Dennis leaned over and whispered to him. But Braden was somewhere else and didn't look like he'd even heard him.

"We are here today for the matter of Braden Toby v. the State of Utah, case number 224267, and Judge Boyce has recused himself due to a conflict. My understanding is we're here to determine whether Mr. Toby should stay in juvenile court or whether the Court will grant the plaintiff's petition to certify this case an aggravated offense, and transfer jurisdiction to the district court. I have read both counsels' briefs on the matter and consulted with Judge Boyce. Are there any issues before we begin that either side wishes to bring to my attention?"

"No, Your Honor," Solomon said.

"One thing, Judge. The sudden departure of Judge Boyce was rather unexpected and committed over our objection. I would like it noted on the record for appeal that the defense objected and believes that the recusal prejudices my client."

"So noted for the record. Anything else?"

"That's all, Judge."

"Okay, well then, Mr. Shepard, the floor is yours."

"Plaintiff would call Dr. Ruth Fuller to the stand, please."

Dr. Fuller was sworn in and took her seat in the witness chair, briefly straightening her suit. Her face was stern but held confidence and intelligence; she'd been doing this long enough that she was no longer intimidated by being cross-examined in court.

"Please state and spell your name for the record," Solomon said.

She did, and he went through a few preliminary questions before saying, "And what is your position now, Dr. Fuller?"

"I'm the head psychiatrist of the Children's Justice Center, where I oversee the counseling for troubled youth."

"Have you met the respondent in this case, Braden Toby?"

"Yes, multiple times."

"In what capacity?"

"Yourself and the Court asked for an evaluation of his mental faculties and cognizance of the crimes he's accused of. This was in an effort to help determine if he is fit to stand trial as an adult or should be held in juvenile court."

"Did you only talk with him, or is there more to it?"

"Oh, quite a bit more. I interview family and friends, I go through their entire medical history, I'll order sleep studies and blood work, CAT scans or MRIs if I suspect brain injury, and several other measures to give me a complete view of the child."

"Did you do those things in this case?"

"Yes, I was asked for a complete evaluation."

"Let's start with organic origins. Did you find any evidence of brain injury?"

"Yes."

"Is this the MRI result here?" Solomon said, holding up an image of a brain, milky white on x-ray film.

She looked at it and said, "Yes, that's it."

"And you took this yourself?"

"Myself and the radiologist."

"Your Honor, we would move to introduce plaintiff's exhibit one through eight for the record."

"Any objection, Mr. Yang?"

"None, Judge."

"Then the items are introduced. Please have them marked by my clerk."

After getting them numbered, Solomon said, "Now, Dr. Fuller, what does this first image show us?" Solomon hung the image on a whiteboard so the judge could see it more clearly.

"May I get up?"

The judge said, "You may."

Dr. Fuller went over to the whiteboard and spoke to the judge as she said, "In a normal functioning brain with no severe trauma, we would expect a homogenous coloring on the MRI. That's the blood flow to the brain. It should flow to each section in more or less uniform patterns, meaning that this should all look the same," she said, pointing to an area on the image.

"But you can see these two black spots here. One of them is larger than the other. I surmised that these two areas suffered injury when Mr. Toby was younger. In consulting with his mother, it was revealed he was climbing a tall fence and slipped, fell, and landed on his head. The other injury, the smaller one, is from an older student in school hitting him with a baseball bat during some altercation in gym class. The injuries damaged the front and occipital lobe areas of the brain. That's the two black marks. They're areas that did not receive oxygen for a prolonged period and have, for lack of a better term, died."

"Regeneration is not possible?"

"It's documented in the literature occasionally, but if I had to guess, I would say these areas were not going to be repaired."

"What would someone with these injuries generally behave like?"

"The frontal lobes are the seat of reasoning. They control things like language, the ability to pick up on social cues, and the brain's executive functions, such as higher reasoning and logic. They've also been shown to have a strong correlation to regulating the emotions."

"Could damage to the frontal lobes lead to mental disorders?"

"Yes, absolutely."

"Disorders like malignant narcissism?"

"It's difficult to say with medical certainty, but many of those who suffer from malignant narcissistic personality disorder have received some sort of brain damage to their frontal lobes, yes."

"What about psychopathy?"

"That's controversial right now. Many of my colleagues still do not believe psychopathy is possible and that there are other explanations for the behavior of those with antisocial personality disorder. But it is generally accepted that if the frontal lobes are no longer functioning properly, the patient would have difficulty in many areas of social life. This would include feeling empathy for others, the ability to regulate their emotions, to stay in control of their temper, and to be able to accurately judge the consequences of their actions."

"Given all this, what is your opinion as to Mr. Toby's diagnosis?"

"It was difficult to draw too many conclusions as he doesn't like to speak, though he did open up a small number of times. But the likely diagnosis is antisocial personality disorder with a concomitant malignant narcissistic personality disorder."

"And when you say antisocial personality disorder, you mean what used to be termed a psychopath, correct?"

"That is the closest popular term, yes."

"What are the traits of a psychopath?"

"It runs the gamut, but there are certain characteristics they all share. Lack of empathy for others, artificial charm, frequent lying, and an inability to take responsibility for one's actions are the most common traits."

"Violence?"

"Many psychopaths do leave a pattern of harmed individuals behind them, but not necessarily through physical violence. We find a sizable percentage of psychopaths in business, medicine, and law enforcement, for example, who never actually violate the law enough to lead to incarceration. In a small percentage, however, we would deem them as being in an active psychotic state, and this can lead to the formation of violent fantasies, which can lead to a killing compulsion."

"What about Braden Toby?"

"He would be in the latter category. I've spent many hours interviewing friends and family and poring through records, and certain patterns emerged in his history."

"Such as?"

"Such as an ingrained sense of pathological lying. When an average person lies, they feel uncomfortable. Their heart rate elevates, they begin to perspire, and have a host of physiological reactions. For the pathological liar, we have the opposite scenario. They have lied so much that they have rewired their brains, and now when they tell the truth, it is uncomfortable for them, in the same way telling a lie is to a person without the disorder."

"What other patterns did you see?"

"He seems to have an inability to take responsibility for his own actions. For example, in an interview with me, we went through his medical records. He had a broken arm from a car accident, and he blamed the other driver's actions. However, in going into Mr. Toby's juvenile record, I saw a pattern of—"

"Objection!" Dennis said, shooting to his feet like he were an athlete. "She cannot testify about what she observed in my client's *sealed* records, Your Honor. Otherwise, what's the point of getting them sealed?"

"I agree. Doctor, please do not refer to or describe anything learned through sealed records. You are given special permission from the Court to view those and must ask the Court's approval before discussing them with another person."

"I understand. I apologize, Your Honor."

"Mr. Shepard, go ahead."

Solomon watched Braden, who hadn't pulled out any hair today. Instead, he stared down at the table without blinking. A strand of drool trickled down his lip and left droplets on his pant leg.

Braden turned and looked at him as quickly as a snake. The motion startled Solomon, who hid it just enough for no one else to notice. But Braden had noticed, and he smiled and turned back to the witness.

"Mr. Shepard? Do you have any more questions for this witness?"

"Yes, Your Honor, sorry. Dr. Fuller, let's cut to the chase. In your professional opinion, is psychopathy, or antisocial personality disorder, a valid diagnosis for Mr. Toby?"

"No."

Solomon couldn't speak for a moment. He glanced down to the other questions he had, and they all relied on a yes to this one. A question she had answered affirmatively every time they had talked.

"What do you mean?" Solomon asked, unsure what else to ask.

"We use the terms interchangeably, but they are not the same. For example, for antisocial personality disorder, the child must have been diagnosed with conduct disorder in youth. It's considered unethical, and therefore is unrecognized, to diagnose a child with psychopathy or antisocial personality disorder. For the same reasons, we don't use the word *defendant* or *jail* in juvenile court proceedings."

"So, what would be your diagnosis?" Solomon said, thinking he'd just been thrown off by the wording and not the substance of what she had said.

"I believe Mr. Toby suffers from severe narcissism and conduct disorder. Brain damage is likely a contributing factor, but genetic factors can play a part. There was some abuse involving a boyfriend of his mother's, but it didn't last long as his mother left the boyfriend afterward."

"Do you believe he can be treated?"

"Anyone can be treated; the question is whether it will help or not. With the severity of the conduct disorder Mr. Toby displays, I'm afraid treatment may not be effective. However, we won't know unless we try." She glanced at Braden. "I believe it is unethical for Mr. Toby to not get that chance. That's why I recommend he be kept in juvenile court and—"

"Objection!" Solomon shouted.

Dennis rose. "He can't object to his own witness."

"The hell I can't."

"Your Honor—"

"Mr. Shepard, you may not shout at a witness just to get them to stop talking. Please allow the witness to finish her statement."

"Your Honor, I can't sit here and allow her to commit perjury on the stand and mislead this court to—"

"How dare you?" Dr. Fuller said. "I have a reputation in the community for fairness. That's why I'm hired by both prosecution and defense. I am giving you my diagnosis and opinion, which is what you asked me to do. I'm sorry if now you disagree with it."

Solomon stood there in shock. His mind was blank, and he couldn't think what to say. She was saying exactly the opposite of what she had told him in private she would testify to. It had been a ploy. She knew he would get a second opinion if she'd told him she was recommending that Braden Toby stay in juvenile court.

The only thing that would happen by continuing his questioning was to make things worse.

"I'm done with this witness."

"Very well. Mr. Yang, any cross?"

Dennis rose to his feet with a small smile and looked at Solomon before saying, "I have no questions for the doctor," then sat back down.

"Then we will take a brief recess and reconvene after lunch. Thank you, gentlemen."

Out in the hall, Solomon waited by the courtroom double doors. Billie stood next to him and said, "Don't do anything you're going to regret."

The doors opened, and Dr. Fuller came out. Solomon immediately said, "You sandbagged me."

"I did. And I'm sorry."

He hadn't expected an apology, and it confused him enough that the anger dissipated, which confused him more.

"Why?" he asked.

"That boy deserves a chance at treatment. If I can't believe a child can change, then my entire career has been a waste. I knew if I told you that, you wouldn't call me to testify. So I thought it was the lesser injustice to lie to you."

He tapped his cane against the floor. "What happens if you're wrong? What if the second he gets out he kills again?"

"Then I'm going to feel guilty for a very long time."

52

Solomon hardly slept that night. Lying in bed with his hands behind his head on the pillow, he fell asleep once and woke up twenty minutes later. The anxiety was overwhelming, and he felt old compulsions coming back. Chewing on a pen was only the tip of the iceberg. He thought back to prescription pills and whiskey bottles that had taken up all his time and made the days tolerable. He didn't want to go back to that, and the thought that it was even a possibility frightened him.

After a cold shower, he left. He stopped in front of Kelly's apartment and listened. He did that almost every time he came or went into his apartment now. Hoping that the next time he would hear her voice and that she had just run away and decided now to come home.

When he heard nothing, he summoned a car and left the building.

In court, the judge was announced and seated before she whispered a few words to her clerk, who nodded. "Okay, we are here on the record for the continuing matter of Braden Cunningham Toby. The plaintiff may proceed."

Solomon didn't move. Last night, his mind ran through iteration after iteration of what he could have done to prevent the doctor from pulling the rug out from under him. He couldn't think of anything. He'd done everything he was supposed to do and still came up short.

His only hope was that the judge was convinced the crimes were heinous enough that the doctor's recommendation was inappropriate.

He pictured Braden stabbing Kelly, an image he'd been fighting. The idea made him nauseated, and he leaned his elbows on the plaintiff's table.

"The plaintiff rests, Your Honor."

"Very well. And the respondent has no witnesses?"

"Just one, Judge. We would recall Sheriff Elizabeth Gray to the stand."

Billie looked surprised as she went to the witness stand.

Solomon chewed on a pen while she took her seat. He ran through different scenarios of why Dennis would call her and couldn't come up with anything. Billie had nothing to add, and the defense could only be harmed by having her up there.

"Sheriff," the judge said, "I would remind you you're still under oath."

"I understand, Your Honor."

Dennis got up to the lectern and laid a laminated sheet of paper down in front of Solomon. Then he asked if he could approach the witness, and the judge said he could.

While he gave Billie a copy, Solomon read the first sentence on the paper, and his heart dropped.

This is Reaper speaking.

"I received this letter under my door last night, Sheriff," Dennis Yang said casually.

Solomon nearly shouted, "Request to meet in chambers!"

The judge didn't respond to his raised voice and calmly said, "Very well, the court will take a five-minute recess."

Solomon stormed over to the respondent's table. "What the hell are you doing?"

"I'm not doing anything. I'm just telling the truth."

"You're telling me now about the letter? You should have notified me last night, not let me go through my case and then pop it on me for maximum surprise."

"You're crazy, Solomon. You see conspiracies everywhere."

"Gentlemen," the judge said, "please keep up."

They followed the judge back through the door behind her bench. A few clerks sat in cubicles, and Solomon saw more than one poster of a cat hanging off something with the words *Hang in there* across the top. A half-eaten birthday cake sat on a table.

Judge Covey's chambers were clean and free even of books. Nothing personal. He'd seen many judges do this in an attempt to separate work and homelife, to try to somehow turn off what they saw in court with how they lived in the real world. A task that Solomon knew was impossible.

She took her robe off, revealing a beige pantsuit underneath, and sat down at the desk. Solomon and Dennis each took a chair. Dennis was calm and waited patiently for the judge to speak first. Solomon felt like he was about to either vomit, or pass out, or both.

"I was never given this letter," Solomon said, barely able to contain his anger.

"This letter was slid under my office door late last night, Judge. I immediately made copies and brought them to court for everyone."

"That's not enough notice. He didn't even tell me about it before court, when I could have gotten a continuance. I need to analyze the letter and ensure its authenticity. I'm willing to bet this is just some member of the public trying to stick their nose—"

"The handwriting looks plenty authentic to me," Dennis said. "But I, of course, stipulate to a continuance of this matter while Mr. Shepard has his handwriting experts compare."

"No, it's too late. We're nearly done with this hearing, Your Honor. There's no reason for this letter to come in. The district court can use it as exculpatory evidence, but it doesn't pertain to whether Mr. Toby should be tried as an adult."

"So we have a letter from the real killer, and we're going to ignore it and put this boy through hell? *Hoping* the district court gets to it fast enough before he gets killed in custody? That about right, Mr. Shepard?"

"You just happen to get this letter when we get a judge who isn't in your pocket, then—"

"Don't be upset with me because you're rusty in court and couldn't convince Judge Boyce to see things your—"

"Gentlemen," Judge Covey said, agitated now, "please remember decorum. I don't appreciate insults between counsel. Now, Mr. Yang, you're willing to go on the record under oath that you received the letter last night, correct?"

"Correct."

She tapped her finger against her desk. "How long would you need for your handwriting expert to analyze this, Mr. Shepard?"

"At least a week."

Dennis scoffed, "My client's life is in jeopardy every moment he's held in custody. If the expert can't examine this letter by Monday, let's find someone else."

"That's agreeable with me," the judge said. "Let's get out there and put it on the record, and we'll reconvene on Monday. Mr. Yang, I assume you will want your own expert to examine the letter as well?"

"Yes, Judge."

"Then I will grant extra time for both experts to get an opportunity to examine the letter, and we'll hear from both of them at the next court hearing. Now let's get back, please."

They quietly followed the judge out. When back in the courtroom, the judge described for the record what they were planning on doing. Solomon looked over to Dennis and said, "If this turns out to be fake—"

"I have no idea if it is or not. I'm telling the truth. It was slid under my door sometime after I went home."

They rose as the judge left, and before Solomon could turn to confront Dennis again, he was already out the doors.

Billie came up to Solomon and said, "What the hell was that about?"

"It's about me just getting my ass kicked."

53

Solomon stared out of the passenger side window at Dominic Vasili's house. The man had a plethora of businesses, social media personas, and bank accounts, though none of them seemed to make any sense. He owned a horse stable in Beaver, Utah, that held no horses and a bed-and-breakfast in Idaho that had closed three years ago. The businesses, Solomon figured, were probably to move money around to avoid taxes. A common scheme among people who wanted wealth but didn't want to share with Uncle Sam.

Billie sipped a soda out of a bottle as a Brazilian death metal band played on the lowest volume possible through the speakers. The front man screamed, "Bloody roots!" at the top of his lungs with pounding drums and buzz saw guitars behind him.

"You know this music really is meant to be turned up," Solomon said.

"I have a headache."

"Stress headache?"

"Life headache."

She took out two ibuprofen from a bottle in the center console and popped them into her mouth before taking a drink of her soda. "I remember in high school, relationships were so easy. You either liked the guy, or you didn't. Black and white. There weren't all these shades of gray between like and dislike."

"I wouldn't know. I was barely there."

"Seriously? You seem the bookworm type to me."

He grinned. "Why do you say it like that? Like nerds grew up on a different planet?"

"I don't know. You're just so . . ."

"Normal?"

"Yeah."

He looked back out the window at Dominic's home. "No one's normal. There's no adults in the world, Billie. We're all just faking it."

They were silent awhile, the violent, yet somehow melodic, hum of screaming English and Portuguese filling the car.

Billie turned off the stereo and rolled down the windows. She stared out at the home. "You don't think she may be selling herself for this guy, do you?"

He shook his head. "I don't know. I don't think so. If Braden didn't take her, something happened to make her run away, but I don't think it would get that dire for her. She's got other family in the area from her dad's side."

He checked the time on his phone. "You sure about this handwriting expert?"

"Best in the state. I've used him at least a dozen times on letters and suicide notes. He knows what he's doing."

Solomon felt a headache coming on and rubbed his temples. "What if I'm wrong? What if it's really not Braden? What if the Reaper is still out there and it's been him all along, and we got this poor kid in custody who—"

"All the evidence is pointing to Braden Toby. The sweat, the admissions, the mental health history, it's all there. So if we're wrong, we're wrong, but we did nothing anyone else wouldn't have done."

Solomon took a big breath and puffed his cheeks as he blew it out. "I never should have agreed to this. I should have left it to Knox."

"You're assuming it would've turned out different. He would've wanted this out of the media as quickly as possible and given Dennis anything he wanted. That boy would be free in a couple years."

"He's probably going to be anyway."

"Hey," she said, touching his arm to get him to look at her. "Whatever happens, you did everything you could."

While staring at her eyes, he thought something he hadn't considered before. She didn't want this as much as him. She would move on to other cases. This would be something to be brought up over beers with other officers, reminiscing about the close calls and the ones that got away. For him, there would be no other cases. This would be at the forefront of his mind every day for the rest of his life . . . especially if there were more killings.

"Billie, I need you to set something up for me. And I can't have you ask any questions about it."

"That sounds like the type of favor I'm not going to like doing."

"Might have more severe repercussions than that. So no questions. For plausible deniability."

She exhaled loudly and glanced at Dominic's house as a girl in a bikini top and a jean skirt stumbled out and got into a Mercedes, checking her makeup and hair in the rearview before pulling out.

"What do you need?" Billie said.

54

Solomon had never done anything like this. Not once. He had always believed that pure process led to pure results. But there was no choice now, no other direction to turn. Nothing else to do. It was either this or go to court in a couple of days and watch Braden Toby be held as a juvenile, have Knox work out a commitment in the state hospital, and have the boy back on the streets to kill again when he was older.

The secluded room at the jail was off the beaten path. Somewhere no one went. Billie had asked the guards to clear it for him and asked the custodians to stay away for a few hours. Staff at jails liked doing favors for cops: you never knew when you might get pulled over and need a little leniency.

The room smelled like floor polish, and empty mop buckets lined the walls. A calendar of landscapes was up near him, and it had been expired for two years.

The door opened, and a guard brought Braden Toby in. Braden was sat down, and then the guard shut the door, leaving the two of them alone.

"You gotta take it easy on the eyebrows," Solomon said. "It's too noticeable if you're trying to fit in without looking out of place."

"Is that what you do? Fit in?"

"No, I don't think I've ever fit in anywhere."

"Me neither."

He plucked out a bit of hair from his eyebrow and placed it on the table. "I'm thinking you're taking a pretty big risk talking to me without my lawyer."

Solomon nodded, staring at the way he was arranging the hairs. "There's a line in a book that says something like 'If you want to catch unusual beasts, you have to go to unusual places.'"

"I'm a beast? Most people think I'm just a screwed-up kid."

Solomon noticed him staring at the lion's head on his cane. "We both know that's not what you are."

A smile came to his lips, but he didn't look up from the cane. "You write a lot about category zeroes, but you never say if you ever met one. Have you?"

Solomon nodded. "I think so. Only one, though."

"Who?"

"I was prosecuting him for accidentally killing his son, manslaughter. I just got this . . . feeling from him. Being in the same room made me uncomfortable for a reason I couldn't describe. So I dug a little deeper, and it turned out he was a war criminal from Rwanda. He was in charge of a death squad that killed a lot of people."

"Do you get that same feeling from me?"

Solomon didn't respond for a moment. "Yes."

Braden grinned and said, "My mother thinks this is her fault. That she did something to make me."

"Did she?"

He shook his head. "No."

The air conditioner ticked on, and stale, warm air came through the only vent in the room.

"Why the Reaper? There's murderers that have killed a lot more people. Out of everyone you could've imitated, why him?"

He shrugged. "I don't know. There was something about the way he did it. So . . . clean. I remember reading a chapter in a book about him and thinking he was more than human. He'd abandoned morality

263

and was beyond anything anyone could understand. None of the other killers I studied were anywhere near him. They didn't know why they did what they did." Braden tore out a bit more hair from his eyebrow, though it was more skin than hair this time. "Do you know why he did it?"

"No."

"I bet you have a guess. I wanna hear it."

Solomon leaned back in the chair. "He thought that for each person he killed, he increased the odds of his survival a fraction of a percent. It's bullshit, Braden. He would've survived just fine without hurting anyone else. And he did want something, just like every other killer."

Braden nodded. "Death."

"Yeah, death. Is that all you want, too?"

He stopped arranging the hairs and didn't blink. It seemed almost like a shadow came over his eyes. Solomon told himself it was only the way the light in the room hit his brow.

"If I could kill every person, I would."

"Why?"

"Why not?"

"That's not an answer."

He chuckled, and the sound was awful. No mirth or joy, just an expression of hatred in the form of a human response.

"It is an answer. I thought you understood, but maybe you don't."

Solomon looked down at his cane. He tapped it against the dirty floor and thought for a while as Braden ripped more hair out.

"Does it hurt when you do that?" Solomon asked.

He nodded as he ripped another chunk out of his eyebrow. "Does where you got stabbed ever hurt?"

Solomon hesitated. "I wake up sometimes and feel the shank going into me again."

"Do you see him places you go? The guy that did that to you?"

"Yeah, I do."

For the first time, Braden didn't seem interested in the hair on the table and let his hands rest on his lap. "I had something like that. We were camping when I was in the Boy Scouts. We were all sleeping outside in sleeping bags, and I felt this pain in my face. Just in my face, nowhere else. I looked up and saw these two eyes looking at me, and they were . . . beautiful."

"What was it?"

"A wolf. It pulled me by my face and tried to get me away from the campsite."

"What did you do?"

He shook his head. "Nothing."

"You didn't scream?"

"No. I thought he was the most beautiful thing I'd ever seen. One of the scout leaders heard the growling and woke up and scared the wolf away, but I'd see wolves wherever I went. Hiding around corners. Wanna know why I'm not dying in prison or anything? 'Cause that wolf is gonna kill me. I'm going back to those woods, and one day he'll sneak up behind me and kill me, just like I do."

Solomon had thought he would be curious what Braden had to say, that he was some type of sociological puzzle. But all he felt toward the boy was revulsion. A deep revulsion from somewhere in his reptilian brain, as though he were looking at a creature with an unbearable deformity.

"Did you take her?"

"Who?" he said with a grin. He was enjoying the pain.

"I'll do anything to get her back. Just tell me if you took her."

"Anything?"

"Yes."

"Kill yourself."

"What?" he said with disbelief.

"Kill yourself, and I'll tell my lawyer where she is."

Solomon watched the joy in his eyes. The boy was enjoying his pain far too much. Then why hadn't he brought up Kelly? If Solomon hadn't mentioned her, it didn't seem like Braden would have.

"She had a scar somewhere on her body. Somewhere only someone who saw her from up close would know about. So you tell me where that scar is, and I'll do it."

"You'll kill yourself?"

"Yes."

"She means that much to you?"

"She's in this because of me. It's my responsibility."

He shook his head. "Do you know how stupid you sound? The only duty of an animal is to survive. You're doing the most unnatural thing in the world if you die for someone else."

"You're stalling. Where's the scar?"

For the first time since coming here, Solomon thought he saw confusion on Braden's face. It was a flash, a quick drop in his defenses, but it was there.

"You don't know, do you? You don't know because you don't have her."

Braden's lip curled as he felt control of the conversation slipping away from him. Solomon used his cane and rose.

"You're not a category zero, Braden. You said it yourself. You want something. You *want* to be a category zero. That means you can't be. You're just a damaged little boy hiding in the dark." He put his hands on his cane and waited until the boy was looking at him. "And I'm going to make sure you die in a cell, not by a wolf."

———

The truck stopped outside a small home in a quiet neighborhood overlooking the valley. No toys or basketball hoops. It was a retirement community and looked like it.

Solomon and Billie got out and followed the paved walkway to the front door and knocked. A man in light blue pajamas slid open the curtains and looked outside. It took a moment for him to recognize them.

"Sheriff?" he said as he answered the door. "What are you doing here? Do you know what time it is?"

"I need to know right now if Braden Toby wrote that letter," Solomon said.

"What? Who are you?"

"This is Solomon Shepard; he's prosecuting the Toby case."

"I need to know right now, Doc. Tonight."

He looked at Billie. "You said I have until Monday."

She shook her head. "This is important, Fred. Please. Have you looked at it?"

"Yeah, but I haven't even written up a preliminary report."

"Is it him?" Solomon said impatiently.

"Mr. Shepard, I can't just say that. It's going to take several more hours of analysis, and the best I can do is say whether the handwriting is consistent with his handwriting or not. So I can't say it's him with any real certainty."

"I know you got a reputation to protect, and this is how you make your money, but cut the bullshit. Is it him or not?"

He sighed and glanced at Billie before saying, "Come in. I want to show you something."

55

Dennis Yang got to court and looked grumpy. Like someone had roused him from a deep sleep. Solomon sat at the plaintiff's table, and Billie sat behind him.

He hadn't slept after leaving Fred's home two nights ago and didn't sleep more than a couple of hours last night. Instead, he sat on his couch with Russ and watched the sunrise as he let his thoughts take him where they wanted to take him. Sometimes, that was the only way to really see what you were thinking.

He reread the Reaper's letter to the media from eight years ago, and then reread it several more times.

There was beauty in it, purity, but also underlying insanity that could only be detected between the lines. The man could hide in plain sight, but if someone paid attention, they could see what was underneath . . . nothing. Duality incarnate: something human but not human at the same time.

In some sections, Solomon could see the hints of a man with the gift of words, one who could speak smoothly and quickly and get what he wanted. In other sections, he saw the instability and the rage. He wondered if the Reaper could see the differences or if he was oblivious to himself.

And there was one thought of the Reaper's that Solomon could never shake. The same thought that he had shared with Braden Toby.

Every person that I kill, the Reaper had written in his letter, *increases my chance for survival slightly. The more I kill, the more resources there are for me and everybody else. People should be thanking me, and instead, they call me* monster.

"All rise," the bailiff said. "Third District Juvenile Court is back in session. The Honorable Judge Lisa Covey presiding."

The judge came out holding a mug of coffee and sat down. She booted up her computer as she sipped her coffee.

"Okay, we're here for the matter of Braden Toby, case number 224267. Mr. Yang is here for the respondent and Mr. Shepard for the plaintiff. Bailiff, please bring out the respondent."

The bailiff brought out Braden, who didn't look at anyone. His face was turned to the floor, and when he sat, he stared at the table without blinking.

"Mr. Shepard, the floor is yours."

He rose. "The plaintiff would call Dr. Fredrich Zheutlin to the stand."

Fred stood up from the back of the courtroom and made his way over. The clerk swore him in, and he took a seat in the witness chair. Solomon sat on the edge of the table facing him and folded his arms while waiting for Fred to settle.

"Dr. Zheutlin, what is your specialty, sir?"

"I'm a professor of communications at the University of Utah, specializing in graphology."

"What is graphology?"

"The study and analysis of handwriting and calligraphy."

"How many cases have you testified in, Doctor?"

"I would say over a hundred in the past twenty years."

Solomon held up the laminated letter Dennis had sandbagged them with. "Did you analyze this letter?"

"I did."

"What is it, Doctor?"

"It is a letter allegedly written by the perpetrator of these crimes and given to defense counsel. I was asked to analyze whether it matched the handwriting in the letter of the original Reaper case, as well as the letters purported to have been written by the respondent in this case, Mr. Braden Toby."

"Move to qualify Dr. Zheutlin as an expert in graphology, Your Honor," Solomon said.

"Any objection?"

Dennis rose. "Your Honor, though we had notice that he may be testifying, we've had minimal time to prepare. I need to interview the good doctor and thoroughly prepare for cross-examination. I have no idea if he's qualified or not."

Solomon jumped in. "Dr. Zheutlin, do you recognize the defense attorney in this case?"

"I do."

"How?"

"I was hired by him on several occasions to analyze writing samples for veracity."

Dennis blushed for the first time Solomon had ever seen.

"He's the defense's own expert they turn to when they need a handwriting analyst. That's why they don't have one testifying. I don't think he needs time to qualify his own expert."

The judge thought a bit. "I agree, but Mr. Yang, I will note your objection for the record should you wish to appeal the issue. Go ahead, Mr. Shepard."

"Dr. Zheutlin, what did you find upon analysis of this letter?"

"Well, it is a decent, I would perhaps even say moderately good, replica, but I believe I can say with confidence that this was not the handwriting of the original Reaper letter from eight years ago. There were twenty-two points of contention, which we in graphology use to describe samples that don't match. For example, the word slant, the direction the words lean, was completely different, as was the spacing, which are two attributes that are very difficult to fake. If I may bring up the slide?"

"Sure," Solomon said, nodding to the clerk. She pressed a button, and the projector turned on, shooting the image over to the white screen the bailiff had pulled down. It revealed a close-up of two letters: one from the original Reaper and then the letter Dennis had just received.

"You can see here the word spacing is completely different. The original Reaper was organized and methodical, some would even say obsessive, about symmetrical words and letters. This most recent letter, however, is all over the place. You can see that the distance between the letters and words has no symmetry and, in fact, differs even from the same letters, a situation we call *disorganized agreement*. You can also see some unusual formation of words. For example, in the Reaper document, the word *never* has a slant to the *V* prevalent in every *V* the author used. However, in this most recent letter, if you look at the *V* in the word *very*, which is used twice, you can see that the *V* actually slants the opposite way. I found another twenty-one points of contention similar to this where the handwriting differed."

"What does this tell you?"

"It tells me, one, that this is inconsistent with the letter of the Reaper that I was given for analysis. Every paragraph I read in the original Reaper letter was consistent in its slants and spacing. I couldn't find a single exemplar—the term for the writing being analyzed—across the eighty or so paragraphs written that had disorganized agreement."

"And what else?"

"Typically, these points of contention, taken together, are a sign of simulation."

"What is simulation?"

"It's where one person is trying to copy the handwriting of another person. It's actually quite easy to decipher if you know what you're looking for. Both authors of the most recent letters are attempting to imitate the letter of the original Reaper."

"'Both authors.' Because I also asked you to take a look at the note Braden Toby handed me in the museum. A note he does not deny writing." Solomon gestured to the clerk, who advanced to the next slide, a side-by-side comparison of all three letters. "So there are three different authors?"

"I believe so, yes."

Dennis objected again, though they both knew it was a losing battle for him. This was his own expert he relied on, and it was difficult for him to convince the judge he didn't believe in Dr. Zheutlin's skills or qualifications.

"In other words," Solomon said, wrapping up, "two different people tried to copy the Reaper's handwriting, and one of them was presumably Braden Toby?"

"Correct."

"Thank you, Doctor. No further questions."

The judge said, "Mr. Yang, any cross-examination?"

Dennis rose and approached the lectern. "Doctor, what are the Hitler diaries?"

Fred cleared his throat and poured some water out of the jug into a plastic cup. "A man named Konrad Kujau came forward several decades ago and stated he had found some lost diaries written by Hitler. So handwriting experts were brought in, three reputable ones from Europe. They analyzed the diaries based on exemplars known to be written by Adolf Hitler."

"Three of the best handwriting experts in the world, correct?"

"Correct."

"And what did they find?"

"They agreed that the diaries were not simulations and they were in fact written by Adolf Hitler. The diaries were then published in the *London Times*."

"But they weren't written by Hitler, were they?"

"No, sir. Two professors, a reputable graphologist and a forensic analyst, worked together years after the diaries were published and determined that the ink and paper used in the diaries were not consistent with the ink and paper used before 1945, when Hitler died. Furthermore, under ultraviolet light, it was shown that the paper held an ingredient that was not used in paper until 1954, and that, in fact, the ink had been applied to the paper after 1954."

"So the diaries fooled three of the best handwriting experts in the world."

"Yes, sir."

"Is it possible you're being fooled, Doctor, and these exemplars were in fact written by the same person?"

"Yes, of course, it's possible. But we're talking about probabilities."

"Do you know the probability of these exemplars being faked?"

"Well, no, that's difficult to determine with the brief time I had to analyze them. You're asking me to predict the probability of an unknown variable. Any number I give you without thorough research and analysis will just be a guess."

"A guess? So really, with all the fancy words and explanations, you're simply taking a guess that these documents weren't written by the same person."

"Yes," he said, unsure. "I suppose you could say that. Though it's a very good guess based on my decades of experience, but yes, it is just a guess."

"Thank you, no further questions."

Solomon rose. "Just a few redirect questions, Judge."

"Of course."

"Dr. Zheutlin, do you have an ultraviolet spectrometer?"

"Yes, I do. At the laboratory at the University of Utah."

"Did you submit the exemplars to ultraviolet analysis?"

"Yes, at your . . . vehement insistence, I went to the lab yesterday and compared them."

"And?"

"All three papers are made up of different fibers. In addition, the ink is not the same across the exemplars. Same colors, same *type* of pen, but we can say with some reliable degree of certainty that they were not created by the *same* pen. This type of ink is based on soybean oil and petroleum as a solvent. We can date when the oil was broken down to form ink. Exemplar one is at least five to eight years older than exemplars two and three, which we would expect, but exemplars two and three were also definitively written with different pens on different types of paper. It would be a proper conclusion to make that they were written by three different authors using three different pens and types of paper."

"So it's your professional testimony today that the pens used in the three exemplars are not the same, the paper is not the same, and the handwriting of each does not consistently match the other two?"

Fred hesitated a moment and thought. This was the question that would make or break the case. If Dennis created enough doubt in the judge's mind that Braden was the killer at all, she'd have a hard time consigning him to the adult justice system. But Solomon also knew experts didn't like saying things with certainty, because if they turned out to be wrong later, there was a court record of it.

"I would say that it is my opinion that these three different exemplars were likely, but not unquestionably, written by three different people."

"Thank you, Doctor. No further questions."

56

The judge said she needed a break to take the testimony under advisement, but Solomon knew she was likely consulting the other judges in the building, which frequently happened on complex issues.

Solomon sat outside the courtroom on a bench. He leaned forward with his elbows on his knees and listened to a family whose loved one had just been released from custody. They were crying and hugging, and he was saying he would never go back.

Dennis Yang strolled over and sat next to him on the bench with a groan. He leaned back against the wall and said, "He didn't take that girl."

Solomon watched the family as they stood around and talked about things the man had missed while incarcerated, including the birth of a granddaughter. "Yeah, maybe. I doubt we'll ever know without finding her."

Neither of them spoke for a moment.

Dennis finally said, "So what's next for you after this?"

Solomon shook his head. "No idea. You?"

"Depends what happens here, I would think."

"You know, you're at retirement age. You don't have to do this anymore."

"Not for me, thank you. My father retired and died two years later. Work gives me purpose." Dennis looked at him now with a mixture of curiosity and fatigue. "What's your purpose, Solomon?"

"Wish I knew."

Dennis leaned forward in the same posture as him, and Solomon was sure he'd done it intentionally. Studies had shown people were more likely to listen to you if you held the same posture as them. Something about the unconscious identifying with them in a way the conscious might not.

"Five to life with parole," Dennis said.

"Twenty-five to life with parole."

"Far too severe. That's probably what the judge would give him if we lost at trial."

"Not *if*. There's admissions all over the place, Dennis. Your client *wants* people to know he's the killer. And when it gets to trial, I'll be introducing his little notebook with all the pleasant pictures he drew, and everything he's said since he was in custody. You'd have zero chance of a win. The only reason I'm even considering dealing is because I want to spare the victims' families a trial."

He nodded. "Fifteen to life, and we'll let the parole board decide how long to keep him."

Solomon thought a moment. After Braden had served fifteen years, he knew the parole board would keep him at least another fifteen. Though murderers did get released on parole, it was usually when they were much older and not considered a threat to society anymore.

"I can do that," Solomon said.

Dennis watched the family who had been weeping leave and get on the elevators. "I'll speak to him and his mother. I'm certain I can get them to accept."

"I'll let the judge know."

Dennis stood up and said, "Are you coming back to the CA's Office?"

"Anything's possible, I guess."

Dennis nodded. "You will. Everyone needs a purpose."

Solomon waited until Dennis had gotten on the elevator and left before he went to the courtroom. He asked the bailiff to take him back to the judge's chambers. The judge sat at her desk on the phone, and Solomon chose to stand. When she got off, she said, "Mr. Shepard, I can't speak to you ex parte without the permission of Mr. Yang."

"I have his permission."

"Oh, I see. So then I assume you have a resolution?"

"Yes. We're transferring the case to the district court, and Braden will be pleading to fifteen to life."

She nodded. "Well, that saves me some research. I appreciate you letting me know."

Solomon turned to leave, then stopped. He turned back to her and said, "Since we've resolved it, out of curiosity, hypothetically, which way would a judge lean on a case like this, do you think?"

She looked out her window and sighed. "I think a judge has to believe that if anyone can be reformed, it has to be a child. If the judge didn't believe that a child could change, then who can? As Dr. Fuller said, a child would deserve a chance."

He nodded. "Have a good one, Judge."

"You too, Mr. Shepard. I hope to see you again in my court."

"I think . . . that's not outside the realm of possibility."

57

Billie was leaving the sheriff's station when she heard two deputies outside speaking. Word had gotten around that they had locked up the Reaper copycat, potentially forever. One of the deputies said, "Didn't think she had it in her."

She couldn't suppress a grin as she headed out to her truck.

Solomon was waiting for her on the curb in front of his apartment building. He had a smile on his face as he got in.

"What are you so happy about?" she said.

"Just a nice day."

"It's a hundred and seven."

"Better than freezing."

They drove down State Street and got onto the on-ramp. Billie rolled up her window and turned her air-conditioning all the way up. "You feel good about it?"

"I do."

"Seems like he could get out at some point."

"When he's in his forties probably. Who knows what the world will be like then? You and I will be gone anyway."

She glanced at him. "I never said thank you."

"No need."

Dominic's home had several cars in the driveway. It was early enough in the morning that Solomon was confident most of those inside the house were still asleep.

In exchange for terminating probation early on a drug case she had pending, Cammy had agreed to let them know when Kelly was back. The text had come at six in the morning.

Solomon knocked and rang the doorbell impatiently. Dominic answered in a robe and squinted from the sunlight like a vampire.

"What the hell do you want?"

"She's here. Move."

They walked by a few bedrooms and noticed people passed out. Billie had seen more than one party house belonging to an older man who was wealthy but had no family. They let the young stay over and impressed them with fine clothes, drugs, and expensive cars. It always struck her that having people like that around, those who were only using you for what you could give them, would be more lonely than being alone.

Cammy came in from the pool, already in a bikini. She smiled at them and said, "You'll remember me, right? If I ever need you?"

Billie nodded and handed her a card. "Don't get in trouble again, and I'll talk to your probation officer about early termination. *If* I don't see you again."

"You won't."

Solomon said, "Where is she?"

"She's outside, by the pool."

The pool was large and trimmed in dull, fake gold. The shrubbery was neatly clipped and the grass manicured perfectly, hardly a single blade taller than any of the others.

"Man," Solomon said, "could this guy be any more insecure?"

"Jealous?"

"Totally."

Two other girls lay by the pool. Neither of them was Kelly, and Solomon looked around before saying, "Where is she?"

"Right there," Cammy said, pointing to one of the girls.

"That's not Kelly Greer."

"No, that's Kelly Garcia. That's what you said, right? Mexican chick with long black hair. That's what you told me."

Shit, Billie thought. She saw the color drain from Solomon's face.

"I need you to drive me somewhere right now," he said with something in his voice she hadn't heard before: rage.

———

The truck stopped in front of the large grocery building where Travis worked as a pharmacist. Solomon hopped out, and Billie followed him. He had butterflies in his stomach, but the anger overrode his nervousness. There was still the chance that he was wrong, and he hoped like hell he was.

A clerk at the pharmacy desk inside said, "Can I help you?"

"Travis Wilks, please."

"And you are?"

"I'd prefer he didn't know," Billie said, holding up her badge.

"Oh, okay, well, he's over at the deli having breakfast. Straight back past the produce. You can't miss it."

"Thanks," she said.

The grocery store was upscale, with clean floors and a pleasant scent coming from the plant nursery.

Travis sat at a table eating some eggs and bacon. It took only a moment. A brief pause where the world seemed to slow down and their eyes locked, and Solomon *knew* that *he* knew.

Travis jumped up and ran.

He sprinted through a door by the deli while Solomon shouted, "Hey!"

Every other worker turned toward them and watched in shock as Billie took off after Travis and Solomon went outside to cut him off. He had planned on only speaking with him, so they had brought no other officers with them, and he deeply regretted it now. If Travis got away because of his stupidity . . .

Outside, he looked from one end of the parking lot to the other. The door Travis had run out of was on the south side of the building, and the parking lot was on the west. He didn't see or hear anything but a few shoppers going in and out.

He had seen Travis drive away from their apartment building before and knew he drove a Volvo. The car was parked near the middle of the lot. Before Solomon could even take a step toward it, Travis popped up behind him and smashed him in the back of the head with his fist.

Solomon flew onto his stomach. The blow had been entirely unexpected and caught him unprepared. While Solomon was on the ground, Travis rammed his heel into Solomon's face. He heard his jaw crunch and tasted so much blood it made him gag. By the time Solomon managed to sit up, Travis was already at his car.

Solomon grabbed his cane and forced himself to his feet, spitting out globs of blood. The car rumbled to life just as Billie's truck came flying past them. She slammed on her brakes behind the Volvo. Travis hit the pedal and flew backward in reverse. He smashed into Billie's truck broadside, and his airbags went off. Solomon hurried over, pain flooding his face and jaw as the shock of what had happened wore off.

Travis jumped out of the car, covered in blood from cuts caused by the impact. Billie tried to open her door, but the crash had set off her airbags, too, and she couldn't press them down fast enough to get out in time.

Travis made it only a few steps before collapsing. He shook his head and tried to stand again. Blood was pouring down his face from a gash across his head.

Solomon got there first and jumped on him, using his body weight to pin the man down. But Travis was bigger and stronger. He flipped Solomon over and smashed his fists into him, over and over. Solomon brought up his arms to protect himself, and the blows were powerful enough that they would hit his arms, slip off, and his face would take the impact. Then, when Travis lifted his right hand to bring his fist down again, Solomon grabbed his neck and pulled his face toward him. He bit into the muscles of his jaw as hard as he could, tasting blood as Travis screamed. The pain of biting made Solomon nearly pass out, and he knew his jaw was broken.

The man wrapped his arms around Solomon's throat, and he felt the air instantly cut off. Colorful swaths appeared in his vision, and his eyes bulged. It amazed him how quickly his body went limp, and he felt his life leaving him.

He couldn't get breath anymore and thought his windpipe might be crushed. Then, darkness started squeezing into his vision from both sides.

The crackle of the Taser was only a distant sound. He was somewhere else. Somewhere from a long time ago, a young boy in a sandbox. He remembered the sandbox and the toys he kept in there, but he couldn't remember where it was or if it was even his memory.

Travis screamed, convulsed, and rolled off Solomon. Sirens weren't that far, and the last thing Solomon heard before passing out was Billie saying to hold on.

58

Hospitals all smelled the same. Antiseptic, bleach, and sickness. Solomon had always believed illness had a smell, and humans were able to pick up on it. An evolutionary adaptation meant to weed out those potential mates who might not produce the best offspring.

As he woke up in the hospital bed, it took him back to four years ago with doctors telling him he might never walk again, and the pain pierced him like a needle in his heart.

Billie sat on a chair in the corner. In her arms was Russ. She set him down on Solomon's thighs and said, "I brought a friend."

Solomon grinned, and it hurt, but he managed to lift his hand and rub the cat's head as he purred. Solomon was about to speak when Billie said, "Don't talk, your jaw's wired shut."

She watched the cat slink down and close his eyes.

"They had to put you under to wire your jaw. Luckily your windpipe didn't get flattened, but it was cracked. It's going to take some time before your voice gets back to normal, but since your jaw's wired shut, I don't think it matters too much. I think this will be a new experience for you, not talking." She took out a small whiteboard and a marker from a Walmart bag she had set on the floor. "Thought you might at least like to be able to tell the staff when you need to go to the bathroom."

Solomon took the board and marker and wrote the words, "Is she dead?"

Billie looked away, and he knew the answer. He closed his eyes and inhaled deeply.

"I'm sorry, Solomon," she said, running her hand through Russ's fur. "Travis said it was an accident. That he was drunk and she was pushing his buttons, and it got out of hand. He apparently only hit her once, but she fell back and fractured her skull on the wooden headboard of her bed."

He wiped the board clean with his palm and wrote, "Where's her body?"

"They panicked and didn't know what to do. They dumped her body in Small Creek Canyon, then made up a story about going to dinner and a movie and bought tickets right then. We've got both of them in custody, though I'm not sure Knox will bring any charges against the mother. She already has an interview tonight, and she'll appear like the battered and abused victim." She rubbed Russ's back. "What is wrong with people, Solomon? How could you let that happen to your own child, then dump her body like trash?"

He stopped petting Russ but left his hand on the animal. He could feel Russ's heartbeat and smelled his pleasant cat scent, and it took him back to his childhood and the sandbox he had seen when unconscious. He had a cat when he was that age, too. Rainforest. He'd been killed when he was run over by a neighbor, and it was the first time Solomon realized that not everything had a happy ending. Life itself ended in tragedy for every human being who had ever lived and ever would live.

Russ purred in his lap, and he thought about how sweet the cat was . . . to him. To mice, he was a monster who played with them and took enjoyment from their fear before tearing them apart. Solomon had never seen Russ that way, and it surprised him that he thought of it now, in this place, while the pain coursed through him and made his face feel like it was on fire.

Billie picked Russ up in her arms and said, "You should be outta here by tomorrow. I'll come by and pick you up." She let out a sigh and said, "I'm so sorry I brought you into this. I never should have come to your door."

Slowly, he shook his head, and wrote, "I'm glad you did."

The cat looked at ease as his eyes drifted from consciousness into sleep. He could fall asleep anywhere at any time, perfectly content no matter where he was. No past, no future. Just the pleasure of the moment.

Solomon envied him.

The cat stretched out in Billie's arms, opened his eyes just enough to see Solomon, then closed them again. Delighted where he was. People spent the majority of their lives figuring out how to be happy and a sliver of it actually being happy. But Russ was happy now.

Solomon decided cats were wiser than people.

He closed his eyes and let sleep begin to crawl its way over him, and soon he was back in the sandbox. A smile on his face as the sun shone on his bare legs, the sand warm against his skin. He recalled a stream behind that house and rumors he'd heard that a boy had drowned there once. After that, the stream had taken on an ominous appearance, and he wouldn't go near it. His child brain was telling him it was a place of evil where things went in good and came out bad. But now he saw that the stream was just a stream. It didn't kill purposely, and it didn't bring joy purposely either.

The stream didn't care.

59

Melinda Toby hated the prison more than the juvenile detention facility. There was something about the juvenile building that at least attempted to make it seem like a school, probably so the children didn't feel ostracized. The prison had nothing like that, nothing comforting. Everything from the floors to the lights to the doorknobs was about cheap efficiency. It gave the place a Frankenstein-like appearance. Like it had been cobbled together from pieces of other decrepit buildings.

Braden was already seated in the visitors' area when she arrived. He had some cuts on his face and a fat lip. The bald patches on his head and eyebrows were more noticeable. His lips were dry, and the nails on his fingers were bitten down to the point she could see dried blood. But his eyes looked the same. Indifferent. Like he didn't care whether he was in here or in his room.

"Are they treating you well?" she asked as she sat down across from him.

"No, Mom. They're not treating me well. Do you care?"

"Of course I care."

"Or maybe you don't want to feel bad that your little boy turned out like this? But you visited and don't need to feel guilty now. You can go."

A deep breath escaped her, and her eyes drifted to the carvings on the visiting room table. Mostly profanity with a few names inside heart shapes.

Braden waited until she looked up before saying, "I'll be older than you when I get out of here, and you'll be dead." A movement made his wrist cuffs rattle. "This place is like a time machine. I have no idea what's going on out there and won't see it change, but when I leave, it'll be totally different."

"Is that what you've been thinking about? All the time in the world, and that's the only realization you've had? The world will be different *if* you ever get out?"

"What did you expect to hear? That I feel bad? I don't. It didn't really feel like anything. Everybody makes it seem like killing someone is the worst thing you can do, and the sky's gonna fall on your head if you do it, but nothing happened. It was actually kinda . . . boring."

She shook her head as she felt the tears in her eyes. "You destroyed the lives of those poor people and their families, and all you can say is that it was boring?"

"That's not all I could say. I could say a lot more. Like how the best thing in the world is to watch someone's eyes as they die."

A woman at the visiting table next to them stopped speaking and looked over. When Braden glanced at her, she quickly looked away.

"I'm so sorry, Braden. I did everything I could to keep you out of here. I wasn't strong enough or smart enough, and I am so sorry." Melinda smiled sadly at a thought. "When you started being violent as a child, I used to think that if I'd given you up for adoption, you would've turned out better. That this was my fault, and if you hadn't been raised by me, things would've been different. But now I know that's not true. There's nothing I could've done for you, and I'm sorry I didn't recognize that sooner."

He watched her with a tilt of his head, and it reminded her of an animal. She wondered why she had never seen that in him before: a creature of pure instinct. No more able to deny his instincts than a fish or an ant.

"I'll deposit some money on your commissary card," she said before standing. "Goodbye, Braden."

As she turned toward the exit, Braden said, "You're not going to ask me why?"

She faced him and wiped tears away. "No. I already know why."

———

By the time Melinda got home, there was a fresh spatter of paint on her door. It wasn't as bad as the last time. This time, the paint was white, which at least was more pleasant than red. The frequency of the vandalism had diminished since Braden had taken the plea deal but hadn't entirely stopped.

Forget it, she thought. *They'll just ruin it again if I clean it.*

The home was silent and had a mildew scent to it. The water heater had burst a few months ago and soaked everything in the basement. Despite days of cleaning up, she couldn't get rid of the mildew smell. It had even started invading her dreams.

There was one room in the house she didn't like entering. After moving in, she didn't recall going into it more than a handful of times, and she knew, or at least had hoped, Braden would never even know about it.

The room was above the garage. After pulling down a thin piece of thread taped to the ceiling, a set of rickety stairs fell out with a snap as the wood hit the cement of the garage floor. Dust and cobwebs covered the steps. She got a broom and brushed the spiders off while repeating, "Ew, ew, ew."

When the steps were clear, she took the first few, fearing, like always, that the stairs could collapse at any second. As slowly as possible, she took one step at a time until she reached the top. Then hurriedly jumped off the steps and onto the solid wood floor as though the steps were on fire behind her.

The room contained a few piles of junk covered in white sheets. Old mementos that served no purpose anymore. Not that she liked thinking about her past. In fact, almost nothing up here was hers: it was almost all Braden's. Almost.

Braden's old homework assignments from elementary school, paintings, poetry, a trophy for setting the high school record on the bench press, and one for winning a wrestling tournament, along with dozens of other mementos in boxes. She had wanted to display some of the items in his room, and she'd set up a row of weight lifting trophies as a surprise when he got home from school one day. When Braden saw it, he shouted, "Are you stupid? Why would I want to stare at a trophy? You're lucky I don't shove it down your throat."

The memory pained her because that was when she'd realized her son was never going to get better. There was not going to be a happy ending. For his life, or hers.

She moved aside the piles as she searched. There was one thing up here that was hers. One thing that no one else in the world knew about. Something she had never even shown Braden or her fiancé, who she'd had to leave because Braden had threatened to kill him.

She had never told anyone about this and never would. Everyone had one secret they took to the grave with them, and this was hers. It gave her a sick, heavy feeling, but there was nothing she could do. It wasn't like she had asked to have this secret.

A locked wooden ottoman with a plush cover sat in the corner with a white sheet over it. The ottoman was perfect for storage because it didn't look like it could be used as a container. Melinda took out her key chain, and her hand shook as she inserted the key into the keyhole.

Inside was a thick accordion file overflowing with papers and trinkets. The sight of it made her feel physically sick, and she had to look away to ensure she didn't vomit right there.

Once her heart had sufficiently calmed, she picked up the folder and went downstairs.

The den had a fireplace that turned on with the push of a button. The flames hissed to life. She removed the protective screen and sat cross-legged in front of the fire with the folder in her hands. The heat warmed her face. It made her uncomfortable because it made her think about hell. Was there really such a place? Would the universe truly be so unjust as to torture people who had no say in who they were born to, or how they were raised? It was too complex a question for her to answer, she decided. It was enough to be alive. Asking for more answers than that was pointless.

The first things she took out of the folder were letters her father never sent to the media.

When he died, she had been by his side at the hospital. Melinda had pictured the last conversation she would have with him for a long time: there would be apologies and tears and reminiscing—but there was none of that when it happened. Instead, her father said that he had something to tell her.

He told her he had an urge that he had been fighting since he was a child but that he couldn't beat it, and it had taken over when he was twenty.

He told her where she could find everything, and she'd sat there in shock, listening to her father recount horrific details like they were casual musings. It appeared that he felt remorse, but looking back on it, she knew it was a lie. He *wanted* to be remorseful but didn't know how.

She took out the first letter. It was beautifully written in the eccentric handwriting her father had practiced since she was a child, resulting from being a lover of Japanese calligraphy and taking inordinate amounts of time with each stroke of the pen. She'd never asked herself why he spent so much time practicing calligraphy since she'd never seen him use it.

This is Reaper speaking.

The words were like an icy finger sliding along her spine. The fire flickered. Her first thought was that her father was here, and it made her shiver.

She tossed the first letter in the fire, then the second, then the third. Some jewelry was there, knickknacks from victims who would never be found. The police thought the Reaper had started killing in Utah eight years ago, but that was the tip of the iceberg. He had been killing since the age of twenty, beginning in San Francisco, until he died at fifty-seven. How many he had killed, how many families he had destroyed, how much suffering he had brought into the world, would never be known. Not really. He'd taken that secret to the grave.

When Braden started displaying disturbing behavior at an early age, she'd thought it was the result of his father not being in the picture, or her parenting, or them always struggling to pay the bills back then, or a million other things, but it was soon apparent that wasn't what it was. Braden was born with hatred and rage. An uncontrollable rage. How was a child supposed to cope with hate and rage as their first emotions?

For a long time, Melinda thought she could change him. But after her father's confession, she knew: his rotten genetics had infected her beautiful son. He would never be healthy, not on the inside. Not in the parts that counted.

It didn't matter anymore. She had done all she could.

Copying her father's handwriting and sliding that note under Dennis Yang's door to convince them they had the wrong person had been an act of desperation. A mother's last instinct to try to save her son, but trading her own soul to do it. That's what mothers did, she believed. Gave their lives and souls to their children.

She lifted the file and tossed the entire thing into the flames.

For the first time, she understood why it was said that fire was cleansing, but she also knew the feeling wouldn't last. The dark phantoms inside her were still there, and would be until the day she died. Just like they had infected Braden and somehow led him to admire the insanity of the one man Melinda had most tried to protect him from. But there was no protection. Before Braden was even born, he was going to do what he'd done. Her father's decay had been passed to her son, and it broke her heart in a way that would never be healed. There would be no closure for her, no resolution.

Inside the file were a handful of family photos. Some had slipped out onto the floor when she'd thrown the file into the flames, and she began tossing them in, stopping on one. It was her and her father. She was maybe thirteen in the picture, and they were holding up a fish by a lake, her father's arm around her shoulders. Both of them wearing broad smiles. Her father had loved fishing, said it was good for the soul to be out in nature without other people around. He had taught her to fish, gave her life lessons, talked to her about her mother's death from breast cancer and how she was still with them. She had told him to remarry once, and he had gotten quiet and didn't respond for a long time before he said, "No. I don't want to bring anyone else into this."

She hadn't understood what he had meant then, but she did on his deathbed. Her father, as monstrous as he was, didn't want his corruption to spread any further. That's why she was an only child. But he had never considered that *she* would have children . . .

She tossed the last photo into the fire and watched it burn.

ACKNOWLEDGMENTS

A huge thank-you to everyone at Thomas & Mercer; my agent, Amy Tannenbaum; and my family and friends, who make the lonely profession of writing a little less lonely.

ABOUT THE AUTHOR

 At the age of thirteen, when his best friend was interrogated by the police for over eight hours and confessed to a crime he didn't commit, Victor Methos knew he would one day become a lawyer.

After graduating from law school at the University of Utah, Methos cut his teeth as a prosecutor for Salt Lake City before founding what would become the most successful criminal defense firm in Utah.

In ten years, Methos conducted more than one hundred trials. One particular case stuck with him, and it eventually became the basis for his first major bestseller, *The Neon Lawyer*. Since that time, Methos has focused his work on legal thrillers and mysteries, winning the Harper Lee Prize for *The Hallows* and an Edgar nomination for Best Novel for his title *A Gambler's Jury*. He currently splits his time between southern Utah and Las Vegas.